NANCY HOWARD

THE ALLEY OF EVIL

NANCY HOWARD

THE ALLEY OF EVIL

The Alley Of Evil
Copyright © 2020 By Nancy E. Howard

This book is a work of fiction and all people, places and events are the result of the author's imagination. Any resemblance to places, or events, or people living or dead is purely coincidental.

All rights reserved. No part of this book may be reproduced or transmitted in any form or by any means, including electronic or photocopying without written permission from the author/publisher.

ISBN: 979-8-6737-9177-6

Cover Art; From Book Cover Zone: By Old Rose #2538

Websites: nancyhowardauthor.wordpress.com—Books by Nancy Howard
nancyhoward93.wixsite.com/nancyhoward—Nancy Howard Author
Facebook Author Page; Nancy Howard - Author

NANCY HOWARD

THE ALLEY OF EVIL

NANCY HOWARD

"There is no force more powerful than a woman determined to rise."

-Girl Power Quotes-

THE ALLEY OF EVIL

NANCY HOWARD

THE ALLEY OF EVIL

THE ALLEY OF EVIL

NANCY HOWARD

ONE

February 5, 2124, New Rotterdam, New York

It is eerily quiet—silent, as I walk down ages old city streets of broken sidewalks and crumbling curbs. On both sides of the street are ancient apartment buildings that rise above me and into the darkness. It's three a. m. as I round a corner, alone. I stop—looking over my right shoulder to see if I'm being followed. I'm not. I'm well known around here—people know who I am. They see me often, and call me the enforcer, because I'm a bounty hunter.

I don't hunt people perse, I collect money owed to my clients. But now and then I do have to search for someone, and hunt them down. But it's for the same reason, because he also owes my client money, too.

This winter morning as I journey home it's miserable, damp, and freezing cold. A steady mist of rain falls from the sky, accompanied by a stiff easterly wind that blows directly into me. Adding to my anguish about life in general. I begrudgingly pull the hood of my sweatshirt under my leather jacket up over my head, turning my back to the rain and the wind.

THE ALLEY OF EVIL

I'm guided only by the street lights and the flashing signs above me on the rooftops, blinking their debauched messages brightly into the night. They glare gaudily into my eyes when I look up —causing me to turn my eyes away from them.

And there's the graffiti—everywhere graffiti—even in the darkness I can see it, when the light hits it just right. Tonight it's wet from the rain, giving it a spooky sheen, that seems to make the messages it conveys, shout louder. It's painted everywhere and contains the tidings of the artists that painted them. A few of the messages are of hope—but most have no vision at all. Heralding nothing but hopelessness—mocking life as it is today.

Everywhere I walk, every step I take I see hundreds of people who live on the streets with nowhere to go. I see it every night. On most nights they're restless, shuffling here and there in the darkness, creating ghostly shadows on the building walls —but not tonight. Tonight they're huddled up next to the buildings on this cold, wretched, rainy night, just trying to stay dry, trying to stay warm. It's the grimness of life as it is in New America.

I finally reach my apartment building and trudge disconcertingly up the old concrete steps, that are broken and crumbling badly. I open the door and walk in—no key is required. It's a rat hole like everything is nowadays. I go up the stairs to the second floor where my apartment is—number two twenty four. I unlock it—a key is required. I enter and turn on the overhead light, and for once the crummy little place I call home is warm—the heat is actually on and running.

I'm beat. I left at ten this morning, looking for some dude

who owes my client money. I just want to go to bed. But before I crash, I remember that my phone had pinged earlier in the evening, so I decided to check the message. It's from my client, Colin Lampoor.

The message reads: "Sasha, there's been a change of plans." He says that instead of me looking for the guy I did this night. I need to get my associate, Charley Bill and visit a gambling establishment owned by a man named Diego Sanchez. He gives me the address where we're to go. In addition he says that Sanchez owes him ten grand, and for me to collect his money for him at all cost—then bring it to him immediately.

I reply: Will do.

I send Charley Bill a text to meet me at the fountain square on Hawk Street at noon the next day.

I take off my leather jacket, and hooded sweatshirt—both wringing wet from the mist. Then my guns, boots and the rest of my clothes, throwing them over my one chair. I turn out my light and crawl into bed to crash and burn. I lay there in my underwear, under two blankets, shivering. Trying to get warm—trying clear my head and fall asleep. Hoping that tonight I don't have that horrific nightmare that continues to haunt me. Often it rouses me out of a sound sleep, and robs me of much needed rest.

The dream is always the same. I'm in this very dark scary alley and there are five shadowy figures, behind me, that seem to be chasing after me. I can't get away from them, but it's the alley and what lies in it that really frightens me. Right now though I just want to sleep, something I need badly.

THE ALLEY OF EVIL

TWO

The next morning comes all to fast, I look at the clock and it says ten thirty-four. There were no nightmares—a good thing. The first thing I do is look out the window. I do it every morning, and for the life of me I don't know why. I guess what I'm hoping for, is that something might change the view. But of course that is totally unrealistic.

I lay back down and think, I'm so over this fucking place—sick of it—the whole city. I live in, no, I actually exist really, in this tiny dingy little place—an apartment they call it, that's smaller than most bedrooms. I don't have a bed really. I sleep on a mattress on the floor. I have an electric lamp on a small table, and one metal folding chair. Two closets—one for what clothes and few belongings I have. The other is like a walk-in closet and serves as a kitchen with a tiny stove, sink, and mini fridge, with a cabinet up above.

There's a laundry room in the basement with washing machines and dryers that work...sometimes, but not always. They're decades old and seem to be broken more that they work. But really when it comes down to it the bathroom is the most disgusting part about living here. I hate it, but I have no other choice but to use it. It has lavatories, toilets, and shower stalls, but it's used by both men and women, which is not good at all.

Girls have been raped in there, as many as five since I came here to live two years ago. So when I go in there, I'm armed, and will kill anyone who tries anything with me.

I live on the second floor of this grungy old building smack in the middle of New Rotterdam, or Rottendamn as I like to call it. It used to be called new something else until it got changed before I was born. Anyway, the place is rotten to the core, thus my nickname for it. It has violent crime and poverty on every corner. The bad thin is that there is very little if any real law enforcement around because all the cops are private. Which means if you don't pay your premiums to the city, you don't get protected.

The whole country is this way, overridden with trash and poverty, because years ago it drastically changed. Not only did the name of the country change, but it became a place run entirely by plutocrats who care about nothing but their own wealth.

I guess I should be thankful that I have a roof over my head and I'm not living on the streets, like those I see at night. Though I did that for a time when I was a kid. But when it comes right down to it, I'm not a girl who is thankful for anything. I have no reason to be. I don't care about anyone, or anything. I never have. I learned very early to be self sufficient, so all I want to do is stay alive.

I set up, finally, with my legs straight out, and drag myself up to put on my clothes. My jeans, boots, and shirt, all that I wore the day before, and the day before that. I grab my old hair brush and run it through my hair to get the tangles out. I don't know why, my hair is dirty, and it's in bad need of washing.

I lay hair brush back on my table and reach over to my chair for my guns, and strap them on. Two of them, one for each leg. They're replicas of Glock 17 forty-five caliber semi-automatic pistols. I had them specially made for me by a gunsmith on the south side of the city. He made them of a special light weight metal alloy, which makes them lighter and easier for me to handle—without them losing their muzzle velocity or power.

I carry them openly in two leather holsters, that I wear mid thigh right where my hands are so I don't have to reach for them when I draw. I strap them to my legs in two places, securing them with leather straps. On my belt I have five magazines, each with twenty rounds. So with what is in the two guns—fully loaded, I have a hundred forty rounds on me. They are deadly weapons, that I am deadly with.

I pull my hoodie on, then put on my leather jacket and gloves on, and go out locking my door behind me. I head down the old wooden interior stairwell. The steps are old like the building is, and they creak and groan with every step I take. The hallway is not well lit or is the building secure, thus allowing vagrants to wander in at night and sleep off whatever their poison is. This morning is no different than any other, and just to reach the door I have to step over two bums that are sound asleep at the bottom near the door.

Outside on the crowded sidewalk, I see the usual. People, lots of poor people, with empty looks on their faces who are wandering aimlessly to wherever—lost. They're just looking for a place to light on this cloudy, cold, disagreeable day. Some are probably the same ones I pass unknowingly at night, when I'm on my way home. They're all familiar with me though, or at least most are, they know my reputation and why I carry the guns. Being armed openly is allowed today, but still most don't carry openly like I do. Concealed carry is common, and I have to be aware of that every time I walk into a situation.

The client that I work for is a man named Colin Lampoor. A slimy little bastard—a loan shark. I only see him when I take a collection to him. To put it frankly the man is disgusting in every sense of the word. He's an unshaven nasty little pip squeak, that I would kill if he didn't pay me so well.

I take the money to him that I collect from all the business owners, that owe him for the favors he's done for them. It's a simple process. He loans you money in advance—for say your rent. Then if you don't pay him back, it's my job to go and collect his money for him.

And that can get very messy sometimes—people don't want to pay him back. Even though that was the agreement they made with him in the first place. They balk when Charley Bill and I come to collect. When that happens violence usually breaks out, and he and I simply kill them and take the money anyway. Problem solved.

Besides the people I do have to kill are usually just slim balls themselves—just like Lampoor. I have to work this way. I do it to survive out here, and to stay alive. I know Lampoor has people all over the streets—snitches that watch me, too. And I really don't know them or where they are, so I do his bidding and get his money no matter how I have to do it. If I have to shoot and kill someone to collect, then so be it. That's what I do.

Today before I meet Charley Bill, I'm on my way to talk with my snitch. A drunk I only know as Cooch. I don't know how he got that name, and no one has ever asked me, and I'm glad because I don't know and don't care. But that's what he told me his name is and I leave it at that. Hell for all I know he may be working for Lampoor, too. It wouldn't surprise me. But the fact is he's helped direct me many times to people that are trying to avoid me.

He's supposed to meet me in an alley near an old rundown watering hole, called Kegs, at eleven. It's about a half mile walk from my apartment. He got a message to me yesterday that he has something to tell me. I go into the alley next to Keg's and there's no Cooch. What else is new? I pull my cell phone out of my back pocket and look at the time, it says eleven right on the nose. So I decide to wait and see if he shows up.

It's not all that unusual for him to not be on time, because he's nothing but a drunk, who hides in the shadows and hears things. He's not usually noticed because most of the toughs and thugs out here on the streets don't consider him to be any kind of threat. But there are those that do notice him, and he's had the hell beat out of him a few times because of it. Some of the punks out here think he's watching and listening to them. And that he presents some sort of threat to them. Of course he's listening, but he's no threat to them. He's just a drunk, but he usually gives me is reliable information—that's why I'm here.

After about five or six minutes waiting, I start to wonder if he is going to show at all, and I think about leaving. Just as that thought races through my mind I see him stumble out of Keg's. He's loaded to the gills. He's having so much trouble coming down the entrance steps he stumbles and he nearly falls. He grabs hold of the railing catching himself. That steadies him. If someone as drunk as he is can be steady. But that keeps him from falling flat on his face. Watching him I shake my head in pity, and try not to laugh.

He hasn't seen me yet so I walk over to him. He's a scrawny man about my height, in his early sixties, I think. He wears an old beat up fedora hat that covers his wrinkled and drawn face, a trench coat, and scarf. All of which are dirty beyond belief. He reeks of liquor and cigarette smoke, and his bad body odor is atrocious, so I do everything I can to stay up wind of him.

I walk over to him and say, " Hey Cooch."

He looks up at me and mumbles something that is slurred and completely inaudible. After he rights himself and gets steady on his feet, I ask him if he's got anything for me. Anything pertinent to my work.

He ignores me for a second time—he's looking for a place to sit. He then staggers over to a couple of near-by wooden crates. He grabs hold of one and sits down on it gingerly trying not to fall over. He looks at me with glassy eyes, weaving around. Then he mumbles, "I ain't got a thing for you today, little girl."

"So why did you want to meet? I have work to get done and I have to meet Charley Bill at noon."

As I turn my back to walk away from him, he says, "be careful out there, Sasha. I heard some rumblings that there are people out to get you. They want a take you down."

I turn and walk back toward him, with a curious look on my face. He's still staring at me with glassy eyes, like a blind person would who can't see me. Then he looks away and begins to fumble around in his jacket, looking for his smokes. He finds them and puts one in his mouth, and drops the rest of the pack on the ground, spilling them all over the place, cussing when he does it.

"Who is it that's looking for me now, Cooch, and why," I ask? This is nothing new. I've heard this kind of crap before about someone looking to take me out.

"The Seventh Street Gang is what I heard." He pats his pocket looking for something to light the cigarette with.

"Again? I didn't know I had a quarrel with them."

"The source I was listening to Sasha was pretty reliable. They say you been hornin' in on their turf, they want to stop you," he pauses. "You don't happen to have a light do you?"

"No," I snapped. "Do you know the name of this source?" This is where it gets good because he's going to want money for that information. So I reach into my back pocket and pull out my wad of cash, take a twenty and hand it to him.

He takes it and looks at it, then at me, like it's not enough. I just stand in front of him and raise my eyebrows, my arms folded in front of me, shaking my head. Waiting for him to give me a name.

"All I heard was the name Tyler Baines. Not sure he's the one that's after you, though." He says, gagging on his words. He takes the twenty from me and looks at it, figuring that was all the money I was going to give him. And if he figured that, he was right.

"I don't understand what their beef is with me. And what the hell do they mean by their turf. I go where I damn well please to collect for my clients. Then I leave."

"Don't know, maybe they don't like you coming over to their part of town," he says.

"Their part of town. Fuck them," I say sarcastically.

I stand there and wonder if I should take what he's telling me to heart. Though I've never heard of anyone named Tyler Baines, and Cooch is usually dependable in his assessment of things no matter how drunk he is when he hears it.

"You have anything else for me?"

He shakes his head no—violently burping at the same time.

Then he does something that completely repulses me. I notice that he's suddenly turned white as a ghost, and the cigarette falls out of his mouth. Then he bends over, gags violently, and vomits, with puke spewing out of his mouth and all over him and the pavement below. It turns my stomach completely, grossing me out. So much so, that it makes me want to hurl, too. But there's nothing on my stomach to vomit. So I turn away in disgust and march quickly out of the alleyway. Walking past the door of Kegs where I nearly get run over by two more drunks stumbling out of the place. It's time to meet Charley Bill and get to work.

THREE

I approach and see him standing next to the old fountain just as we agreed. Charley Bill is a big man, six-four/five, I figure. I know he's at least that because he towers over me and I'm five-eight. He's somewhat muscular and is much bigger than most people, so it's nice to have him along to help collect. Because the very sight of a man that big carrying big guns like he does, tends to scare the holy hell out of people.

He sees me coming and gives me a slight wave, I walk up to him.

"Hey boss."

"Hey," I say. Returning his greeting. One thing about Charley Bill is that he's reliable—always on time. He's been my shadow for nearly three years now. I met him one day in a bar, as he was beating a couple of punks half out of their wits. I'm not sure what they'd done to anger him, all I know is that I remember standing by and watching in awe, as he turned them inside out. And just when it seemed like he was going to finish them off, they both got up and ran for their crummy lives. Of course I would have done the same thing if I had a man that big mad at me.

After he gathered himself that day I approached him,

taking a seat at the bar next to him, and took up a conversation with him. After introducing myself to him, I told him I was in need of an associate. He knew who I was of course, and I ask him if he'd like to work with me. His immediate response was he would, but he wanted to know more about the work. So I told him about how I go about collecting for my clients, plus how much he would get paid—forty percent if my take. He said it sounded like a gig he could have some fun with, and that was the beginning of Charley Bill becoming my associate.

I always pay him on time, too, because I don't want to end up in the position that those two punks were in that day. Since then I've seen him take out lots of men who threatened us, fighting them off, tossing them around like rag dolls. He's vicious when he's angry, though he tells me he's just earning his keep.

"Everything okay," he says. "You look kinda anxious." He evidently noticed that I was looking around as I approached him. Something I usually don't do.

"Ah it's nothing, I just came from talking to Cooch, and it seems as though he overheard a conversation where the Seventh Street gang is after me."

"What else is new they're always looking to take you out. What's it for this time?"

"I guess they think I'm getting too far into their turf."

"Their turf, my ass," he responds. "That's always their excuse for wanting get at you. The Seventh Street gang—their nothing but a bunch of street punks, toughs—without the balls to challenge anyone they don't have outnumbered. If they bother you I'll gladly help you kill them all."

I smile and shake my head. "Have you ever heard of a gang member over there named Tyler Baines?"

He thinks for a second before speaking, "No I haven't. You know Sasha I thought I knew most of those clowns. But no, I've never heard that name. He might be somebody new."

"Yeah, maybe an enforcer or something from out of town to help them hold onto, what they think is their turf. Cooch said he wasn't sure if this Baines guy was the one who was out to get me."

"Well, we'll keep our eyes and ears open. You know, be vigilant."

"Yeah we're always that way. And speaking of Seventh Street, that's where we're going to collect from that gambling crap hole Sanchez's. So we'll be on their turf."

He motions for me lead the way.

******

It is now past twelve thirty as we walk down Seventh Street, slowly and deliberately making our way through the chaos of the crowded human condition as it exists today. Every street is a market place, where each and every merchant steps in front of you to sell you something. It's the only way they have to make a living. The only way they can feed themselves and their families without starving to death. They're out here everyday in the cold—begging. They're also the ones who remember being told years ago, that things would be great in the federation, and they bought into it. Now they know it was all a pack of lies from a bunch of crooked, rich politicians.

After a walk of more than thirty minutes and nearly freezing from the cold damp wind, we duck down an alley and look for a door on our right painted green. It's about half way down the alley—we walk up the four risers, and I stand behind Charley Bill as beats hard on the door. There's no immediate answer, so he does it again. This time with results, as the door is opened, first by a couple of inches and then wider.

The man who opens the door is a goon. He has short hair and is wearing sunglasses inside on a cloudy day. Go figure. He's unshaven, of course and has on a jacket, sweater, jeans, and wingtip shoes. What is it with goons and wingtip shoes? I notice right away he has a Beretta.9mm holstered under his left arm.

Charley says, "We're here looking for Diego Sanchez. He around?"

"Yeah, who the hell's looking for him?" He asks back, using a gruff tone.

"She is, Sasha Cain, and I'm Charley Bill Brown. So again, is he around?"

"He's busy, so leave." The goon says bluntly, and starts to close the door.

Charley stops him. Then he pushes the goon and the door out of the way forcing himself inside. I follow him in.

"Hey you just can't barge in here like that," he protests sullenly. Then starts to reach for his gun.

"I wouldn't do that, and we just did," I say. Walking by him, looking straight into his eyes.

THE ALLEY OF EVIL

I follow Charley Bill into a large room with gaming tables for blackjack, roulette and other games of chance. There are four round tables for playing cards in the back. We walk past the bar, and toward them. Another goon is at the bar with a drink. He stands up when he sees us walk in, and begins to intently watch us. I see at least eight other people in the room. Four are at one of the round tables, all men, playing cards and they don't even look up as we enter.

The other four are sitting in two separate booths in the back. Two men and two women. The windows are darkly tinted and have heavy curtains for window coverings allowing for little natural light to get through. Which is usual decor for rat hole places like this, that reeks with the smell of stale cigarette smoke, which I hate.

I've never been in here before, nor do I know which one these men is Sanchez. So I decide to take a wild guess and look at the man to my left at the back table. The woman setting next to him is a hooker—she's nearly sitting in his lap. The other two people sitting in the adjacent booth, noticed us right away when we came in. I glance at him just to note where he is—he's watching me closely.

I walk over to the booth, toward who I believe is Sanchez. Charley Bill is keeping his eyes on the two goons that are behind me—keeping them occupied. We have to be careful, because if this thing gets out of hand, I'm sure the men at the table playing cards will defend Sanchez.

"You. Are you Diego Sanchez?" I said.

He dosn't answer me immediately, then looks up, "What if

I am? And who in the hell are you, lady?"

Bingo, I got him right.

Lady?

"I'm Sasha Cain, and I think you know why I'm here."

"Is that so. Well I don't know why you're here, Sasha Cain. I ain't never seen or heard of you before until now."

He's a liar on both counts. He knows damn good and well who I am. Anyone and everyone with any kind of connections on the streets knows my name and what I do. He also knows he owes Lampoor money, and doesn't want to own up to it. So he lies.

"Well Sanchez to refresh your memory. I'm here to collect a debt, on a loan that was made to you a month ago by my client, Colin Lampoor. The agreement was that you would pay the loan back to him today with interest. The loan was for five grand and the interest on it is the same. So you owe him ten grand."

"You got the wrong place. I don't know, nobody, named Colin Lampoor. Now get out." He says.

"Well…you see Diego—no I do have the right place. Lampoor sent me here, so you do owe him money. So let's make this easy. You just give me the money owed to him, and me and my associate will be on our way."

"I don't give a fuck about what this dude Lampoor told you. I don't owe him no money, especially ten G's. Now I remember telling you to leave, and while you're at it take Goliath there with you."

I can see this not going to be easy. It never is. Now the people at the card table have stopped playing, and are listening to our conversation. I glance over at them, sure that they're associates of Sanchez and not just friendly patrons.

I again tell Sanchez to pay up that I'm not leaving until he gives me the ten grand. And again he refuses, and tells us to leave, going so far as to threaten us. Saying he'll have is muscle throw us out.

At this point I'm done with his BS and I walk over to the table where he and the hooker are setting. She looks at me her expression is one of being fearful of me. Sanchez looks at me, too. I reach down and grab hold of the table and lift it up, flipping it sideways, sending their drinks and ashtrays all over the floor. He stands up along with the hooker and she moves away fast, sensing trouble.

Just then out of the corner of my eye, the goon at the other table reaches inside his jacket, going for his gun. I see this, and adjust to his action quickly. I draw the gun on my right out of the holster and I fire—killing him. Then Sanchez gets brave, and reaches for me. I back away out of his reach, at the same time I hear gunfire go off behind me. Charley Bill has engaged the goons. I point my weapon at Sanchez just as he pulls a small caliber pistol from behind him. I fire, and he dies.

That leaves the table of card players who've turned their focus on Charley Bill after he killed the two goons. They're firing at him and are now engaging me, too. Charley has taken cover behind a column and is taking and returning fire with them. I'm behind the table that I turned over for cover, and it's not the best cover but it'll have to do. They're firing at me and I shoot back.

The round card table they're behind is big and heavy,

possibly made of oak, which makes it great cover—good at stopping bullets. But not this time, I fire relentlessly, unloading my Glock at them. I pull my left one and begin firing it. Two of them are shooting at me and two at Charley Bill. Then I see two of them get up to escape through the back door. I fire and hit them both. Charley takes out one still behind the table. He continues to shoot, giving me cover as I move to the bar to get a better angle on the last man. He's the only one left, and then he gets up and bolts for the door, to get away. I shoot and kill him.

The shooting has stopped, but the two hookers got away, which is not good, because they can ID both of us. A lot of gunfire was exchanged in here today, and New Rottendamn's private finest will be showing up soon. That is if Sanchez has paid his monthly premium for police protection. So there's little time to waste. I still need find the ten grand that Sanchez owes Lampoor, and we need to get out of here, soon. But the question is where does he keep the cash in this place?

I look around almost frantically. And Charley Bill asks me what I'm looking for?

"A safe maybe. Like, where in the hell does Sanchez keep his stash. Did you see a safe or anything in that back room?"

"No, but I'll check again." I hear him rumbling around for several seconds, then he calls out, "Sasha."

"Did you find his safe?" I said going over and standing in the doorway to the backroom.

"No, but you'd better come over here and have a look at what I did find."

He's standing in front of a large cabinet that is wide open

and is loaded with cash. More than I've ever seen in my whole life. It makes sense because Sanchez runs a gaming joint.

"Damn, we hit the jackpot, Sasha."

"We did!" I exclaim with a big grin, as we high five each other.

So I reach in and begin to count out the ten thousand that Sanchez owes Lampoor, and I look at Charley Bill, and say, "help yourself. Hell, he ain't gonna need this now, and nobody will even miss it."

"Except the cops maybe." He laughs.

"That's okay. I like to piss them off."

After counting out the Ten G's, Charley Bill and I help ourselves to as much of the money as we can carry, stuffing it into cloth bags. We hear sirens in the distance, their sound growing louder as they get closer. Charley motions that we should leave now. So we go out the back door because there's less chance of us being seen running away. We head down the alleys that form a labyrinth of passage ways behind the old apartment buildings, going this way and that. Making it impossible for the cops to find us once we leave Sanchez's place.

By the time we hear the sirens stop we're long gone, and heading back to Hawk Street where Charley Bill and I split up. Half an hour later I returned to my apartment, with the money bag. I unlock my apartment door and go inside, and put the bag of cash in my dresser for the time being. I will count it out tonight when I get home, right now I need to go see Lampoor and give him the ten grand that Sanchez owes him. I head back out of my apartment building, and I can still hear sirens wailing in the distance. All of them racing to the carnage we left behind. Evidently Sanchez paid his premiums.

THE ALLEY OF EVIL

FOUR

I walk slowly and nonchalantly down the street after I leave my apartment, so I won't draw any unwanted attention to myself. Not only do the people around here know who I am and what I do, so do the cops. They know where I live. Just as I thinking that, up ahead of me and coming in my direction I see one of their patrol jeeps. I don't look at them, I don't want to make eye contact with them. I keep walking and ignore them as they drive slowly past me, taking a long look at me. It's one of those that gives you the creeps. But they don't stop, they continue on by and don't come back around and drive by me again.

I'm glad they didn't stop and hassle me, because I would have killed them both if they would have tried to arrest me. Evidently they weren't looking for me specifically—not right now anyway. Which is what Charley and I want. But then there's the two hookers that got away. I'm sure they're snitches for the cops or someone—maybe even Lampoor. I'd bet my last dollar on that. I know that somewhere along the line they'll rat us out to somebody for a price.

Getting to Lampoor's place is a pain. He lives clear the hell on the other side of Rottendamn. And I have to ride the dilapidated old subway to get to him. Even if the train is on time, which it never is, it will take me two hours to get there and two hours back. It sucks, but when he pays me my cut, it makes it all worth the aggravation to ride the train.

I get off the subway—two hours exactly, and I walk the three blocks to his building where he lives. It's not in much better shape than mine, it's just that he has a real apartment with real rooms—not one room like I live in. But not for long, that bag of cash that I took has enough money to take care of me and make my life a whole lot better. I enter and go up the stairs to the second floor, and walk down the hall to apartment two fourteen, and ring the bell.

A young woman about my age answers, I figure it's Colin's latest and greatest conquest. Though I admit, she's better than most of the ones he's had in here.

"Can I help you Miss?" She asks me.

"I'm here to see Colin. Is he around?"

"Yes, may I tell him who you are?"

"Yeah, Sasha Cain."

She invites me in and I stand in the foyer where I wait for a few seconds, while she tells him I'm here. This is a usual occurrence, it's like a big deal, like he's some big executive or something. I have to laugh when I think that. In just a few seconds she returns and leads me through the apartment and into his study. I've made this walk at least ten times so I have it memorized, too.

The walk through the place is a journey in itself. The place is trashed. It has junk everywhere you look and boxes stacked on top of boxes. There's absolutely no place to set—anywhere. The walls are drab, and the place hasn't been painted in what looks like since before I was born. The blinds are broken and have missing slats and are closed, making it dark and cold feeling inside.

The girl and I follow a narrow path through the junk to what is called his office. An office for what? I laugh to myself again. Lampoor is a slim ball, and criminal.

I've been in it before, and like the rest of the place, it's depressing, even more so than my little hole in the wall place, if you can believe that. The woman turns and invites me to sit, and asks me if I'd like something to drink, and I say no, I'm good. I look around and think to myself this chair I'm sitting in, it must be the only free one in the apartment, except for the big office chair I see behind his desk.

Lampoor of course, likes to make me wait, it gives the little bastards ego a feeling of power over me.

Soon he comes into the room and sits down behind the desk. It's covered with piles of paper, and is in the same messy condition as the rest of the apartment. I doubt if he even knows what all the stuff laying on top is, and has not looked at it in ages. He has an old desktop computer terminal on it that looks older than he and I are. It is near him and he looks past it and at me, it must add to his feeling of self importance.

He relishes the idea that he gives Sasha Cain orders, that I work for him. It makes the squeamish little bastard feel superior to me. It only makes me want to kill him.

"So Sasha, I hear you've been busy lately," he comments sharply.

"I got what you wanted," I responded. Not lingering on his curt tone of voice at me.

"All ten grand?"

I shake my head yes.

Then he reaches out over the desk with his right hand, palm up, and snaps his fingers at me. Speaking in an ordering tone, "give it to me, now. Let me see it."

I don't like him ordering me like that, but I reach into my back pocket and pull out the wad of cash and hand it to him. He yanks it away from me, then he leans back in the chair and begins to count it.'

"It's all there," I say.

He looks up at me like he doesn't believe me and continues to count anyway. Done, he slams the money down on his desk and glares at me.

"So, where's my cut," I ask? Getting to the point. I want to be paid. Twenty percent means two grand, and I have to give Charley eight hundred of it.

"There is none, Sasha."

"What the hell do you mean? There is none." I retort, loudly.

"There is none Sasha, because you're sloppy. You fucked up! After you killed Sanchez and his gang you and that buffoon, Charley Bill, that you call an associate, decided to steal as much cash from the place as you could possibly carry."

"So what the hell is that to you? He won't miss it."

"Yeah, you're right, he won't, but you were sloppy as hell. You let people get away. Why didn't you kill them, too?"

"Well, Lampoor."

"My name is pronounced pour, not poor. I've told you that before." He snaps at me.

I sneer at him, curling my lip at his comment. "Like I started to say, we were kinda busy getting our asses shot at, and they left just as the shooting started."

Those two whores that got away did the squealing on me and Charley, just as I figured they would. They're in his pocket, too. He's right though, I should have killed them. Like I should kill him right now.

"Well since you were the one who took out Sanchez and his gang, and you stole that money, those witnesses ID you and Charley Bill. Besides, you were there working for me, to collect a debt and got greedy. So, you, my dear, owe me that money you took, too. It's all my money. What you took and what Charley Bill took, is mine.

"You seem to have forgotten that you were working for me. It's all over the streets that the enforcer killed Diego Sanchez and his gang." He pauses. "You know Sasha one of these days your crazy shit is gonna come back to haunt me. And we don't want that to happen, now do we?" He's smirking at me and enjoying his little tirade.

"You don't own me, Lampoor," I declare. Not pronouncing his name like he wants.

"Yeah, well when you're on a job and working for me, I do. Remember that. And I will tell you now, I will not tolerate what you did." He says this and leans forward, pointing his finger at me.

NANCY HOWARD

It doesn't matter what you won't tolerate dickhead. Someday I'm going to kill you anyway.

"So you need to bring me my money that you took by tomorrow, or I'll turn you little ass over to the police. Promise. It's that simple.

"Don't you threaten me you son-of-a-bitch." I say, angrily. Thinking of killing him right now.

"Don't even think about it," he says. Glaring at me—reading my thoughts.

I look at him and sniff slightly. "Well I am thinking about it, dude. But I won't do it today, because it would be too messy for your girlfriend to witness. And I don't want to have to kill her, too. But someday, Lampoor, someday, I will kill you. I'm not going to forget this. You know you shouldn't poke the tiger."

He laughs slightly at my comment.

"Do you find me funny, Lampoor?" I snap at him.

"Just bring me my goddamn money, by tomorrow, Sasha." He shouts at me.

"Don't you shout at me, you sick little bastard," I yell back. "I've had enough of your shit for one day." Then I use my middle finger for an obscene gesture at him, and get up and leave. I hear him laugh as I stomp out of his grungy apartment, slamming the door behind me.

When I get outside his building, to say I'm furious is putting it mildly. I'm shaking with anger. I'm so pissed off at what he just did. The little bastard stiffed me out of my share of the money I collected. Two grand and he wants the other money I have at home. I want to kill him so bad, but that'll have to wait.

Right now I have other issues. He told me the cops are looking for me, because the little fucker instigated it himself. I wonder why the two I saw patrolling earlier didn't apprehend me then. Maybe they didn't know, or word hadn't gotten out yet, that they were to arrest me.

So that makes two, the number of organizations, if that's the right name for them that are looking for me. The Seventh Street gang and the Rottendamn cops. And they really aren't any better than the Seventh Streeters, because both groups are all just a bunch of thugs on the take.

It's nightfall when I leave Lampoor's place, dark, as I make my way back to the train station. I'm in an unfamiliar setting and don't really know what to expect around here after dark. I suspect it's just like where I live. Bad. But it still makes me anxious walking down these streets that are strange to me at night. I'm not well known around here and I usually come here during the day. But Lampoor wanted the money I collected right away.

As I walk I slide my right hand gun out of the holster to protect myself. It's now at my side, ready to use if I have trouble of any kind. There are few people out as the darkness deepens. I turn around and look every now and then to see if I'm being followed—it's a habit of mine.

I approach the rail station, and I see three people standing around, all men. I assume they're waiting for the train. It's hard to see what they look like, but that doesn't matter to me. I don't want to get too close to them. So I stand back and off to the side in the shadows, giving myself plenty of space between me and them should they try something. I can't tell from my vantage point if they're armed at all. But I figure even if they are, my gun is drawn and loaded and they can see that, too. I think I would have enough time to react and kill them if they tried to attack me.

For several minutes I'm in this situation, as I wait for the train, which is late as usual. Then it begins to rain, adding to the tenseness I feel standing here in unfamiliar surroundings, not knowing what to expect. I'm not afraid, but I am cautious. Soon I hear the train's horn.

******

Two hours later I walk into my apartment building, then up the flight of stairs to my apartment and unlock the door. It's still locked, just like I left it, which is a good sign. Indicating to me that Lampoor didn't have anybody come around here to break into the place looking for the money. The first thing I do is turn on the light and then walk over to the dresser and reach into the third drawer for the money bag. It's there, so after taking off my jacket, I decide it's safe enough to sit down on my mattress and count it out. I close the rickety blinds that cover my window, sit down spill the money out of the bag and start counting.

After five or six minutes, I count eighty-eight grand, enough to get me out of this fucking fire trap, rat infested, building I been living in for the past two years. But I need to keep this money in a safer place than the dresser drawer. I need to keep it to myself where I hide it. I won't tell a soul. Charley Bill knows I have it the money, but I won't tell him where I hide it either. I have think of a better place, and I know just where that place is.

******

I wake up the next morning and don't immediately pull back the blinds as I usually do, to see what it's like outside. I can hear it. It's raining cats and dogs. I was late falling asleep last night after racking my brain to find a place to hide the cash safely here at home. I remembered that I had an empty container in my cabinet that I used to keep sugar in, but stopped doing that because the roaches got into it and I had to put the sugar in the fridge. So I stashed the money in that container and taped the top shut, because I don't want the rats to get into it and chew it up either. Then I put it on the shelf in my cabinet. I lay back down and try to rest and listen to the pouring rain outside. Hoping it will stop by tonight, so I can go hide my money in the cover of darkness.

    I must have drifted off to sleep because I wake up and it's nearly eleven in the morning. I'm supposed to take Lampoor my stash today. That ain't gonna happen. He can go fuck himself if he thinks I'm stupid enough to do something like that. And without muscle he won't come after it by himself, because he'd never get it in the first place. He knows all too well that if he tried that I'd kill him in an instant. But he will tell the cops, and he has a lot of them in his pocket. I fully expect them to come here and get me, but they won't do so until Lampoor tells them to.

My phone rings interrupting my thoughts, it's Charley Bill asking to be paid.

I answer: "Hey Charley."

Charley Bill: *"Hey. Did you get our money?"*

Me: "No, you ain't getting paid, bro, because I didn't get a dime for what we did. Simple as that. That little bastard Lampoor stiffed me."

Charley Bill: *"You're shittin' me."*

Me: "No I'm not. He wants me to bring him the money I took out of the cabinet. He wants yours, too."

Charley Bill: *"That ain't gonna happen."*

Me: "Well he plans on getting it from you. And if I don't give him mine he'll turn me over to the cops. Who by the way are looking for both of us."

Charley Bill: *"What are you gonna do with yours?"*

Me: "Hide it, where only I know where it is. You should do the same."

Charley Bill: *"Yeah, you're right I should."*

Me: "Stay alert."

Charley Bill: *"Will do you do the same."*

We disconnect the call.

I wish I could pay him his cut for the work we did. But hey, I saw him take a bundle of cash yesterday morning just like I did, so he ain't broke.

I notice the rain has let up. I look out the window and see that it's just cloudy, cold, and gloomy now. A tap at my door. I think the cops are here. I grab one of my guns and go look through the peephole. Damn it's Drago. What does he want? If it's a quickie he wants he's in for a rude awakening. I open the door and let him in.

"Hey," he says, greeting me.

"Hey to you. What brings you over here?" I let him in.

Drago is a tall skinny dude, with long black hair, long as mine. He's unshaven as usual. It must be some sort of look men enjoy or he's just too lazy to shave regularly, which is most likely the case. Drago usually visits me when he doesn't have anyplace else to park himself. I have no idea what kind of work he does, if any. And he comes around once in a while, because we bang each other now and then, but not on a regular basis. I'm sure he brags to all his buddies, if he has them, that he's banging Sasha Cain, the enforcer. It makes me laugh to just think about it.

"I didn't think I'd catch you home," he says.

"I don't have a gig today, so I stayed home."

"Me neither, like you, no work," he says. Sitting down on the one chair I have. I set back down my mattress, Indian style.

After a second he says, "it's a good thing Sasha that your stayin' in today.

"Really? Why?"

"Word has it all over the street that the cops are after ya, for killin' some dude by the name of Sanchez yesterday."

"Yeah, I know all about the cops looking for me. And If they want me, they know where I live."

"Seventh Streeters, too. They're mad as hell now. From what I hear, for you and Charley Bill killin' Sanchez."

"Well now, that's just tough, ain't it?" I respond. "So did you come all the way over here just to tell me crap I already know."

"Na, I was just worried about ya that's all. Wasn't sure ya knew. Besides you need to be careful Sasha you're makin' a lot of enemies."

"I've done it before. And listen, you bring up a good point. Since you know all of this, it may not be such a good idea for you to be here right now, ya know. I know people, the wrong people that know you're acquainted with me. That we've been together. You know what I mean?"

He shakes his head that he does.

"So maybe you should just be on your way. I'm not trying to be mean to you. I'm protecting you, Drago."

"I know that, Sasha, I just thought I'd take a chance and find you home. Which I have, and if you wasn't busy, we could spend the day together. You know, gettin' it on."

"No. Not now, not today, Drago. Listen to me it's too dangerous for you to be here. I need to let all this crap settle for a while. You need to not be here right now. I need to lay low for a while, then we can get together. Okay?"

He shakes his head reluctantly, and then slaps his legs with his hands and gets up. I get up, too. Then he grabs me and kisses me, and at the same time starts to run his hands into my pants. Which I remove.

"Go. Stay away, I don't want you to get hurt because you know me."

He shakes his head and leaves as we stretch out our arms as

a last touch."

I close the door and lock it, shaking my head in relief that I got rid of him so easy. I set down on my bed and shudder just a bit at Drago reiterating stuff to me I already know. I know the cops are after me and they know where I live. I know I've been ratted out by those two hookers—Charley Bill and I both have. Of course I know why they haven't come to arrest me yet They're waiting on the word from Lampoor to tell them to do it. That's why. He's waiting on me to bring him the money and if I don't. Then that's when he'll sick the cops on me. He can wait, it ain't gonna happen.

With the rain stopped my thoughts return to the canister of money that is in my cabinet. I need to take it out and bury it. Because when they do come to arrest me they won't find it here, when they search my apartment. I need to hide it soon or I'll never see it again.

******

I put the canister of cash in the bag that I brought the money home in and I slip out the back door of the building and into an alley under the cover of darkness, like I'd planned. It's not raining, it's just cold, windy, and disagreeable. I know exactly where I want to take this, to the old vet cemetery that is just a couple of blocks away.

My walk over to the Vet is quiet, no trouble, and no cops. I climb over an old fence that is rusted and falling apart. I brought my little spade to dig with. I used one time to try to grow a potted flower in my apartment. it died and I threw it out, but kept the spade. I don't want to be here a longtime, the ground should be super soft from all the rain we had this morning and will making it easy to dig and bury the money.

Over the fence, I begin to walk through the graves, most of them are very, very old. The place is eerily quiet, and while I don't believe in ghost—they may reside here. The place is spooky, which is one main reason I decided to bury the money out here. Nobody ever comes here anymore, to pay homage to these great soldiers. Who fought so valiantly and died, defending a lost cause all those decades ago.

I walk down what's left of an old asphalt path that is broken and overgrown by the dead grass of winter. The wind is blowing harder, howling through the bare trees around me, causing them to sway wildly back and forth when a big gust catches them. The swaying of the limbs causes them to create spectral shadows in the light of the moon that has emerged from the clouds. The whole scene gives me goosebumps, I tell myself, keep going Sasha, there are no such things as ghosts. I look around as I always do to see if I'm being followed or watched. I'm not.

I know exactly where I'm taking the money to a large monument in the center of the cemetery where it will be easy to find, when I come back for it. It has the name Carter in big bold letters on it. It's one that has been here a longtime, possibly, since a war called World War One.

I find it easy enough and go around behind it and start digging. Just as I do, I'm startled, suddenly by a bird that flutters wildly right in front of my face. Scaring me half out of my wits, causing my heart to skip a couple of beats.

After taking a few seconds to get myself settled down from that bird, I resume my digging. I must carefully remove the sod, so I can replace it, not giving any clue that it has been disturbed. I dig, and dig, and dig some more, the ground is muddy and soft. Finally I shine my phone light on the hole I've dug and see that it's deep enough to cover the bag. I put the bag with the canister of money in the hole and I fill it back in, replacing it with the muddy soil and sod as best as I can. I leave the vet quickly, going home the same way I came. Looking around me to see if anyone saw me.

I go upstairs to my apartment, it's late as usual. But my mind is at ease for the money, it's safe now. And if and when the cops come by to arrest me, they won't find the money in here. And I will not tell them where I hid it no matter how much they threaten me. I laugh even though the cops will come, eventually, but Lampoor sure as hell won't get his filthy paws on my cash.

******

The next morning I get up, it's only about eight, early for me. I sent a text to Charley Bill—he didn't respond. I wanted him to meet me at the fountain, but that won't happen if I can't raise him. I don't use the phone for calling much, because I figure someone may be listening in. Someone out to get Sasha Cain, someone other than Lampoor.

I'm dressed, my guns are on, I'm running my old brush

through my dirty hair. When suddenly, without warning my door gets kicked in. It flies open and hits the wall with a loud bang. Startled at the sudden intrusion I drop the brush and reach for my gun. But before I can get it out of the holster two big burly cops are on top of me. They grab hold of me and pull my arms behind me and handcuff me. I squirm violently trying to get out of their grasp, but it's no use they're much to big and strong.

I look in the doorway and see a woman cop coming down the hall toward me. She's heavy set with a round face—her hair pulled back in a tight bun. She walks into my apartment, stands directly in front of me, and says, "Sasha Cain. You're under arrest for the murders of Diego Sanchez and his five of his associates. We've already taken care of your associate Charley Bill Brown."

"What did you do to him," I shout at her.

"He chose not to come with us peacefully. But it doesn't matter, you're who we want." She speaks using a haughty tone.

She's still standing right in front of me and I utter, bitch, through clenched teeth. Then I spit in her face. She wipes my saliva away with the sleeve of her uniform, sneering at me. Then she back hands me hitting me across the face. As I'm still being held by the two muscle bound cops who first grabbed me.

"Get her out of here." She screams at them.

"You shouldn't have done this." I say to her.

"You," she yells at me. "Are in no position to threaten me or anybody else, anymore. Get her out."

I said nothing as they hauled me out of my apartment, down the steps and out the door. I hear her tell some of the other officers to search the apartment for the money. Good luck with that I say to myself. But this whole scene is Colin Lampoor's doing. I didn't bring him the money yesterday, so he had the cops come and arrest me. That little fucker gave me up to the cops, like he said he'd do.

Outside they shove me into the back of a police jeep that has a cage across the back. A large crowd has gathered around the building where I live. All of them with astonished looks on their faces. I hear them say, "They've arrested Sasha Cain."

FIVE

The ride to the police station took only about ten minutes. They stop and park the car and get out. The cop driving comes around and watches as his partner take me out of the jeep. He's standing close, I guess he figures I might try to do something to get away. They turn me around and start to walk me inside, but are stopped by the commander. Her car has pulled up behind the jeep I was in. She's out, walking toward us, and begins to immediately start barking orders at them.

She stands in front of us, her glare meeting mine, a look that tells me she's enjoying the hell out of this. She's arrested Sasha Cain. She says to them, "book her. Then when you're done doing that, take her to interrogation room nine, and come and get me. She's mine." I continue to glare at her, thinking how much fun it would be to kill her. The cops jerk me away as she turns her back on me and proceeds to walk on into the building.

Inside I see a lot of other cops, men and women, mingling around in this big room. Doing what looks like busy work or nothing at all. I can hear them talk about me as they bring me in and we walk through the room. All of them staring awkwardly at me. They all know who I am and my reputation, but their gawking at me makes me feel like a zoo animal.

I'm taken me into a room where there's guy that finger

prints me and takes a mug shot of me to put in this decades old computer. This is all useless and just a show, to make me believe that what they're doing is official. It's all bullshit. These guys are not real cops anyway, not it the sense that they're public servants like they once were. No, these clowns won't lift a finger to help anyone, for anything, unless they've paid their premiums.

Done pretending like they booked me, the two cops lead me out of that room and down a long hallway deep into the building. Which looks like it once long ago served as some sort of factory. Now it serves New Rottendamn's private buffoons with badges.

The halls are dimly lit, and old like the building. The old paint on the walls, which looks like some sort of gray is peeling badly off of the concrete block. We turn right and down another hallway that leads past several doors, I count at least ten in all. They lead me to one of the two on the end and on the left, with the number nine on it.

They unlock and open the door and shove me inside. Then one of them puts his hands on my shoulders, and forces me to sit down in a chair at a table. I notice the chair and table are both bolted to the floor, so they can't be used as weapons. He takes the cuffs off my hands behind me and then he cuffs me to the table. They leave without a word and I sit alone in interrogation room nine for what seems a longtime. It's a small dimly lit room with no windows and has the same drab gray paint that is peeling off the walls, like I saw in the hallway. I need to pee.

Then the door opens with what seems like a sudden burst. In walks the woman commander. She's not at all attractive. She's in her early fifties, I guess and she very much overweight. She walks around like she's important, making me want to laugh at her, but I don't.

She sits down in a chair across from me, she has a manila folder in her hand. I see her name plate says, Cmdr. Par. She's also accompanied into the room by a male armed guard. He's a big burly cuss, with arms bigger than my thighs, and of course he hasn't shaved. He stands by the door. And I think to myself what the hell is he in here for? Do they think I'm stupid enough to try escape or something? Besides, how could I do that, escape when I'm handcuffed to this table.

Commander Par looks at me with a smirk on her face, that says to me she can't wait to tie into Sasha Cain.

Then I say, "what did you do to Charley Bill? And I need to pee."

"We took care of him. You see, he didn't want to give up all that money he stole from Sanchez, so we took it from him. After he was dead."

"You killed him! You fucking..."

"Ah, ah, ah," she says. "Remember where you are." Then she laughs a dirty laugh.

I glare at her.

"So tell me, Sasha, where did you hide the money that you stole from Sanchez. And don't lie to me, we have it from credible witnesses that saw you and Charley Bill fill at least two bags with money. We checked your apartment, and didn't find it there. So where did you hide it, Sasha? It's only a minute detail we need to clear up, anyway."

"I thought you arrested me for murder. What happened to that all of a sudden.?"

"Well, that is what got you arrested, but we need to have you tell us where the money is."

It's funny how the money in this is so important. After all I did kill five people, which doesn't seem at all to matter to her that much. This whole thing reeks with Lampoor.

I look at her with a defiant little grin on my face, and say, "well if you want to know where it is, then find it yourself. Cause I ain't telling you a damn thing. Bitch."

I see the expression on her face change, after I said that. And without warning she reaches across the table and back hands me hard across my cheek again. Causing my head to jerk to the right. That's the second time she's hit me while I'm cuffed, I won't forget this.

"You sassy little bitch." She remarks.

Then she stands up and puts her hands on her hips, where she can look down on me, giving herself a feeling of superiority over me. "Sasha, where did you put that bag of goddamn money?"

She's leaning in close to me, enjoying her little show of being tough. She's close enough that if my hands were free I'd rip her throat out. I can smell her cheap perfume and her nicotine stained breath. She's disgusting. But I don't answer her.

"Tell me where it is, because, it's only a matter of time until I beat it out of you." She's still close and in my face.

"Didn't you hear me? I told you I'm not going to tell you. So go ahead and try to beat it out of me. Because I will not tell you where I put it," I said.

I can see she's boiling at me. Then she rights herself and draws back doubling up her fist, and hits me as hard as she can, in the side of my head.

"I've wanted to do that to you for longtime, Sasha Cain." She hisses, with an evil grin on her face.

After she said that, I thought that she was going to hit me again, but instead she ordered the guard, "take her down to piss. Then to holding block two and cuff her into a cell by herself. I don't want her roaming around in the cell I want keep her away from the other prisoners, she's too dangerous to trust."

Then she gets in my face again and says, "it doesn't matter about the cash you stole, sweetheart. I've been ordered to make arrangements to have you transported under guard to Westerville Prison tomorrow. You think I'm tough girly—you just wait until you get there," she says. "I know the warden there and she's tough as nails. She makes me look like a choir girl."

"Who ordered you to do that? Send me to Westerville. Lampoor?" I said to her defiantly. "I know he ordered it, the little bastard."

"It's none of your concern," she snaps. Choosing not to confirm what I know, as she leaves. But by not telling me she told me I'm right.

After she's gone a second guard comes into the room, and uncuffs me from the table. He doesn't cuff my hands behind me, but instead grabs me by the arm and jerks me ruffly through the door and out into the hallway to the restroom where he follows me in. He turns his back while I pee. I'm led back into the hallway and cuffed, then to a door that says, 'Stairs' and we go down one flight.

The hallway down here is very long and has holding cells on both sides. All filled with people, male and female. They begin to yell at us the minute they see us. Reaching through the bars trying to grab us as we walk by, which they can't do because the corridor that we're walking down is too wide for them to reach us.

The guards take me all the way to the end and open the last cell which is empty, and deposit me in it. Then another guard comes inside and cuffs me to the cell bars, per Commander Pars' instructions. They've at least attached me below the cross bar so I can sit on the floor.

The people in the cells are still yelling at the guards. We were followed by a third man, and the guards tell him not to put anyone in the cell with me. They close and lock the cell door, and leave to the continued yelling of the other prisoners in the adjacent cells. The third man yells back at them as loud as he can, "shut up!" Going so far as to take the stick he's carrying hitting the bars of some of the cells, where people are reaching through, causing them to jerk back not wanting to be hit.

After the guards leave the yelling suddenly stops, and the whole place grows so quiet you could hear a pin drop. The people in the crowded cells around me just look at me, gawking. Then one man whose leaning on the bars in the cell across from me says, "she must be real dangerous. They cuffed her to that empty cell by herself. Funny, she's just a little girl—she don't look dangerous at all." Then the yelling and screaming began again, as people looked at me and literally demanded me to tell them my name.

I'm sitting on the cold hard floor and I just look away, turning my head toward the wall. Not answering them.

Then a man in the cell next to mine pushes his way toward me and says, "go ahead sweetheart, tell them who you are. It won't hurt that much, now will it? Because I know your name."

"Then if you know it, why don't you tell them," I said, looking up at him.

"Okay I will. Folks," he begins, looking at me with a wry smile. "We are so honored to be in the company of Sasha Cain. The infamous enforcer of New Rotterdam. There, satisfied." He looks at me. Then he starts to turn away as everyone continues to stare at me from all the cells.

"Wait. How did you know my name," I ask? He stops for a second and looks over his shoulder.

"It's not important, Sasha."

"It is to me."

"Like I said, it's not all that important. I just know who you are, that's all."

"Okay. So what's your name?"

"That's not important to you either, but I guess it's okay to tell you. FYI it's Baines, Tyler Baines," he says.

Tyler Baines, that's the name Cooch gave me yesterday. He said the guy with the Seventh Streeters was named that.

I say, "my snitch told me that a guy with the Seventh Street gang has that name and my be looking for me. That true Mr. Baines? Were you working with them—looking to take me out?"

THE ALLEY OF EVIL

He says, "no I wasn't. Now I have a question for you."

"Yeah, what's that?"

"How did you get yourself arrested?"

"Well, it's really none of your business now Mr. Baines. But I was double-crossed, by my client."

He looks at me for a second then disappears behind all the people in the cell he's in. I yelled over to the cell trying to get him to talk to me some more, but he didn't do it. I stare at the cell for a few seconds and then look back at the people in the other cells, who are just staring at me, like I'm a zoo animal again.

******

Mealtime comes and none too soon. It dawns on me I haven't eaten at all, not since the day before. Meaning I'm starved out of my mind. I see the guards coming down the hall with people in aprons, that I assume are kitchen crews. They're carrying large servers, with bowls on them. I don't know what it is for sure, but it smells delicious. It takes a long time but they finally get to me, and when they do a guard unlocks the door to my cell and comes in. Before he does he hands his gun to his partner. He uncuffs me then then a man in an apron comes in and hands me a bowl full of soup and a small plate with a huge chunk of bread on it.

"What is it," I ask?

"Vegetable soup. Eat." The guard commands.

Then the man and the guard go back out of my cell, locking

the door. It's quiet, as everyone is busy consuming their soup. Which tastes as good as it smells. Lots of veggies and the bread is fresh.

I scarf down the first bowl of soup and ask the guard for seconds and a kitchen helper gives me another bowl, which I also consume. I'm now full to the gills, and think that even a cold blooded killer like me needs nourishment.

After eating I am again cuffed to the bars. Where I set down again and begin to drift off to sleep. But before I do I can hear some of the conversation about me from the people in the other cells. None of it good. I hear them call me names when they think I'm asleep. Some of the things they're saying about me is just plain crazy. I can handle being called names, but the stories they're telling about me are insane. Stories of how I killed ten people on one job, all by myself, which I have never done. Four/five maybe, but I always had Charley Bill's help.

Charley Bill. Dammit! I will never see him again, because these bastards killed him. He wasn't just my associate. He was my friend, too. He protected me with his life, many times, and loved doing it. He loved being Sasha Cain's associate, just as I loved him being that. As I sit here on this cold hard jail cell floor I think of him, and a tear sneaks down my cheek, that I wipe away. I will miss him. And if I get the chance, I will someday avenge his death.

The next morning my cell door opens, jolting me awake. A guard comes in and gets me up off the floor, and shakes me to wake me up more. I'm groggy and tired, still half asleep. I can't feel my right arm at all as he stands me up and cuffs my hands behind me.

    The people who were in the cells next to me are completely gone, including Mr. Tyler Baines. During the night I would wake briefly, and hear them being shuffled out by the guards. There are three men and one woman that have arrived to get me this morning, I figure to take me to Westerville.

    They let me pee before leading me back down the hallway and up the stairs. I was escorted into the restroom by the woman guard—a big burly gal. Who helped me pull my pants down. She seemed to delight looking at me, and enjoyed watching me piss even more, freaking me out. She seemed to be fighting the urge to touch my genitals. I would have kicked and fought her with all my might if she would have tried to do that.

    She helps me pull up my pants and we leave the restroom and she hands me over to two male guards. One grabs me tightly by the arm as I'm escorted out of the building. Where they put me in a police vehicle in the back just like the day before, and then we drove off and away from Rotterdam.

SIX

The trip up to Westerville shouldn't have taken all that long, but the two guards made a stop to lollygag, at a bar/cafe with a couple of hookers. This made the trip a lot longer.

When we stop, I tell them that I have to pee again. They look at each other and shrug. Then one relents and grabs my arm and pulls me out of the car. And instead of taking me inside the cafe to the restroom, the idiot leads me into the woods behind it. There he takes the cuffs off of me and tells me to drop my pants and pee. I did as he instructed me, I had to, before I wet in my pants. He didn't watch me. When I was done he put the cuffs back on me, and returned me to the car. They locked it and went into the bar. I had seen the two girls waving at them, as we arrived.

For two hours I sat in the car handcuffed, as it got colder and colder inside. Finally, I see them come out of the place, with the two women. They evidently told them about me, because they immediately brought them over to the car. They all stand outside stupidly looking in—gawking at me. I'm shivering and freezing cold. My teeth are chattering and these fools treat me like a zoo animal. Wanting to show these hookers Sasha Cain.

The women are making stupid faces through the glass.

Which included pursing their lips, and doing shame, shame, with their fingers. Shaking their heads—cooing at me like they were scolding a ten year old kid. I tried not to laugh at the stupid bitches or look at them, but it was impossible not, too. I even made a sudden motion toward the window, causing one of them to jump back from the car, as she feigned being frightened. Then they all laughed at me like the stupid fools they are and walked away.

With the two cops, or guards, or whatever they are, having gotten their juices off. They leave the women bidding them good-bye, with big hugs and kisses. A fake display of affection that makes me want to gag—causing me to turn my head.

Before we proceed on our way to Westerville, one of the men walks behind the car and opens the trunk, then closes it. I turned around as best as I could to see what he was doing. When I see him I notice he's carrying some sort of bag. The other man opens the door and reaches in and grabs me by the arm tightly, yanking me out of the car. His grip so tight it hurt. I yell at him and tell him. He yells at me to shut up. Then the man with the bag puts it over my head.

"Why are you doing this?" I question, trying to wriggle free of them and what they're doing to me—not wanting the hood over my head.

"This is where you don't get to see where we're taking you. Miss Enforcer," he says. Mocking me. They laugh at his comment, as he forces the hood onto my head.

"But…" I start to say. And again, he yells at me to shut up. Then he shoves me back into the car and I fall over on my side. I right myself as I hear them get in and start the car. I feel us moving as we proceed to this Westerville prison that I've only heard stories about. But what I wonder, is what its purpose is, really. I know what prisons are for, but why is this one so much a secret that they don't want me to see where it's really located. At this point I don't even know what direction we're headed in. My senses have gone completely bonkers right now, because of the hood on my head.

Some time passes before I feel the car stop and hear the window go down. I hear what sounds like big metal gates open. Then after a few seconds we are on our way until I feel the car stop again. This time I hear the locks on the doors release. The two guards get out, and say nothing to each other, nor to me.

One opens the door in the back and reaches in and grabs my arm, clutching it tightly again, but not as hard as before and pulls me out. Then he yanks me to my right with the hood still on my head, and we proceed, walking into what I assume is Westerville Prison.

I'm led through doors and into a building. I know this because it's warm in here, indicating that the place still has heat that works. There is still no talking as we walk for a long way. We get on an elevator and go up, the elevator stops and get off. We walk some more, then I hear what sounds like doors opening, and the man holding my arms yanks me hard in that direction, through them. Inside wherever I am, they finally pull the hood off of my head. I stand for a minute, blinking my eyes so I can see more clearly.

I see that I'm in a large room filled with other women all

sitting at school cafeteria style tables. All of them are looking at me. The guard takes the cuffs off of me to my amazement. Making me think that there can't be any other person, man or woman in this room that is more dangerous than I am. He pushes me toward a table off to the side, and all alone. He puts his hands on my shoulders and forces me to sit down. Then before they leave, two female guards walk from the front of the room to replace them, standing close to me. They're both armed with semi-automatic rifles, as are all the other guards I see. I count twelve in all.

Then I think about the location I'm in. At a table with no one else, and it's off by itself. Making me wonder is this all a setup? Does someone know that I was coming here? I guess I'm going to find out whether I want to or not.

After a few seconds looking around I notice a you woman about my age at an adjacent table. She looks at me briefly, and I look back at her. She's pretty I think.

All eyes still are on me and have been since I came into the room. I feel like a zoo animal again. The girl who first looked at me, looks again. I nod to her and she nods back.

There must be at least two hundred women sitting at tables in prison garb. As I scan the room I notice something. No one in the room is older than me. Some look to be much younger, which is strange. They're all races white, black, brown, so that doesn't seem different. But it makes me curious as to what this place really is. Where are the older women prisoners? Don't they have them here?

Soon the doors at the front open and everyone turns their

attention away from me and in that direction. A heavy set woman, appears and walks in to the room. She reminds me of Commander Par of the Rottendamn cops. Same stature and just as obese, maybe even more so. She marches with authority over to a podium and stands there pausing for a minute, while everyone notices her. She looks over the room trying to eyeball each of us, like she's sizing us up. She seems to not want to start speaking until she has everyone's attention.

She looks in my direction, and I notice she lingers just a bit longer on me, with a slight smirk on her face. She of course is the one who knew I was coming here, and she knows who I am. I am at this table to serve her purpose. Just what that is, I'm not sure of yet.

"I am Warden Cynthia Behar." She begins speaking, sternly and bluntly. "From now on, women, I will tell you when to eat, when to sleep, when to shower, and yes, even when to have sex. You are prisoners after all. You have no rights except when I say you do. You will always do my bidding whether you want to or not. That, women, goes with being a prisoner. Some of you will be here only a short time." *Hmm. I think.* "Some of you will stay longer. Do not cross me, or you will pay the consequences. When you talk to me you will always address me, as yes warden." Then she finishes with the usual bullshit warning of make sure you understand me, because I will not let insubordination go unpunished.

Fuck her.

Finished with her little diatribe, and rather than release us to go back and be locked up in our cells. She walks away from the podium and steps off the platform. She begins to walk slowly around the room, up and down the aisles, looking at everyone. Like she's dressing us down with her look, which frightens some of the girls because I see them look away. That's what she wants, to frighten them. Again making me wonder. Wouldn't women prisoners look back at her in defiance?

It's obvious, she's looking for an easy mark to make an example of before she lets us go. She wants to prove to everyone how tough she is. And she's doing it all to get at me.

The room is dead silent as I watch her. And from time to time I catch her glancing over at me out of the corner of her eye. I still have my street clothes on having just arrived in time for this little get together. Everyone else is in prison attire. Tan jackets, like a blouse that hangs loose and pants the same color. Both are drab in appearance and not intended to win a fashion show. The girls all have a number on the jacket over their left breast that signifies something. It all seems so dehumanizing.

After a few minutes the warden stops at the table next to mine and glowers down at the young woman who had looked at me when I first sat down. The girl looks away from Behar wanting her to move along. But she doesn't, she lingers, then tells the girl to stand up. She does so, snapping up like she's at attention.

"What's your name? Five, six, six, three." She orders the girl.

"T...Tori," she says in a small voice. The girl is scared to death. Trying to free herself from Behar's intention to humiliate her.

"Tori what? Speak up, girl." Behar orders her again, this time loudly so everyone in the room can hear her.

"T...Tori Nicks, Warden," she says, just a little louder.

Behar gets close to her and says, "you just got here didn't you?"

"Yes, Warden, yesterday." The girl Tori responds in fearful voice. Looking away.

"Well what crime have you committed that got you here? Tori Nicks." The bitch is mocking the poor kid.

"I...I stole something, Warden."

"Stole something. What did you steal? Tell us." She demands.

"A loaf of bread and some meat to feed me and my little brother, warden."

"So you're nothing but a common little thief. That right Tori Nicks?"

"No warden, it wasn't like that."

Oops, wrong thing to say to her, Tori.

"So you're disputing what I'm saying?"

"No warden," Tori says, fearfully.

She's no match for Behar, but the woman is not done berating her in front of everyone. Just so she can get at me.

"You have dark skin Tori Nicks, just what the hell are you?" Behar sneers getting into the girl's face.

"I'm...I'm native, warden," Tori stammers.

"So what you're telling me is that you're an Indian, and a thief. That right."

You mean, bitch.

THE ALLEY OF EVIL

"No warden that's not what I meant."

"Then what did you mean? Spit it out girl."

All Tori could do is look down. She's scared to death.

"So you're disputing my assessment of the fact that you're a common thief, and a savage. Is that true, Tori Nicks?" She grabs Tori under the chin. The girl is crying, and I'm sitting there helpless to do anything about how this Cynthia Behar is demeaning this poor girl. I look around the room and many of the girls are not watching this, it's to painful for them.

The girl tries to shake her head no, and at the same time free herself from Behar's grasp. And it's really me she wants to challenge, not Tori. She's using her to bait me. Tori is being used to get the ball rolling. She releases her chin hold on her, then draws back her left hand, backhanding Tori with a hard blow that knocks her to the floor. She's laying in front of me, at my feet. Tori looks up at her through tears and says, "I meant no disrespect to you."

"You challenged my authority," She says, leaning over the girl. "What did I just say up front?" Then she draws back her right leg, she's wearing heavy military style boots with a steel toe. She kicks Tori, hard in the stomach. Thus causing her to cry out in pain. I hear the other women in the room gasp and groan as Behar does this. The guards just look ahead, not willing to stop her.

Tori is laying at my feet weeping loudly, and holding her stomach, as Behar is readying to kick her again. Without thinking I get up from where I'm sitting and bend down to aid Tori. That's when I feel Behar's huge boot come into the side of my head, sprawling me onto the floor.

She finally got what she wanted. Me. I look up at her, trying as quickly as I can to gather my wits about me after being kicked in the side of the head.

She turns to the room full of women to gloat, "prisoners, meet Sasha Cain, better known as the enforcer. She interfered, and now I will make an example of her and Tori Nicks."

I shake off the pain and get up quickly to go and aid Tori, again—to help her up. I see Behar's boot to kick me in the head again. But this time I'm ready for it. I grab her leg, forcing it up, pushing hard, and sending her flailing violently backwards and into a table behind her. She lands hard. Then the two guards who were standing by me make a move, but I'm too quick. I jump up and shove one into the other, causing them to go down in a pile. Now all of the women in the room are standing and watching. I look for Tori, she's up and she hits a female guard that is trying to join the fight.

Behar has gotten up and grabs me from behind. I elbow her in her gut and she doubles. I turn and grab her hair and throw her forward head first, against the wall. She goes down again. The two women guards are up, and get behind me grabbing my arms. Then male guards arrive, to help subdue me. Behar is up, she turns around and locks her glare on me. She's furious as well as embarrassed. She walks toward me, and before she lets the guards take me away she gut punches me several times as hard as she can. Causing me to grimace in pain. I can see that a guard is holding on to Tori, she's okay.

Then Behar, orders the guards, "take this fucking little

bitch downstairs to solitary, and while your at it put that savage in with her."

On the way out I see Behar glaring at me, and I somehow manage a sneer at her, and say, "Fucked up that little party for you didn't I? Cynthia."

Then she shouts, angrily at me, pointing her finger, "I will be dealing with you, Sasha Cain, for what you did here today. Count on it."

Tori and I are led quickly out of the room and down a long hallway to an elevator that goes down one levels. The cells down here are empty, I could see there are only three.

The guards shove Tori and I hard into a cell, causing us both to stumble forward, nearly falling down. The door closes with a loud clank. Making me think. If someone is in here with me then it's not really solitary confinement. Is it?

SEVEN

The cell is small, no more than twelve feet by seven feet. It's like every room I've been in the last two days, no windows, and dimly lit. This place though has a musty smell to it and is spartan as hell. There's a wash basin, a toilet, and a cot that is attached to the wall, for one person to sleep on. A small desk and one chair. Obviously this cell is meant for only one, but this one has two occupants.

Tori and I set down next to each other on the cot.

"You okay," she asks me? "She gut punched you pretty hard."

"Yeah, I'm good. But are you okay? That bitch kicked you with those big boots."

"It just knocked the wind out of me. And she kicked you, too, in the head."

"I have a hard head," I say. Then we chuckle.

I looked at her and then offered my hand. "By the way I'm, Sasha Cain.

"Tori Nicks."

"Nice to meet you." We both said at the same time, then giggled.

"I've heard of you," she says.

"Well I hope that doesn't scare you."

"Na...I want to thank you for sticking up for me up there. I didn't know how to handle that kind of situation at all."

"You did great, you popped that one bitch, and Behar was baiting you to get at me. I played right into her hands. But I wasn't about to let her abuse and humiliate you like that. I had to do something. Anyway we have the satisfaction of knowing that we spoiled the hell out of her little party. She knew I was coming here and couldn't wait to show me how tough she is, and I made sure it didn't work out for her."

"Are you scared of her?"

"No, not at all. Someday, maybe I'll kill her."

Tori laughs, "I cannot wait for that."

I smile. "So what you were telling about how you got in here, was true."

"Yeah it is. Me and my little brother were starving and I stole some bread and meat from this butcher and bakery shop. And the man who owns the place called the cops. He told them I was stealing from him all the time, and I wasn't Sasha. I asked him if he could spare some food for me and my brother and he refused. He said gruffly. Go get a job and pay like everybody else, that he's not a charity. So I took the stuff. Maybe stealing is wrong, but we were hungry."

"What happened to your brother?"

"I don't know. The cops came and hauled me off while he wasn't home. I'm so worried about him."

"So let me get this straight. You were just brought here against you will, for trying to feed your brother and yourself. No court hearing."

"Yeah. I can't afford food let along those stupid premiums."

"Me neither."

I set and pause after I listened to her tell me her story of how she got sent here and said, "Do you have any relatives that he could have gone to."

"An uncle, but he's not a very nice person, but if Davy went there he'd treat him okay."

"Let's hope that happened." I paused and looked at her. "How old are you?"

"Twenty-three. You?"

"Twenty-four."

"You know you may not be scared of Behar, but I am."

I turn to her, "don't be. I want you to stay close to me. I doubt she's stupid enough to try that shit she just did again so soon. And remember it's me she wants to make an example of, not you. I can take anything she dishes out."

"What if she tries anyway, to do something to me."

"Then I'll kill the bitch right in front of everyone. It'll take the strength of three male guards to pry my hands from her fat neck, and then they may not be able to do it."

"Why are you doing this for me, Sasha? I mean nothing to you after all. And we just met under very crazy circumstances."

"I don't know why I'm doing it, honestly. But I want you to just know that I am, and I want to do it for you."

I pause and look at her. "Tori, I ain't a good girl by any stretch of the imagination. I can kill someone at the drop of a hat. I want you to know that, so does Behar. She knows I call myself a bounty hunter but the moniker that I have, *The Enforcer.*"

"Yeah?"

"It fits me to a tee."

She looks at me, not fearing me at all, but with an admiring look. "I'm not afraid of you at all, even though I know all that about you."

"I don't want you to be afraid of me Tori. We gotta survive while we're here no matter what. And if that means you and I stick together, then we will. So stick close by me, even if she gets her revenge with me, which she will."

"She was pretty mad at you and me. How long do you think she'll keep us in here?"

"I don't know. She wants us in here together in the hope that we'll start to argue and hate each other. She going on the fact we don't really know each other, and will not get along."

We look at each other after I say that. "Na! Ain't gonna happen." Then we giggled again, obviously starting to enjoy each other's company in spite of our circumstances.

"Besides like you said, if we did that we'd be playing right into her hands," Tori says.

I shake my head in agreement, then I suddenly think of something that dawned on to me. I look at Tori and put my fingers over my mouth, making a soft, shush. She looks at me mystified as to what is going on and I mouth, "bugs."

"Bugs?" She questions me, in a soft whisper.

"Electronic listening devices," I whisper back.

Then we get up off of the cot, and I get underneath it and

run my hands along the bottom of it everywhere, covering every inch of it. Tori is up, too, looking at everything she can. Then I find it. Near the front of the bed. I pull it off and get up and show it to Tori. Then I walk over and throw it in the toilet, and flush. Then we look at each other and break out into a loud boisterous girly laugh. That has us both in stitches thinking about old iron boots, sitting in her office listening to the bug being flushed down the toilet.

"You think she' been listening to us all along?"

"I'm sure of it," I said. "And I'm sure the stuff she heard us talk about has rankled her ass even more. I hope it did."

"That was funny, Sasha."

"Yeah it was, I can't wait to do it again."

We look at each other and laugh again, and sit back down on the cot next to each other, and we are quiet for a few seconds each of us alone with our thoughts. I just met this girl and we seem to be becoming fast friends. And I'm questioning why I am doing what I am for her, just like she did. And the truth is like I said to her I can't answer it, because I don't know why. I protected her this morning, and now am taking a liking to her as she seems to be with me.

I think the reason I protected her, is she doesn't belong here. She needs a strong friend, me, to make sure she survives while she's here. Tori isn't at all like me, and if I have to protect her then I will. As long as she doesn't object to me doing so.

And of course there is our situation here with the warden. We, both of us really didn't get off on too solid of footing, with her. But it was all her doing, she provoked that situation. I know she's fuming and embarrassed after what happened in the chow hall this noon. I embarrassed the hell out of her, rather than the other way around. It was her intention the minute I walked into that room, to make an example of me and it backfired on her. She will have to rectify that situation, she has to. She'll have to regain her stature of authority with the other girls that are locked up here, as the supreme authority. And the only way she can do that is to get back at me, by making an example of me.

Tori looks at me and says, "can I ask you something?"
"Shoot."
"Did you see the other girls in this prison? I mean all of them are about our age, or younger even. Like, where are the old gals here? There's got to be old gals that are prisoners here, too. Don't you think?"
"Yeah, you noticed that same thing. I looked around the room and all I saw was young women, girls even. A lot of them looked like teenagers. So yeah, it makes me wonder what may be going on here."
"And another thing. When we got into that fight, and got bashed, I could hear the gasps from them. You'd think that prison gals would be tougher than that."
"Makes me wonder, Tori, what kind of prison are we in," I said. Then I aked her. "Question did you see me when I first came into the chow hall?"
"No, I didn't turn around when you came in. I kept my head down,"
"Well, the reason I ask you is, the guards that brought me here, put a bag over my head about halfway up. So I couldn't see

where they brought me, and I was wondering did they do that to you?"

"No, they didn't do that to me, but I was brought up in a van with two other girls and no windows in it. So I couldn't see out and I have now idea where this place is."

"Yeah, me neither, that's why I asked you. I wonder what all the secrecy is about the location of this place."

"I does make you wonder."

"Well we're gonna be here for awhile so I'm sure we will find out."

She looks at me shaking her head in agreement. Then asks me, "so how do you want to handle this?"

"Handle what?"

"I'm talking about sleeping arrangements I'm thinking about taking a nap. This bed is built for only one you know."

"I know, you can have it, I'll just sleep on the floor."

"Nonsense," she argues. "You will not. We can make this work. Come on, let's take a nap and see how it works. I'll sleep here and you can sleep next to me."

"You sure?"

"Of course I'm sure, I wouldn't be suggesting it if I didn't think we could do it."

She already has the blanket that was folded at the foot of the cot, and is pulling it over her. I get in next to her, and lay down, she shares the blanket. I'm on the outside, she's next to the wall. We're on our sides facing each other.

"You're cold," I say.

"Yeah, it's clammy down here, Sasha."

"Yeah, you're right about that."

"Are you cold?"

"No, not really."

After a brief pause she says, "So how is it? I mean, are you okay with this?"

"Oh, yeah," I say. "I thought it would be more uncomfortable than it is. Especially for you."

"It's not comfy, but it's the best we can do. I wasn't about to let you sleep on the floor."

"I would have, you know."

"I know you would." She says with a soft little smile that I just seem to already take in. What's the matter with me? She's pretty. I've never looked at a girl like I'm looking at Tori, and we just met.

"Have you ever slept with a girl before," she asks?

"Nope. This is my first time."

"You?"

"Yeah I had a female lover once. You straight?"

"I always thought that about myself, but.... I already like you, Tori."

"I like you, too, Sasha."

I look at her and she's looking back at me with her beautiful big brown eyes separated by a little turned up nose.

I want to kiss her!

"So are you nervous about sleeping next to me?"

"Kinda, but it doesn't have anything to do with you, it's about me, I've never been friendly or close to anyone, let alone slept with them for any length of time."

"I understand," she says. "The enforcer doesn't have time for relationships."

"Yeah, but it's not to say that I don't want them. I do."

"I know that already."

She's smiling at a girl she only met and is taking a nap with her, locked in a solitary jail cell in God knows where. And that girl is a killer—yet she's so understanding.

She closes her eyes, relaxing and I close my eyes, too, but not all the way. I want to watch her fall asleep and listen to her soft rhythmic breathing. She has her right arm thrown over me. I watch her, opening and closing my eyes, looking at her.

I still want to kiss her. Why am I thinking that? I've never in my life wanted to kiss another girl. But I want to kiss Tori and I can't explain why.

******

The next morning the kitchen crew puts breakfast in the opening in the bars, just as they did dinner the night before. Tori and I are awake—having been frightened awake by the alarm that went off in our cell. It's like a fire alarm that makes a loud shrill beeping noise, with a flashing red light. We jumped like we were shocked at the sound, both of us not used to being aroused in that manner.

When the food appears we are setting up on the cot next to each other, close, shoulders touching, feet on the edge of the cot, with our knees to our chest. Talking.

"So how was it," She says quietly, looking at me with a wry

smile. "Or shall I say, sleeping with a girl, and me, since I'm very much a girl."

I pause before I answer her. "I liked it, though I'm sure it wasn't very comfortable for you. Both yesterday afternoon and last night."

"Me! What about you? I'm surprised you didn't fall on the floor, or I didn't push you off. I've been told I sleep restlessly." She giggles.

"You didn't last night. You were…just, quiet all night."

"I wonder what they brought us for breakfast?" She says, turning her attention to the food.

"I'll go see," I said. I go get the food and go back over to the cot. "Let's see a couple of sweet rolls and some juice."

"I'm hungry," she says.

"Me, too."

I hand her a roll and a cup of juice. I set back down next to her, we're quiet for a few minutes as we consume our food. Both of us starved.

Tori asks me, "Sasha, you think we'll ever get out of here?"

"Do you mean this cell or Westerville?"

"Both, really."

"I do, eventually. It'll just take me a little time to figure it all out. But trust me, we will."

"I'm finding out that's something that I need to do already."

"What's that?"

"Trust you."

"You sure, because it can be…well, dangerous."

"If your being dangerous gets us out of this hell hole,

sooner, then I'm willing to take that chance. Besides what choice do I have? I would not survive a week in here without you. I know that even now, and I'd be kidding myself if I thought I could. I'm no match for Behar."

"I know that too, and no matter what happens to me, I want you to stay strong, Tori. Don't ever let that bitch beat you. Whether I'm around or not."

"I hope that doesn't happen, Sasha," she says. With fear in her voice.

"It won't. I will not let that happen if I can help it." I try to reassure her.

She looks at me and shakes her head.

After we finished eating I took the empty tray back over to the slot in the bars, and came back to sit on the cot next to Tori, close, shoulders touching again.

I look at her and reach for her right hand. She doesn't resist, taking my fingers in hers as they entwine tightly to mine, holding on. I say, "you asked me if I liked sleeping with you last night. I want you to know I liked it a lot. I never, thought, ever, of bedding down with another woman for any reason. But it was so nice being next to you. I want you to know…I…wanted to kiss you, but I didn't want you to reject me, since we only met yesterday. And at the same time I was fighting the urge to do it. I'm confused about doing that, you know? I have never in my life wanted to kiss a girl."

"But you could have kissed me. I mean, I wouldn't have rejected you. I think we already know where we're headed—the two of us."

"I just hope you're patient with me if we go down that road together. I'm really new at this type of thing. Like I said earlier I've never been close to anyone. Ever."

"I will be. But what about that guy you talked about yesterday. Uh…"

"Oh, Drago. No. No, no." I laugh out loud. "Drago means nothing to me. He was just a toy, somebody to play with when I got bored. I had no feeling for him whatsoever, other than the thrill of the orgasm."

I pause.

"Anyway you're way more experienced at this relationship stuff than me."

"Me? No. Like you I've had a couple of flings, one with a girl the other a guy. I will admit I was pretty sweet on them, both, at one time. I was pretty close to the girl. The guy not so much."

"What happened?"

"It turned out he wasn't so nice. If I didn't give into his wishes he'd get pissed off and beat me."

"I wish I'd have been there for you then."

"Me, too."

It's funny I think, but for just these few hours we've been together, it's like we weren't in this cell at all. We're just a couple of girls getting to know each other, and at the same time realizing our need for each other. Not just because of our fast developing close friendship for each other, but also because our very lives in this wretched place depends on it.

SEVEN

It's nearing noontime when we hear the door to the cell open and two muscle guards barge in, both of them armed. "Stand up, both of you." One of them orders us sternly. They're followed into the cell by a third guard, a woman, and I see she has two pairs of cuffs.

We stand up.

The guard growls at us, "turn around."

Then the woman handcuffs us both, arms behind our backs. The male guards grab hold of our arms tightly, causing Tori to grimace, and we are pushed toward the door and out into the hallway.

"Can I ask what this is about?" I say.

"Just shut up, Cain, and walk. No talking," he orders.

They lead us to the elevator, without saying a word between them. We ride it up and then they turn us to the right toward the chow hall. I look at Tori and she at me, both of us thinking—what is up, now.

I don't like the feeling of this one bit and I know she doesn't either. I can see the fear all over her face. I figure it's Behar's time to get her revenge with me, I'm just not sure what she has planned. I am sure she's been chewing on the events that happened the morning before. She's had plenty of time—all night in fact to build up the courage to confront me.

I know I can handle anything that she throws at me but I worry if something serious were to happen to me, I fear for Tori. What would happen to her? I hope she has no plans to harm her.

As we're led down the hallway I can see that we are headed straight for the mess hall. A guard opens the doors, and we go in. The place is full of all the other girls, just like yesterday morning when I arrived. They all turn to look as we walk in, and I feel like that zoo animal again. The guards walk us to the front of the room where Behar is standing, wearing that smirk on her face. I notice, too, that she has leather gloves on.

There are two guards on the platform that she spoke from yesterday, but no podium, just a sturdy metal chair. The guard that is holding Tori stops, and the one that has me takes me up to the metal chair on the platform. He turns me around, so I'm facing everyone in the room. He takes my cuffs off me and puts his hands on my shoulders and pushes me down onto the chair. Then he grabs my arms again and yanks them hard behind the chair, locking each hand to the back of it. At the same time I hear Behar tell another guard to shackle my legs to the chair.

She glares at me and I do the same to her, trying to muster all the defiance I can, as it is, being chained to a chair. I figure that she's found a way to make an example of me. I look over at Tori, tears filling her eyes, as she's begun to cry.

Behar looks at her first, then at all the women seated at the tables, and throws herself immediately into one of her verbal outbursts. She draws her authority and superiority from situations like this. She knows she's creating tension with her crap. She has to do this to regain her stature as the authority of Westerville. But just the same she loves this type of situation that she alone creates. It makes the bitch feel important, like Lampoor.

"This morning I have brought you all in here to witness what will happen to any of you when you dispute and disrupt my authority here at Westerville, like she did yesterday. You, all of you," she says, looking at Tori, then to me. "You all saw her total and absolute insubordinate attitude for me yesterday morning. She attacked me. And today we are all in here so I can show you how I'm going to rectify that situation. Let what I am about to do to her, be a lesson to all of you. To never, and I mean never, do what she, Sasha Cain, chose to do yesterday morning." She looks at me and says, "and for that, you are going to pay."

She gets in my face, close, and says, "Sasha Cain, are you ready to admit your guilt as to what you did yesterday? You challenged my authority and blatantly assaulted me for no reason, in front of all of them. There by instigating a brawl, for which you are now, about to be punished?"

"You know what I think? Cynthia." I use her name to show disrespect for her. I hate the bitch. She's nothing but a bully.

"I think you want to beat the hell out of me, no matter what I say. You, started that fight, not me. You were humiliating Tori in front of all of them, to get at me. You knew I was coming here, and you did all that to show everyone how tough you are. Like you're doing right now. So, fuck you, Cynthia!"

After I say that I spit in her pugnacious face, my saliva

splattering all over her. She looks at me, sneering, teeth clenched in anger. She wipes it off her face with her uniform sleeve. Readying herself to castigate me for something she started. I could see her enjoying the anger building in her, and I knew it was about to be unleashed at me. I embarrassed her again.

She knows I'm not afraid of her, by my defiant answer and what I did yesterday. I can take anything from her and she wants very badly to show me that I can't. She's making a point to show everyone she can hurt Sasha Cain. It's like she's making it her mission.

She get close to me and says in a low voice, not audible to the rest of the room. "You fucking little bitch, I'm going to beat the hell out of you. And there's not a damn thing, I mean nothing you can do to stop me. And you know what? I'm going to enjoy every fucking minute of it. You're right, I knew your were coming here, and I cannot wait to make you pay for what you did yesterday. I've waited a longtime to do this."

I glanced over at Tori—being held onto by a muscle guard. Then I felt Behar drive the gloved fist of her right hand into the left side of my face, as hard as she can. Causing my head to jerk violently toward my right shoulder. Just then she drives her left hand into my right cheek. She has brass knuckles on under the gloves. I can feel them when she hits me. She slams me in the face again repeating those blows—quickly bloodying my nose and mouth. Whack! Whack! I hear the popping noise as the brass knuckles crack against my face with all the force she can gather. I feel the searing pain they leave as it streaks though my face, not having time to recover, before she hits me again.

NANCY HOWARD

I hear Tori screaming in horror, "Stop! Stop! Please Stop!"

Behar ignores her pleas as she continues her abuse of me. Now she's slamming her fists into the side of my head. One blow right after another, she hits me again and again. So many blows I lose count. I'm loosing consciousness. My lip and nose are bleeding and my eyes are blackened. She's enjoying beating the hell out of me. I'm defenseless against her—handcuffed to this chair.

I'm slipping away fast, I can barely hear Tori screaming at her, "Stop it! Stop it!" She screams. "Stop it, before you kill her!

I can vaguely hear the gasps of horror from the women seated in the room, as they witness her unchecked brutality against me. Many of them, too, saying stop. I hear Tori weeping loudly. I'm almost completely out.

For a split second I thought she was going to beat me to death in front of all of them, but then she of course she won't do that. She needs me to be her trophy—her whipping girl. She wants all of the others to see that they should not challenge her authority. If she can do this to Sasha Cain, she can do it to them, too.

Just when I think she is going to kill me, I faintly hear a man's voice say, "Stop it, Cynthia. She's had enough."

Finally she relents. I'm battered and beaten to a pulp. My head hangs down. I'm too weak from the beating she just gave me to hold it up. Through my daze I hear her say with haughty arrogance in her voice, "okay. I'll stop. I'll stop, but only after you all applaud and show me the appreciation I deserve. After beating this little piece of scum half out of her wits."

She pauses and then yells at them, "applaud me or I will strap Tori Nicks to this chair and do the same to her."

Then I hear one, then two, followed by all of them joining in. But the clapping is rhythmic, not meant to be an applause of appreciation for what she just did to me. They're mocking her.

She screams at them at the top of her lungs. Stop it! Goddammit, stop it!"

Then I hear her order the guards, "unshackle the little bitch, and take her and her girlfriend back to their cell." I hear her say to Tori, "you two will stay in that cell together until you both rot there. Get them the hell out of my sight."

I feel them unshackle me from the chair. I can't walk, I'm to badly beaten. I feel one of the big muscle guards pick me up and throw me over his shoulder and carry me back down to our cell, like I'm a sack of potatoes. I'm in and out of consciousness, along the way, and the next thing I hear is the door to the cell opening. The guard carries me in and flops me onto the cot. I land hard on my side.

I feel Tori roll me over on my back and I lay there, unable to move. She sits down next to me, weeping, holding my hand. Her face, horrified at what she saw Behar do to me. She looks at me with my bloodied nose, swollen lip and eyes that are black. We clasp our hands and hold tight to each other. Then she leans over and kisses me on the forehead. And I manage a slight smile. "Stay strong." I whisper to her.

She says through her tears, "I will."

Then something plops on the floor that came though the food slot. Someone has given us an ice pack and some sort of pain medication. She goes over and gets it then one of the towels and puts water on it. She comes back and gently cleans my nose and lips and runs it across my face. Then she gets the ice and puts it on my face and wraps the towel around it.

She leans her head into mine, and kisses me gently on the forehead again, "I say thank you."

She says, "I won't leave you Sasha."

I manage a slight smile and then I pass out.

THE ALLEY OF EVIL

EIGHT

I wake up and look around the room, opening and closing my eyes, looking at the ceiling. I'm still dazed. I try to set up but my head won't let me, I get dizzy, like I've been on a merry-go-round too long and I can't get off. Tori notices this immediately and reaches over. "No, no, no, no," she says, "Take it easy."

"I look at her, I know my eyes are still glazed, I ask weakly, "how long was I out?"

"Two days. I think she gave you a concussion. The bitch."

"You, been taking care of me all this time."

"Yeah, she said, "I wanted to take care of you Sasha. But we, you and I could rot in this cell. Though yesterday the guards allowed me to go out into the yard—but by myself. That's the only time, I haven't been in here with you. Except when I took a shower."

I reach for her hand and she takes it.

"I wish I could be more help to you," she says, compassionately.

"You are helping. You're here…with me. Thank you for not abandoning me."

"I won't leave you, Sasha. I want to take care of you."

"It's the same here, I won't leave you either. If the situation was reversed I would take care of you, too."

"I know you would," she says. Then kisses me on the cheek.

I lay there and look at her, still a dazed. But even injured like I am, I can see that Tori is a beautiful girl. Her native black hair is long and flowing, she has high cheek bones, and of course that turned up nose that isn't Indian at all. She's an inch or so shorter than me, with big brown eyes, and soft lovely brown skin. And curves, she has lots of soft curves, everywhere. Not like me and my boyish angular figure.

I look at her, and I'm beginning to realize why she and I are hooking up. And it's not just out of need by being locked in here. We sincerely like each other. Even in our present quandary we enjoy being with one another.

It's still a completely foreign idea to me that I may be falling in love with another girl. I question why? I'm still confused about that, but even now, I want her with me. As she sits next to me holding my hand, it dawns on me, that we, she and I, are all we each have. We are drawing each other into the other, closer, and closer, after just three days. We care about each other. I care about her already, and she does me. Something I have never had anyone do for me, ever—especially so quickly.

"You know," she says. "Her beating you like she did didn't turn out the way she wanted it to."

"How do you mean?"

"Well, if it was her plan she to get everyone's attention, she certainly did that. But not the way she intended. Instead of making an example of you, by beating up on you like she did. It only served to embarrass her further. Her brutality against you only made her out to be more of a monster in everyone's eyes. After she told the guards to get us out of there and back down here, she just turned and quietly walked away. I watched her Sasha, she grew quiet. Like she was sorry for it all."

"It serves her right—the bitch," we chuckle. "You know Tori there's got to be a reason for them keeping you and me, locked up in here and away from from the other women. They don't want us near them to talk to them.

"I thought about that, too. Like they don't want us talking to them because the other girls might tell us something that Behar thinks we shouldn't hear."

"Exactly. That's what I'm thinking."

She's raised up and leaning on her right elbow, I m next to the wall. She smiling and then leans into kisses me on the lips. I kiss her back.

"I've wanted to kiss you too," she says.

I smile and say, "that was so nice. Now if you don't mind I need to go to sleep again. Sorry."

"That's okay, I understand," she says. "Sleep and get well." Then she kisses me again. I smile, even though my eyes are closed, in my mind I know she's smiling at me.

I drifted off to sleep, I have a concussion and it will take time for me to get back to normal. And I'm doing it with only Tori's help, she's in here with me, and I'm very thankful that she is. During this time we get our meals through the cell slot and when I have to go, Tori is right there for me helping me every step of the way.

******

The next two days go by very slowly, and even though we like each other, a lot, this cell is small. It's built to hold one person, not two. So boredom sets in easily, especially for Tori. I'm still sleeping a lot because of the concussion, and she does, too, leaving her especially not doing a lot of sleeping at night. During those two days she goes out in the yard, for exercise time, but not with the other girls. When she comes back inside, she tells me that she hasn't seen hide nor hair of Behar.

This morning Tori and I make our way down to the showers under guard as always. She holds onto me giving me assistance walking. I'm still unsteady on my feet and get dizzy if I try not to turn my head suddenly or move to fast. I am getting better, as I feel my strength coming back little by little every day.

I've been hurt bad before in altercations, but in those I had a chance to defend myself, and I did. I usually killed my assailant. This time though I got the hell beat out of me, and all I could do was sit take it. I got beat up by a bully who was hell bent on making an example of me the minute I got here. She used Tori to do that—get at me. I will remember what Behar did to me. She will one day pay up for what she did to Tori and me.

We go into the shower and disrobe, and during this time we had fun. We're like two school girls having a good time together, each knowing that the other one cares. Causing us to almost forget that we're being held prisoner against our will.

THE ALLEY OF EVIL

There was no need for sexual play though our hands were all over each other. What I've discovered is, how much fun Tori is and how she draws out the girly side in me. Something I've never allowed myself to do much. She is helping this killer, in ways that she never imagined.

The woman who guards us is a big black woman named Chyla and we're getting to know her and she is getting to know us. She lets us do pretty much as we please together. We are glad she does. She doesn't interfere with us—she's no doubt seen girls together before. She is also the one who has helped us, by confiscating things like pain medication and food. She has told us never to worry about anything while she's there with us. Tori and I thank her, because we know when she brings us stuff we need, she's putting herself at the risk of Behar finding out she's helping us. She's told us not to worry about Behar, because she doesn't.

At the end of the shower the water is off—we are dry and our hair is still wringing wet, with towels around our heads. We are still naked. I look at Tori, and I pull her up close to me. I hug her and she hugs me back. She feels so good in my arms, her warm body next to mine. I feel it every night, though until last night I've been completely out of it.

I kiss her forehead, and look at her. She then kisses me on the lips. A light little kiss that just brushes by, tantalizing me. Then I kiss her as we find each other's mouths—tonging each other, for a longtime.

After we break, I say, "that was nice. I want you to know that, like I said, I've never kissed a girl before you, nor did I think about doing it. But I want to kiss you...a lot—I always have."

She smiles and says, "Yeah, I'm like that with you, too. I've wanted you to kiss me since that first day we were locked up together. You told me that you wanted to, and didn't because you didn't want me to reject you, and I wouldn't have."

"You know there's no pluses about being in this place at all, Tori, for either of us. But I wouldn't have met you if they hadn't sent me here. While I still don't like the fact that I'm here, you're here with me and I like that, very much. Does that make sense?"

Tori looks at me with her soft smile shaking her head, and says, "It does, it's the only thing that keeps me sane, I know you're here with me. I was so worried about you after she beat you. They offered you no medical attention whatsoever, except for what Chyla got you. I'm just glad you're getting better, now."

By now we had broken the embrace and were putting on the robes that the prison provides for us. Then the flip-flops for our feet.

"You know I was worried about you while I was out of it. I wondered if you'd be alright. I was worried that I'd wake up and you wouldn't be here, that they took you away. But then I would see you and I was okay.

"Well, no one bothered me."

We left the shower room and Chyla follows us back to our cell as usual. Before she locks the door, she tells us that we are now going to be allowed to eat in the chow hall with the others. And we can mingle at exercise time—something that Tori wasn't allowed to do by herself. When Chyla told us that, we both figured that Behar is behind it—letting us out for recess.

THE ALLEY OF EVIL

Mid morning comes and the cell doors open, this time automatically. That hasn't been the case since we were put in here. The PA blares that it's time for everyone to go outside and exercise. Tori and I walk out into the hall, I still move a little gingerly. She has hold of my arm steadying me, like she did as we walked to and from the showers earlier this morning. We go out the back door of the building—the yard is filling up quickly with the other women. As we appear, they all turn and look when they see us. Some just stand in silence staring at me, gawking. I'm a zoo animal again, but I don't care and it doesn't bother me. My lip is still swollen, and my right eye is pretty black, and there are the scratches and scrape still left on my face from Behar's pounding. I will say I'm not very pretty to look at, but then again Westerville ain't a place one needs to look pretty.

I don't feel much like standing, so I say to Tori, "let's sit down here." Here, is not far from the door, and it's in a shady spot on the walk, where I can sit and lean against the wall. The idea for this time outside is to get exercise, and as we set I see the guards prodding some of the women to not sit, but to walk. Some do, but most just stand around and mingle in groups, looking at, and talking about me.

I've heard that prisons have rival gangs that are part of their societal makeup. Some more dominant than others, but something is out of kilter here. Not right. As Tori and I talked, we both noticed again that the population is very young. Like us, even younger. We're among the older prisoners. The groups of women we see don't seem to be in a rival situation. Some of them are gathering together. Still looking at Tori and me.

Soon I look up and out of the door on the other side of the yard I see Behar. She stops and talks to a guard and then looks across at us.

"What do you suppose she wants to say to you now?"

"Damned if I know."

She strides importantly across the yard and up to us. She stands directly over me, giving herself a feeling of superiority she enjoys so much with me. She glares down at me, wanting to frighten me, which she can't do. She doesn't scare me at all.

She's hovering over me like an albatross. Everyone in the yard is watching to see what happens, walking closer to listen. She knew we were coming out for recess today, because, like Tori and I know, she's the one that authorized it. That's why she's suddenly made an appearance, and decided to come out of her cocoon. She wants to hassle me again for some reason.

"I hope you learned your lesson the other day Cain," she remarks. She's questioning me but with her attention on Tori. She's trying to sound authoritarian. She breaks her gaze at her and looks around seeing that she getting an audience with her crap.

I look up at her and say. "No. I really don't know what your were trying to prove...Cynthia. Except to show all the rest of them how tough you are by beating up on me."

She's looking at Tori again as she speaks to me, "I wanted to let you and the others see, that I will not let insubordination like you showed that first day you got her got here go unpunished. You attacked me." Her tone as she talks is harsh as she glance at me.

"But they way I remember it, Cynthia, you started that fight. And all I was doing was defending Tori. And why are you staring at her and talking to me?"

"You should have minded your own business and stayed out of it. Like now, it's none of your fucking business why I look at anyone."

"Well Cynthia, when it comes to Tori, I will make it my business just like I did the other day. I wasn't about to let you hurt and humiliate her one more minute. And FYI I won't let you do it to her again without it going unpunished by me."

"You haven't learned a damn thing. You're just a fucking hardheaded bitch, Sasha Cain."

"So what was this *hardheaded* bitch supposed to learn from you Cynthia? What was I supposed to absorb from that—getting the hell beat out of me while being strapped the that chair, unable to defend myself. Go ahead, tell me. Tell all of them, I'm sure they'd all love to hear your fucking excuse for doing that."

She doesn't answer my question, and instead says harshly, "you just don't get it do you? You need to learn you place here, Sasha Cain."

"Yeah, and Cynthia, just what the fuck is that place?"

"That you're nothing here, you bitch—you're a prisoner. A nothing. You're not the enforcer—not anymore, not here."

Everyone is gathered around now as close as they can, listening to this. She relishes the fact that she has an audience. She creating tension. And she's still fixated on Tori, making her get closer to me, as Behar's gaze at her, builds anxiety and fear into her.

Then I say, "maybe that's true for you, but you need to know I'm not scared of you. I can take anything you dish out. Your bully and coward, Cynthia. And one day Tori and I won't be prisoners here, and I will be the enforcer again. I will remember everything that you've done. I will get even with you, Cynthia, count on it."

After I said that I really didn't know what she was going to do. She could have had a muscle guard beat up on me, but she didn't. She instead continued to fix her look on Tori. The she did a haughty, hump, and turned away arrogantly, and went inside. Stopping briefly and turning to look at Tori as she opened the door.

"Did you see how she looked at me, while she was talking to you?" Tori says. "It scares me, Sasha."

"Yeah, I know it does, but try not to be scared her."

After a few minutes the alarm sounded and we were herded back into the building. When we got to our cell we looked in and saw that someone had been in it and left us a bunch of books to read. I didn't know the place had a library, only a chow hall and kitchen to feed everyone.

"It's Chyla," Tori says. "She's the one who put ice and medicine in our cage after you were hurt. She told me she did, and now she's got these books for us."

We know that if Cynthia found out that Chyla was helping us out, she would go bonkers. But Chyla is not afraid of Cynthia, and she's told us so. So it is nice to have her on our side.

We spent the rest of the morning looking at what had been given to us.

I said, "I've never read many books, I guess it's time to start, huh"

"It'll help us pass the time," Tori said.

I Looked at her, as she was thumbing her way through a volume, and said, "you probably think I'm dumb, since I've never read a lot of books."

She puts the book down, and looks at me and says softly, "Sasha Cain, I don't think any of those things about you. Stop it. I think you're the strongest and bravest person, I have ever known."

"You do?"

"Yes I do. And you don't have to tell me what you think about me, I already know."

"What do you think, I think about you?"

"You say it."

"You just said for me not, too." I laugh.

"Say it anyway."

"Okay, I think you're the greatest, Tori. You sat here in this cell with me, and nursed me back to health. Without any help whatsoever from those bastards. You, Tori Nicks did that for me. When you could have just as easily not cared and just gone over and sat in the corner and felt sorry for yourself. But you didn't do that. Talk about strength and caring. When I think about what you did for me it blows me away."

"Sasha, I couldn't leave you hurting like that, I had to do something. I care too much for you already."

"I know, I care for you like that, too. I will never let any harm come to you if I can stop it. And I have never experienced the kind of devotion and love that you showed for me. Ever in my life. You are so sweet and caring Tori."

"I was afraid you might die,' she says, blushing slightly at my comment.

"And because of you, I didn't."

Then we smiled at each other and kissed. We are definitely getting on the same page. We are in love with each other. I can't stop it. I don't want to stop it. I already love Tori, and I know she loves me, too.

Later in the chow hall we get our food and find a table in the back of the room and sit down. After a few seconds of looking around at the other girls, we notice five get up and come over to us. They had watched us come in.

One asks, "mind if we sit?"

"Help yourselves," I said.

There's an awkward silence as they look at each other trying to decide which one of them should speak to us first. They all looked to be about our age, and certainly no older.

Then the one who asked if they could join us says, "so what are you guys in here for?"

I say, I'm not sure why Tori's here, but I'm a pretty bad girl."

"Sasha Cain, yeah." One of the young woman says. She's obviously heard of me.

They pause again and then the first one says, "listen guys, I don't know how much you've been told or noticed, but this ain't no real prison by any means. I mean you two are probably the only ones here that they've really incarcerated."

"You're right, we were both railroaded, and put in here against our will, for doing nothing wrong. And, yeah, now that you mention it, we have noticed odd thing aboth this place," I said.

"Well, you're right in you assessment. What I mean is, we ain't prisoners at all. You see we've all been kidnapped."

"Kidnapped?" Tori says, shockingly, with a mouth full of food.

"Yeah, you heard me right. This place ain't no real prison in the true sense of the word. It's not a prison where they send people for being bad. It's a prison for human trafficking. Every girl in this place is going to be auctioned off to the highest bidder, at an auction someplace, and that includes me. They probably would have done it to Tori, but she protected you and they're afraid of you, Sasha. They may not bother Tori because of you.

"That's why Behar put on that little show the other day. She was trying to get a point across to to us, she wanted to show how tough she is. She wanted to show us all that she wasn't afraid to beat the hell out of Sasha Cain."

"Yeah, and Sasha we want you to know that every girl in this place thinks that what the bitch did to you was monstrous and brutal." The girl who knew of me, said.

"But they keep me under lock and key ladies, and as long as I'm like this I'm really no threat to them."

The girl who knew of me said, "they know how dangerous you are. They're afraid of you. They know they can't sell you so they decided find another use for you. Behar's whipping girl."

I agree with what she said, and look at Tori, "so Behar is a human trafficker—a fucking criminal herself, and is not a real warden. That bitch."

"I'm sure they intended to auction you off, Sasha, that was their plan for you, and for Tori before you protected her the other day."

"Yeah you're right, and I know who is behind it all, especially for me."

"One other thing we also wanted to know. Are you looking for a way to escape?"

"Not yet," I said to them. "I've been a little out of it lately, if you've noticed. I really haven't had much time for escape plans, ladies," I said.

"Tori?" The girl asks her.

"No, me neither, I was taking care of her, and without help. Sasha had a severe concussion. And besides I wouldn't know where to start to plan something like that anyway."

"When you were hurt. They didn't take you to the infirmary," the first girl asks?

"They have one?" I ask, sardonically, not at all shocked to learn this. Knowing that Behar wants me to just suffer, and she must be getting her jollies watching me do so.

"Yeah, they do," the girl says.

"Well, they never offered me any medical attention, whatsoever. And if it hadn't been for Tori, and the lady guard Chyla, I would have been in a whole heap of trouble getting my health back."

They pause and then the first girl asks, "if you start looking for ways to get out of here, you would tell us, right?"

"I would. You can trust me on that."

Just then I nod at them, as a burly guard approached us. He walks up to the table and says, "you ladies sure seem have a lot to talk about today. Don't you?"

"We were just talking about what joy it is to be here," I popped off.

"Cain, you're nothing but an arrogant little smart ass."

"Thank you," I say curtly, with a smirk at him.

"Don't mention it. Now shut up and eat. You five move away from them."

Tori and I finish our meal and are escorted as usual back to our cell. The door closes and locks, and we go on the hunt for bugs in our cell. I find it again neatly tucked under our sleeping cot. I show it to Tori and walk over and flush it down the toilet like we always do. And we laugh out loud like a couple of silly school girls.

We set down on the bed next to each other like we always do. Knees up, feet on the edge of the cot. Tori and I take each other's hand, and our fingers entwine and grip tightly to each other. She lays her head softly on my left shoulder and I lean into her. We are just quiet.

After all there's not much room here, not much else to do except read, and we get tired of doing that. So often times we just do this, set on the cot quietly. We are crammed into these uncomfortable quarters, and we both know why Behar is doing it to us. She will eventually come an get Tori and take her from me. She'll do everything in her little book of tricks to to get Tori to crack, and turn against me. Even if that means threatening her or even hurting her. We both know that's a very real possibility, though she hasn't done it yet. But the way she glared down at Tori that day in the yard, I worry that she may be getting close to doing something like that.

As for Behar taking Tori, I know that I only have so much control over protecting her. I'm not armed and without that I can't do much of anything but try to fight them off. They could come and take her away from me at any time, and I will answer them with all the hell and fury I can muster. I don't care what the situation is or how big they are. As the girl up in the chow hall said, they're really afraid of me and what I might do, if they try to harm Tori. But I am little or no threat without my guns.

"Behar wasn't in the mess hall at lunch," Tori observes.

"Yeah I know. It was one less time that we had to look at the bitch."

"I worry about her Sasha. She hates you, but she's not tried to do anything with me."

"Yeah I've thought about that. I'm sure that I consume one hundred percent of her thought's. She hates me to the core of her soul, if she has one."

"Why do you think that is?"

"Well for one thing, I know I've been kidnapped, too, just like all of you. At some point she found out that I was coming here, She knew that I wasn't a girl that they could auction off, so she's decided to make my life as miserable as she can.

"But I make her life miserable, too, because I'm here. I'm a pain in her ass. I've embarrassed the hell out of her, rather than her doing it to me. She wants to use me to showcase to everyone how tough she is, and so far it's backfired on her. Because I won't let her win."

"What about me? Do you think she's gonna try something with me?" She sets up and looks at me, fearfully. "Sasha, she scares the hell out of me. I've told you that."

"I know, and if she does try something with you and I may be not be able stop it, so you've got to remain strong. You can't let that bitch win in anyway, no matter what she tries. You have to remain strong. Okay?"

"I'll try, I just know that I'm not strong like you are."

"But you are strong, Tori. You just don't know how strong you are, because no one has ever told you that."

"You really think that about me, don't you."

"I do. You stayed with me after she beat the hell out of me that day. You never left my side. That is what I call strength."

She smiled at me then she sat back next to me again and we leaned into each other. And we were quiet for a few minutes.

"You're trembling," "I say.

"Just hold me," she says. I put my arm around her pulling her as close as I can, hoping to calm her fear.

After a few minutes she says, "They say that lovers don't have to talk all the time that they just have to be with each other. That they know they love one another."

"I've heard that, too."

"I guess we're lovers then."

"Yeah we are Tori, and I'm glad for it."

"I've loved you since that first night we were put in here

together, Sasha. I felt it somehow, I just knew we were going to be together."

"Me, too. I was confused wanting to kiss you, but now it seems so natural for me," I said. We looked at each other and kissed, causing us to change positions, and our hands began to roam around. First under each other's shirts, finding each other's breasts. Suddenly Tori's fear seemed to be quelled.

I find myself enjoying her, every part of her. Her soft curves and taught but equally soft buttocks. I can't seem to get enough of Tori and she can't seem to get enough of me. I never thought this would be possible of me. Loving a girl—but I do.

That night after loving each other, we curl up and go to sleep.

THE ALLEY OF EVIL

NINE

I'm being chased. Who are those people? Where…where am I? This alley, it's dark, it scares me. I got to run away. My legs, they won't move. It's like they're frozen in place and I can't run. The shadows are about to catch up to me. No! No! Get away from me. I got to get away. Help! Help! I wake up screaming, and roll onto the cell floor. Tori is awake.

She cries out, "Sasha, are you okay?"

"I slowly wake up and get my wits about me, and look at her. "Bad nightmare."

"Well get back up here next to me."

I get back on the cot, we're face to face, "I have those from time to time, Tori."

"Nightmares?"

"Yeah, only lately it's the same one with some variations over and over. Scares the hell out me for a while."

"Well try to forget it, it's just a dream."

******

The next couple of weeks went by without any incidents at all. Behar seemed to make herself scarce at mealtime. And we learned from some of the girls who haven't been auctioned off to beware of her. That she's not only brutal, she's sneaky. She's a snake in the grass, coiled up and ready to strike her victims when they're unaware.

We hear the door to our cell click and open. We expect to see Chyla, but instead it's one of the muscle guards standing in the doorway. He comes in and orders Tori to stand up and come with him. She looks at me, fear written all over her face, as he cuffs her.

It seems that the day we have feared most, has arrived.

I stand up and ask him, "What's this about?"

"It's none of your concern, Cain. So sit your ass back down and shut up." He shoves me back onto the cot, and I get back up and try to get passed him, but he's too big and strong. He shoves me back down, hard, this time.

I shout, "Tori!"

I again I try to get up to go after her—trying to fight him off with all my might. Then he just grabs me and lifts me up by my shirt collar and slams me hard into the wall, "I told you to sit the fuck down and shut your trap Cain." Then he throws me onto the cot like I'm nothing and walks out.

I get up and run to the door and I yell after them, "where are you taking her? You...you son-of-a...." But it's to no avail the cell door closes. Fear runs through my entire soul. I am suddenly alone...Tori is gone.

I don't know where they're taking her. I tried to stop them, but I couldn't. Now I fear the worst. I'm frantic, my heart is racing. What can I do?

I'm shaking with fear I scream out. NO! I'm going crazy with worry. I can't think. I can't set down, I pace, back and forth. No! No! I scream out again and again in anguish, shouting at the top of my lungs—screams that I want to be heard outside of the walls of this cell where I'm being held. I want whoever can hear me that there will be consequences for this.

The hour passes, I set down on the edge of the cot, putting my head in my hands. I'm crying profusely, I can't stop. What have they done with her? Are they preparing her for auction? God, no, that can't be. I say to myself tearfully. I can't, I won't let that happen to her. The thought of her being auctioned off races through my mind again and again. I become even so frantic I begin to hyperventilate. I lay down trying to get myself settled down. But all I can think of is the bastards have finally taken her away from me. I'm never going to see her again. What am I to do?

Another hour passes by more slowly than the first. And now I'm distraught and devastated, thinking that she's not coming back—that she's gone forever. I set like that for what seemed like a longtime, just staring at the wall. Remembering her being here with me. Seeing her in my mind, I cry, and cry. Me, Sasha Cain the feared enforcer now cries for someone she loves.

The third hour passes even more slowly than the first two, I am now resigning myself to the fact that they've taken Tori away for good, that I'm never going to see her again. I'm setting on the edge of the cot when I hear the cell door click, and it opens. I look up with anticipation, hoping to see Tori.

The same muscle guard that came in and took her away, shoves her hard into the cell, causing her to sprawl on the floor on her side. Seeing her I quickly go over to her and pick her up, hugging her tightly to me in my arms. I'm crazy with joy that she's back. I'm crying, she's crying, I hold her and kiss her telling her that I was going insane with fear about what had happened to her. She cries, and cries. Her mouth gaping open, not able to talk. I hold her at arm's length. "Tori. What the hell did they do to you? Please, tell me," I say. Looking into her face that is streaked from tears, she's frightened to death, white as a ghost. I've never seen her in such distress like this before.

After I asked her that she pushes me away gently, and gets up and goes over to the toilet and vomits. Everything coming up, soon leaving her with the dry heaves. I just sit watching her, unable to help her. I don't know what to do.

She finishes and leans back against the wall. I just look at her. We're quiet for several minutes, before I ask her again what happened.

"He....took me to Behar's office."

"And?"

"And she tried to coerce me into turning on you. She.... said she'd let me leave Westerville, if I did turn on you. I...I refused her offer. Then...then she called those two dyke bodyguards of hers, Wanda and Violet, into her office. They closed the blinds, then all three of them stripped me naked. They held me down, and stripped their own clothes off...and gang raped me."

"Fuck! I scream out. "Those fucking bitches."

I start to go over to her and she says, holding her hand out,

THE ALLEY OF EVIL

"no, please, not now, baby I need some space. I'm not trying to be mean. I just need some time."

I retreat and give it to her. She just sits there, dazed. Not moving. Not looking at me. I'm furious inside. All I can think about is killing Behar, and I will kill her, no matter when or where I see her. I will kill her for what she's done to Tori. I will kill all three of them if I can.

Right now my main concern is for Tori. I don't really know what to do, except let her be until she's ready for me to approach her. I'm sitting on the cot, I watched her for a longtime before I got drowsy and fell into a nap.

After a while I am awakened by Tori snuggling up to me. "Hold me Sasha. Just...hold me," she said softly. She's trembling.

I did hold her, up close and tight letting her know that she's safe now. Right now her comfort and safety is utmost in my mind. As I sit holding her, I can think of nothing but killing Behar and her bitches.

******

The cell doors open, it's dinnertime, and Tori still feels like crap after her ordeal with Behar and her dykes. And no one can blame her, it will take time for her to heal—a longtime. She's not hungry. I'm really not either, but I have to go up anyway—I have to. I am going to extract revenge on Behar in front of everybody.

Before I go out she says, "Sasha, please be careful."

I didn't answer her, and only nodded to her and half smiled

as I walked out. She knows me well enough now, that I will not let this go until I've done something to avenge what happened to her. It's like she knew when I left that I was going to do something.

I'm the last one up to the mess hall, I always am. And as soon as I walk through the door all eyes are on me. I figure that the scuttlebutt in the building has already spread about what Behar, Violet, and Wanda did to Tori.

I see Behar, and as usual she's sitting at a table near the front talking to Wanda and Violet. She sees me come in and looks at me with that sneer on her face that I hate. Then she looks away. I don't do anything yet. I go to the food line and get a tray and fill a plate full of food, and get my utensils, then I walk back to an empty table. Every girl in the whole room is still watching me, as I turn to set at the table. I continue to stand—glaring at Behar. She still isn't watching me.

I stand there for several seconds more, thinking about how I'm going to do this. I think about using the knife but it is round on the end—to blunt, and not a good choice. It will not penetrate the skin easily. So take the fork gripping it tightly in my right hand, and point it down. It is all I have to do this with. I will make it the most lethal weapon I can.

I begin walking right toward her—moving quickly. She still hasn't looked at me yet. That's good because I'm about to give her the surprise of her life. I'm less than ten feet from her, when she finally looks up. I break into a full run, charging her table as fast as I can. Her eyes are widened as I hurl myself toward her. The fork in a ready position to stab the bitch. I let out a blood curdling, primal scream, that shatters the utterance of every voice in the room.

I dive over the table. She makes a move to retreat from me, but it's too late. I bring the fork down on her with all the force I have. My teeth are clenched and I'm growling as I push the fork though her uniform near her left breast. Pushing hard into her as deep as I could, hoping to hit her heart. She lets out a loud scream of pain, as the fork penetrates her skin, and we go over backwards.

I fall off over the table on top of her, head first. Then I feel two big hands grab my legs, pulling me up and back across the table. I can see Behar, slumped and holding her left breast. She's taken the fork out of her and is being helped up by Violet.

I drew blood because I can see it on her uniform. She gathers herself enough to come around the table to stand in front of me. She's holding her wound. I'm being held onto by two big muscle guards, and couldn't get away even if I tried to.

I can see the hatred pouring from her eyes at me. She says through her pain, "I will see you pay for this Sasha Cain. You attempted to murder me. I should have them kill you."

"Then why don't you, Cynthia?" I smart off. "What's keeping you from doing that? Killing me. You sure as hell can't sell me."

I can see the rage in her, and she says, "well, little miss smart ass, enforcer. I have better I idea that's why. I will give you and your little Indian girlfriend life in Westerville without ever getting out. I will see that the two of you die old women in here."

"Fuck your life sentence. Tell me Cynthia, who's keeping

you from killing me? That fucker Colin Lampoor. I know it's him."

She's still holding her wound and turns around and back hands me twice across my face, hard.

I take her blows, and look back at her, defiantly, rage pouring out from my eyes, I yell at her, "I got you back for what you and your bitches did to my Tori this morning. You and your bitches, gang raped her today. I don't care what you think of to do to me. But you keep this in mind, I will kill you someday, you and Colin Lampoor."

Then she nods to a guard and with the whole room looking on, she tells him to hit me in the gut. She tells him to hold nothing back when he hits me. He does her bidding hitting me hard three times, causing me to bend double, grimacing, and crying out in pain.

Then he suddenly stops, and she tells him to keep hitting me.

He refuses, too, and says, "No, Cynthia. I could bust her up inside real bad. I won't kill her for you. You're the one she attacked, and you are the one that should punish her for it. Not me or anyone else. So you beat her."

My head is hanging down when I feel her grab hold of my chin, lifting my head. I manage a devious little grin. She hisses, "for now this will do. You've caused nothing but trouble since the day you arrived here."

Then I manage enough strength to spit in her face, and she backhands me across my face again, I laugh in her face. But before she lets the guard take me back to my cell, she rares back and hits me with all her might in my stomach, causing me to double up and groan in pain.

Then she orders the guards, "Get her the hell out of my sight."

The cell door clicks open and the guard tosses me on the floor. I lay there still in a lot of pain from being hit so hard in the stomach. I feel Tori's soft touch on me. She helps me sit up. I can't breathe all that good yet, and my stomach feels like it's about to come out of my body. I look up at her. She's crying.

"I...I need to puke," I said. I crawl over and hang my head in the toilet, hugging it for dear life. It's like Tori had done earlier in the day when they brought her back. Nothing but some phlegm comes up. Then the dry heaves. I sit for a few minutes leaning against the wall, trying to stop from heaving again. As the pain in my gut begins to subside so do the heaves. I look over at her and reach out for her. She takes my hand, and gets up next to me. I lean my head on her shoulder as she wraps her arms around me, hugging me softly.

"My God, what happened? Sasha, baby. What did you do?" She ask me in a small voice

"I stabbed that fucking bitch with a fork. I tried to kill her for what she did to you."

"Sasha, it was crazy to do that, she could have had the guards kill you."

"I know that, but she didn't."

We chuckle lightly even though it hurts for me to do so.

She hugs me and I hug her back. "I wasn't about to let her get away with what she did to you. She raped you. I was trying to kill her, but I couldn't get the fork far enough in. I missed her heart but stabbed her tit. I have the satisfaction of knowing that I drew blood," I said. The words coming out of me weakly.

"She'll really be mad at you now."

"What else is new? She didn't kill me. Lampoor won't let her do that, and she can't auction me off. Oh by the way she sentenced us to life in prison here at Westerville. So I guess we're in solitary again."

We laugh at my comment, even though it still hurts my stomach.

She looks at me. "Sasha, you risked your life for me again."

"I wouldn't have it any other way. When they took you away this morning I was crazy with fear all the time you were gone. I wasn't sure what they were going to do with you. I was so afraid that I'd never see you again, that they were going to put you in another cell, and prepare you to be auctioned off."

"I thought that, too. I wasn't sure what she was going to do to me. I was scared out of my mind."

"I...I want you to know Tori that I wouldn't know what to do without you now." I pause, then say, "Am I smothering you? I'm still kinda new to this relationship stuff you know."

"No you're not smothering me at all."

"I don't want anything to change between us. Except to get us out of this stinking hell hole."

"She looks down at me and says, "me, too. I love you, Sasha."

"I know, I love you, too, Tori."

We kiss and smile and then we just hold onto each other.

After a while I say, "Remember, you asked me about, me?"

She looks at me shaking her head.

"I sigh, "I was born in Rottendamn of course as you know, and was abandoned by my mother when I was ten. She was a hooker and a doper, and one day she just never came home. I don't really know what happened to her to this day. I looked for her for a while after she didn't come home. But I was only ten and didn't know how to go about doing that. I figure she may have been killed by one of her tricks, or she just left. She never really wanted me. I was more of a nuisance to her than a daughter, so I was the daughter her mother didn't want. Oh, she took care of me for a while, but it always seemed like she was doing it out of necessity and not love. You know?

"Anyway, after she didn't come home I was left living on the streets for about two years. I hid everywhere I could, trying to stay out of sight, but I was still beaten and raped. I was afraid, until I met, and was befriended, by an Asian couple named Chen. They took me in and I lived with them until I was eighteen."

"Then what happened and what about your dad, did you know him.?"

"My father? Ha," I laugh, sarcastically. "I don't even know who he was. No idea. My being born was probably the result of my mother's carelessness with one of her tricks, or she was raped by one of them and I'm the consequence of that."

She looks at me shaking her head with pity.

"Anyway I came home from school one afternoon and found both of the Chens lying dead on the living room floor.

Their throats had been slit and the house had been ransacked and robbed. I had no idea who had done this and even less of an idea of how to find them.

"During those eight years when I lived with them, that's how I learned to shoot a gun. I found I could release my anger that way, though I had no intention killing anyone back then. I was already a very good shot, and to make a long story short I eventually found the three culprits who killed them, in a shit hole bar near-by. They were in there bragging about how they'd killed this old Asian couple and robbed them. I confronted them about it, and got into a gunfight with them and ended up killing all three.

"And it felt good to me that I had righted that wrong. So this is what I've done ever since—hunted people for hire. To mainly collect a debt, and kill them if I have, too. I've done it mainly to stay alive Tori, even knowing how dangerous it is for me. It's something I'm not so proud of now, especially since I met you. You are so much better than me."

She looks at me. "You did it because you had to, Sasha. You avenged the deaths of the people that saved you from oblivion after you got deserted by your mom, or whatever happened to her. Those three, they deserved it."

I shake my head.

She asks me, "have you ever been on drugs or anything like that?"

"No, Tori, never. I've never smoked or drank alcohol. I will admit though that I got drunk with a guy one time, and I hated the feeling. I, like, felt out of control, and I swore to myself never again. You?"

"No, not me, never, just like you."

"What about you? You know we've wanted to have this talk for a longtime. What's happened to you?"

She pauses before she answers me

"Like you I was born poor in what you call Rottendamn," We laugh. "But unlike you my mother stayed with me and Davy until she died when I was seventeen. Dad died when I was fourteen. We were poor as hell and I was scraping out a living trying to support the two us, but we still ended up on the street, in the gutter. Then one day I struck up a conversation with this girl, Josie, and she told us to come and stay with her. I was eighteen at the time, and she was maybe twenty-one. And of course one thing led to another and she and I got together, falling in love.

Then one day she went to work and never came home, like your mom. I don't know what happened to her either. I know that she was into drugs and stuff like that, so maybe that's what happened. She was murdered because of her drug use or she over dosed. I don't know for sure.

"I grieved for her for a long time, and during this time Davy had become completely uncontrollable, and he ran off. I couldn't control him at all, Sasha. I would get him home and he'd just run away again. I finally gave up trying. I was afraid for him. I was again living on bare bones without Josie, and that's what led to me trying to take that meat and bread from the shop owner. During this time Davy made an appearance, he was hungry. That's what got me in here. I took the meat and bread so Davy and I wouldn't starve."

I shake my head, then I say, "you got sent straight here. Right?"

"Yeah."

"You know that shop owner is probably in on this, too."

"I never thought of that, but you know, yeah, you're right, he is."

"You know, if and when we ever get out of this place. I want us to see if we can get at whoever is behind this whole trafficking operation. I want to shut it down, Tori, once and for all. And Westerville will be our first stop."

She agrees, and says, "but how do we get out of here?

"I haven't got it all figured out, but it's just a matter of time til I do. Until then we sit tight. I'm curious about something with you though."

"What's that?"

"Your name, Nicks. You're native, so how did you get that surname?"

"My grandfather was adopted when he was real little back in the twenty first century, by a man named Nicks. He kept the name and never used his native name again. My dad never went back to it either."

"And your nose it's cute and turned up not like and Indian at all."

"I got it from my mom. She was only half native."

THE ALLEY OF EVIL

TEN

Days go by, and turn into weeks. Tori and I are still rotting away in solitary confinement, which is Behar's plan. There has been no attempt to punish me further, nor has Behar tried to do any more harm to Tori. I wonder if she's growing tired of the game, realizing that she can really do nothing to me. She can't sell me, like Lampoor wanted her, too. She can't scare me or kill me. Telling me that someone else has got to be involved. Because she hasn't attempted to punish me further for the stabbing incident and my trying to kill her.

While I have my nightmares Tori deals often with Behar, Wanda and Violet raping her. Some times she quiet, sometimes she cries, and there are times she just curls up next to me and wants me to hold her. I do that, just like she does when I have a nightmare. But then there are those times that she is distant, even cold, and pushes me away, as she tries to deal with the rape. It's those time that I feel helpless—I don't know what to do to help her.

But both of us are growing weary and tired of the quandary we find ourselves in, locked into this cell day after day. I thought that by now Behar would let us out, to get her revenge with me, but so far that's not happened. It makes me wonder if she's even here anymore, maybe the boogie man came and got her. It wouldn't break my heart at all if that were the case, or Tori's either.

It has been four months now since Tori and I arrived here at Westerville and we've spent most all of it together in solitary.

Today happens to be one of those days that she and I are close. It's wearing on her very badly, this whole ordeal has been very tough on her. She's been raped and all I can do is try to comfort her. She cries often, and I hold her. She is after all one they intended to sell off, but she got involved with me and she's ended up here. Locked up in a jail cell that is seventy-two square feet, in a basement that's cold and musty. Something that's had its consequences on Tori's health. She has developed another cold, her second one in the last couple of months. She's just now shaking it off, and again she got no help from the infirmary, only the medicine that Chyla gave us.

She takes good care of us. She makes sure that we're not forgotten down here. She gets us meals, showers, and clean prison uniforms. She says she's just doing her job. But Tori and I know that she has now, after all these months got to know the two of us and has come to like us, and we like her, too.

Today we hear the cell door unlock and see Chyla. She says, "both of you come with me."

We get up and follow her out of the cell and to the elevator. We look at each other and wondering what this is about. I figure Behar is up to something, I just don't know what. It's not because I've been causing trouble lately. Hell how can I even try to do that? Locked up in that cell 24/7. We ride up to the first floor to Behar's office. As we approach her she's standing outside of it waiting on us—hands on her hips pretending to be impatient. I look at Tori and she at me, we raise our eyebrows, both thinking the same thing. "Here we go again."

"You two have a visitor it seems." She snaps at us, using a gruff tone.

"Visitor?" I said.

"Yes, you heard me. Follow me," she commands. Hatefully.

We follow her but don't go into her office, instead we go down the hallway and into the room at the end. She opens the door and motions for us to go in.

Inside is a man in his mid fifties I figure. He's about six feet tall, and wearing glasses. He has a mustache and a full head of thick black hair. He well dressed and has on a polo shirt, slacks, a windbreaker, and dress loafers. As I we set down I get a whiff of his aftershave. I look at Tori again and we read each other's minds. Questioning. What could this be about?

After we enter he looks at us, in a studying manner, like he's sizing us up. He tells Chyla to leave the room. A room that is the same drab gray as the whole prison. It has a table and chairs, but no place for handcuffs on the table, and the chairs and table aren't bolted to the floor.

"Have a seat ladies," he says politely.

We sit with me leaning back in my chair, hands folded on my stomach. Tori is straight arms on the table.

"Sasha Cain, right. And Tori Nicks." He looks at Tori.

"Yeah that's our names. So who are you?"

"My name is Raymond Cabot," he says. Seating himself

across from us. There's a manila folder in front of him. He looks at me, "Sasha Cain," he says opening the folder. "From New Rotterdam. Five feet eight inches tall and one hundred twenty-eight pounds, give or take. A bounty hunter, known as the enforcer."

"What do you want with us," I ask? Ignoring his description of me.

"I'm here to talk with you about some things that might interest you, Sasha. You, too, Tori.

"What kind of things," I ask?

"I'll get to that. You see...I'm the owner of this place. Westerville. I've known for sometime that you were in here, because this is where Colin Lampoor wanted you placed when you double-crossed him about the money."

"I didn't double-cross him. It was the other way around, that fucking little weasel railroaded me and had me put in here to be sold. I gave him the money he was owed, but he wanted money I had that he didn't rightly deserve. and I didn't give it to hem he had me put in here. That's what happened Mr. Cabot."

He didn't argue with me, he just sat and looked at me for several seconds. Like he believed me.

"So what is it that you want with Tori and me?"

"Well it's like this, Sasha. You're right, when you were first brought here we had every intention to put you in an auction and to try to sell you, both of you. But it became apparent that wasn't something that would work out for us. Especially with you, Sasha, no matter how bad Colin wanted it. You're just not the type. You're as the sheet on you describes. An enforcer.

You're violent. I also knew of your relationship with Tori. This knowledge of you and your activities became apparent to me when Cynthia relayed her monthly reports on the trafficking. She always wrote what a pain in the ass you were, and how she wanted to be rid of you.

"She beat me and raped Tori. So I'm glad she thought I was a pain in her ass. So you must know I stabbed the bitch. And for that she had me beaten for the second time. Tori and I have been in Solitary, almost since we got here, Mr. Cabot."

"I'm aware of all that, and I'm here to get you out of this situation that is if you're willing to take the offer I have for you."

I immediately sat up straight and raised my eyebrows—looking at Tori after he said that.

"You see Sasha, it's your former work, as an enforcer, that brings me here today. I have a proposition for you, that is if you want to hear it."

"I'm game. What kind of proposition?"

"Well, as it is in my line of work I develop, shall we say, enemies. And I am in need of someone with your talents, Sasha. I need a personal bodyguard and head of security at my estate. I want to hire you for that position."

"Wait, let me get this straight. You want to hire me to keep the creeps off your back, so you can sell girls into slavery? I don't know about that one, you'll have to make it worth my while to do something like that."

"Okay, here's what I want you to do. Understand, Sasha it's just not trafficking, I have other business ventures that as I said creates many enemies. The trafficking creates none actually. So what I want you to do? If you take this position that I'm offering you, is to treat it purely as a business deal. I know you don't agree with any of what we're doing here. But maybe this will entice you. The job pays half a million a year. You and Tori, will be freed today. And you will live in your own quarters—a private residence, on my estate in the Catskills."

He just made it worthwhile. I looked at Tori and she looks back, and then I asked, "so Mr. Cabot, you said Tori can get out of here today."

"That's right, today. Right after we're done here. I knew that Tori would be part of this, so that's why I had you both brought up here to talk to me."

"Glad you did that, because I would never leave Tori here alone to fend for herself."

"Understood," he says.

I looked at Tori again, and said to him, "okay, Mr. Cabot, you just hired yourself a new head of security."

He stands up, "Very good, I was hoping you would take the job. By the way, I've taken the liberty of getting your street clothes and belongings that you had when you got here. So you can change out of those prison uniforms and back into these."

We stand up and he lays the bags with our stuff in them on the table, and says. "I'm going to leave you, but my chauffeur will remain out front with my limousine until you come out of the building. He will drive you up to my estate.

"What about Cynthia," Tori asks?

"She won't stop you, she's been instructed by me to let the two of you leave."

Before he opens the door he looks down at the bench next to it, and picks up another bag. He lays it on the table.

"Oh, I almost forgot you might want these, too, Sasha."

I reach over for the bag and open it. It has my guns and ammo belt inside. I show them to Tori and she breaks into a wide grin.

"I'll see you at the estate then," he says.

"For sure," I respond.

He opens the door and goes out, leaving us in the room to change. Which takes us both less than five minutes. I finish by putting on my leather vest, and Tori looks at me, shaking her head in approval.

"If you think that's cool, watch me put these on." I put the gun belt on and buckled it in front of me, then I put the leather straps around my legs and secured my guns and holsters to them.

"Now that is cool," she says. "They make you look…complete, somehow."

"Yeah they do, don't they. For the longest time I felt naked after the cops in Rottendamn took them away from me. I kept thinking I forgot them and had dreams that I lost them or something."

"Sasha you're one handsome woman, I have to say…wow."

I smile and grab her by the hand, and say, "come on babe, let's you and me get the hell out of this joint."

She smiles widely, shaking her head in agreement. I open the door and follow her out. What we aren't prepared for is the welcoming committee that is waiting below in the mess hall. The metal stairs that lead down are very narrow and circular in nature. As we descend and reach the bottom we see all the guards, armed, with their guns in what appears to be a ready position. Chyla is not among them. I'm sure it unnerves all of them to see the enforcer armed and dangerous.

Cynthia has also allowed the girls being held here against their will into the room to watch us leave. She's is right there at the bottom of the stairs, in our faces waiting to harass us. But then she steps aside.

Tori and I begin our walk to the other end of the room, and the big double doors at the end that will lead to our freedom.

But Cynthia couldn't resist one more jab at me, "I thought you two might like a little sendoff. I want them all to see how fucking unfair it is for you two to be leaving." She pauses. "You know, I don't approve of what Cabot is doing here. I still plan on making you pay for stabbing me with that fork, Cain."

We stop and turn around walking back up to her until I'm in her face her. I smile and say, "well Cynthia, Tori and I don't give a damn about what you approve of. But there is something that I want you to know. We will back, to terminate your job, and to shut this fucking place down."

"Don't you threaten us."

"I'm not making a threat, I'm making you a promise. Oh, and one more thing. Go to hell, Cynthia."

That remark Causes Tori to burst out laughing, out loud, as well as all the girls in the room who are near enough to hear it.

Then I say to the room, "We'll be back ladies—count on it."

Then a cheer goes up, as Behar's face flushes bright red

with my comment. We turn and walk away, striding out of the room, as the throng of girls begins chanting, "Sasha! Sasha! Sasha!" Several times, growing louder and louder with each pronunciation of my name. Cynthia shouts at the top of her lungs. "Shut Up!" They ignore her and continue the chant until we're well out the door.

Tori says, "that was so cool."

"Yeah, it was, except, I wish we could shut this hell hole down today, and free them all. It is unfair, you know."

"But we will be back," she states. I smile in agreement. I can't wait for that day.

We walk out of the building and at the curb is a black stretch Limo. The chauffeur is standing next to it as we walk up to him.

"Sasha and Tori, I presume."

"Yep, that'd be us." I say to him and smile at Tori.

He introduces himself, "I'm Claus."

We smiled and said, "nice to meet you."

We get inside the limo and look at each other giggling like a couple of silly schoolgirls that have just been let out of detention. Then we high five each other and shout out. Yes! Exclaiming it several times as the limo pulls away from the hell hole, called Westerville. The place that has a reputation for being a tough prison. It's a prison for sure, but not one where you got sent here for being a bad person. But because you've been kidnapped and will be sold into slavery.

I can't help but think of all those poor girls that are still trapped inside, against their will. Down inside my heart breaks for them, and I know that I will come back here to do something about that someday.

Now, Tori and I are free and on the way to live at the estate of what we believe is the owner of Westerville, Raymond Cabot. Me to work for him as his personal bodyguard and head of security. It hurts me to do this, in fact it makes me sick to my stomach to do it. I had to take the job really, and it's not just about money. It's about us, Tori and me. At least we will be free, and I won't have to worry another day about her being taken and sold. Plus maybe there will be a way for us to find out who is running this human trafficking operation. Is it Cabot himself? Or some one else. That's what I hope we can get to the bottom of.

The drive up to the mountains was quiet, and uneventful. The chauffeur, Claus, told us it would take about an hour and a half. Sometimes traveling by auto these days can be quite adventuresome. There are people out here called road rats that run around in groups on old motorcycles, and in old souped up cars. They can number up to as many as thirty or more, and they're all armed. People who drive out into the country are often harassed and confronted by them.

But there are no road rats anywhere to be seen today. After we've been traveling for about a half hour, and Tori and I get done celebrating our new freedom, we both sleep the rest of the way.

ELEVEN

An hour later Claus drives the limo goes through two tall stone pillars, that leads to circle. Tori and I are both fully awake and wide-eyed at what we see. In the center of where the drive curves around is a fountain with a nymph that's pouring water out of a jar and back into the fountain. The lawn in front of this huge house is immaculate. It's beautiful—lush and green, with colorful flower gardens adorning it all along the front, and around the fountain.

The house is not a typical house with colonnades in front, but is what I would call modern architectural design. Which is hard to come by in a place like we live in today. The house really reminds me of several boxes stacked on one another, that cantilever out over the edges of the ones below. It has huge windows that span entire walls, that are a tan brick. The window trim and doors are a somewhat darker shade of red. In the center where the front doors are the house has a tower that rises higher than the rest of the place—going up past the second story.

The entire property is in a beautiful setting with wooded hills on three sides, providing for near perfect protection from danger.

Claus stops the car and turns to us and tells us this is it

ladies.

Ladies?

Tori deserves it. She's a true lady in every sense of the word. I'm not so sure that a woman known as an enforcer, that wears guns and is armed like I am deserves to be called lady for any reason.

Before getting out we look at each other and raise our eyebrows. Claus has gotten out and is opening the door for Tori, then he comes around and does the same for me. I can't ever remember having any one opening a door for me except those two goons who took me to Westerville. But it wasn't like this, they treated me like garbage. Tori has come around the back of the limo and is standing next to me. We're just stand gazing at the house in front of us, and smiling widely at each other. We, both of us have never seen a place like this let alone having the chance to go into one.

To our left and right about a fifty yards away sits two other houses on each side of this one, they are much more modest in nature. But they're still better than anything she and I are used too and have ever lived in. Especially after spending the last four and a half months in Westerville, and most of that in solitary. We were growing very weary and tired of the situation we were in. Tori was at her wits end, and I was nearing mine. We were not tiring of each other, but we were loosing hope that Behar was ever going to let us out of solitary.

This, though, is like a new lease on life for us. Even though I don't have a bit of use for what Cabot does, he did show up at the right time. I know he's nothing but a criminal just like

Cynthia Behar, and Colin Lampoor. They're all human traffickers. But for now I will hold my nose and do my job here, because this is better than being held in Westerville.

Out here I am armed, and will protect both Tori and me, even if it means killing Cabot himself. I will kill anyone who gets even close to Tori, and I sure as hell will not let us be returned to that hell place, Westerville.

We pick up our bags that contain our few belongs, like school girls coming home from school. Claus has motioned us to follow him into the massive house, where he opens the huge double doors for us and we enter a foyer and look up. It's open all the way to the ceiling, and is the tower that we could see from the outside. It has window lights all around it at the top. In front of us is a huge stairway that bends to the right and goes up to the second floor, where rooms fan out in all directions from a big landing.

From there we are led through the place, which has huge rooms and high cathedral ceilings. All the walls are ornately decorated with art, and beautiful furniture sits in place undisturbed, facing out more big windows with a view of the Catskills and the lake that is adjacent to the property.

As we walk through the place, Tori and I are quiet, we've both never seen a place like this let alone been in one. I think, too, as we follow Claus, so this is what selling human beings will buy you? A lavish lifestyle, where you live in luxury. I think how do these people sleep at night knowing that they've become rich at the expense of others misery, which they are responsible for.

We walk into a room where Cabot is sitting behind a big

oak desk, with desk lamps and a computer that all look very expensive. He's in a big black leather office chair and behind him the rest of the room is surrounded by bookshelves that go all the way to the ceiling, and are filled with volumes that give the room the feeling and smell of a library. It has lush light brown shag carpeting that goes from wall to wall. And big windows for viewing the mountains and lake on one side of the room.

"Have a seat ladies. I trust your trip up was comfortable as well as uneventful."

We both shook our heads, taking our seats on the other side of the desk. Both of us still awed at this house, even though it has been bought with dirty money.

He looks at us and begins, "I trust that those are the only clothes that the two of you possess?"

Again we shake our heads yes. Then he opens a drawer, reaches into it and pulls out a metal box and opens it. He takes out a huge wad of cash, divides it and hands some to each one of us.

"Don't thank me for that. Consider it an advance on your salary," he says. I want the two of you to go into Roxboro and buy new wardrobes for yourselves, they still have some very nice stores for you to shop in there. You can do that tomorrow," he says, and pauses. "Do either of you know how to drive?"

I looked at Tori and she's shaking her head, yes she does. It's something that I've never thought about asking her. I look at him and say yes I do, too.

"Good because if you didn't I'd have Claus take you into Roxboro. So for now I need to take you down to the house where you'll be living."

"Mr. Cabot?'

"Yes, Sasha."

"I was wondering what kind of stuff you want me to wear, so I'll buy the right clothes to work in."

"What you have on is fine, you can dress as you are. However you should both spend some of that money on the girly stuff if you want, too. You know, a bathing suit perhaps, sleepwear, whatever you want. I have a private beach down on the lake and you and Tori I'm sure will want to do some swimming. While we are down at the house you'll be living in, I want to show you the vintage Ford Mustang, that you can use as your own while you're here to drive to all your errands."

"But before we leave, and do that, I was wondering if either of you knows anything about these damn machines." He's pointing at the computer on his desk. "I just got the thing from an associate. I know the technology we use is decades old, but…I don't have a clue as to how this thing or it's network functions."

"I can help you," Tori says. She looks at me and raises her eyes as a little grin sneaks across her face. I cock my head and smile back.

Hum, I find something else new about my lady.

"I didn't know," I said. "Then again I never asked either."

"No ya didn't, but I never told you that either. I have a lot of skills with those things. I can do about anything with them, including rip them apart and build them."

Cabot, who has been listening to us, says, "good. Then the day after tomorrow Tori, I want you to set this thing up for me.

I'll pay you two hundred fifty grand to be my computer geek. How does that sound?"

She shakes her head and says, "it works for me."

Excellent. Follow me." He says, and gets up from the chair behind the desk.

We get up and follow him back through the magnificent house, and out the front door the way we came in. We begin to walk across the big lawn, to the house that we saw earlier. We say little on the way, but Cabot expresses to us that he wants us to make ourselves at home, even be happy here.

And I guess that could be possible on the surface even knowing how he's acquired all of this. Right now is one of those times. This is someplace I could get used to living and I know Tori can, too.

We get to the house and he unlocks the door. We follow him inside, and look around.

"Nice digs," I comment.

"Yeah, I've never even lived in something this nice," Tori says. She's looking at me.

"You know I haven't," I say. Looking at her.

The house we will be living in is very well maintained. It's a three bedroom ranch with a patio in the back. The exterior is brick half way up and the rest is some sort of yellow colored siding. It has a neat galley kitchen and dining room, two bathrooms, and family room with a fireplace. It's also air conditioned because it's nice and cool inside.

"This is your home while you're working here, which I hope is for sometime. My maids came down earlier and put fresh sheets on the beds, cleaned the place, and put food in the cabinets and refrigerator."

"Do you ever have trouble with the power grid? I mean lights going out like in the city," I ask?"

"No, because a group of us here in the Roxboro area have built our own power station, so that won't happen," he says. "The only request I will make of you is to be sure these doors and widows are all locked at night. As I elaborated to you at the prison, I have enemies. That is why I hired you, Sasha." Then he walks over to a small box on the wall. "You'll find one of these in each room in this house. It's an intercom to the main house, so when you're not present with me Sasha I can get in touch with you right away. To answer, all you do is press this black button. It's the same on all of them.

"Now I want you to see this." He smiles as he walks over to the door in the kitchen that opens to the garage, and motions for us to follow him out. We step into a two car garage with this one car in it.

"This is the Mustang that I told you about a few minutes ago."

Tori goes over to it, she's grinning like a little kid who has just got that dream toy for Christmas. "It's beautiful," she says. I watch her as she touches it running her fingers gently along it, like she petting it.

"Yes I had it completely rebuilt about six months ago, so it is essentially a new car. The only time I've driven it was today when I came down to Westerville. I never drive it though, because usually I just have Claus take me wherever I need to go.

"Well, I'll drive it," she says, enthusiastically.

"I was hoping you'd say that. I want you to drive it."

We both walk around the car, it's a beautiful metallic blue, and has a five speed transmission that no one even builds nowadays.

"I never asked this, but can you drive it? It's a manual transmission."

"You kidding," she says. "I can, and I can't wait to try it out."

"You, Sasha," she says.

"Yeah, it's been a longtime but I'm sure I'll remember how to drive it." I say. I'm smiling. Right now I'm having to much fun watching Tori. I had no idea she had such an affinity for cars. That makes two new things I learned about her today.

"Good, so if you have no other questions for me I will leave the two of you to yourselves. Relax and make yourselves at home. Since you're shopping tomorrow, you can start work, both of you, the day after tomorrow."

He looks at us again and pauses, like he wants to say something else to us, but doesn't then he leaves.

Tori and I watch him go out and she says, "in spite of what he does, he seems nice, at least on the surface."

"Yeah true. I just wonder who those enemies are that he wants me to protect him from."

"He doesn't seem to want to give you names, not right now anyway."

"Yeah, but we just got here, and I'll talk to him about it the day after tomorrow when we start."

"Maybe he doesn't want to give that to you yet, because he still has some sort of trust issue with you."

"I'm sure of that. But if that's the case he needs to get over it, quickly, he hired me to be his head of security. But a man who has built a life and financial empire like he has on the corrupt and inhumane business of human trafficking, has no reason to trust me or anyone else. I'm sure I will have to earn that trust, which is plus or minus with me."

"I know you Sasha, and know that you'll never trust him. Have you thought about killing him?"

"Yeah, you're right, I don't trust him, yet. And to answer your second question. No, and it's funny now that you mention it, I haven't even thought about killing him at all."

She pauses for a second still running her hand across the car, and says, "Sasha I don't want to ever go back to that place, ever."

"Don't worry about that. We're free, Tori, I've got these guns on and it would take an army to get us back there. I won't let that happen, ever. I'll kill anybody and everybody that would even try something that stupid, even Cabot. We ain't never going back to that place—trust me."

"I do trust you," She says.

"By the way," I say to her, with a smile. "We never told each other that we could drive."

"I guess being locked up like we were, it just wasn't something that we brought up."

"So where did you learn?"

"My Uncle Gabe. In spite of him not being such a nice

person he taught me to drive. I was so good that he took me to a place where I raced those old go carts."

"So you'd like to be a race car driver."

"I would...someday, maybe."

I smile at her, as she says that, as our hope for the future seems to be brightening already.

******

That night after a nice quiet dinner of fish and fresh vegetables that we cooked ourselves and ate leisurely. We had already decided that we wanted to spend the evening in the family room, on the big couch in front of the fireplace. We propped ourselves up as we always did knees up holding hands. Tori lays her head on my left shoulder. And for the first time ever, we have the chance to just relax, and talk about our future together. No fears, no interruptions, and no Behar.

Later we're off to bed—yes a real bed. With a soft mattress and equally soft pillows, and blankets to keep us warm. I am so looking forward to finally sleeping with my Tori, where we have plenty of room to hug and cuddle. A place where I can feel her nice warm body up next to mine, and not be crammed onto that damn cot, that wasn't meant for two people to sleep on in the first place. We had no other choice then, but now we have a bed to sleep in. It seems like a month has gone by since this morning when Cabot came to get us, like we were never in that place.

We're going shopping tomorrow to the town of Roxboro. So that is something for us to really look forward to, and get excited about. I have never had the opportunity to just shop, for clothes, and a bathing suit or any of that stuff with the money to do it all. I doubt Tori has either. So it will be fun for both of us after what we've just experienced. We're just going to be two girls on a shopping spree.

After quick, hot showers, we ditch our dirty underwear and decide to just sleep in our birthday suits—naked. Always before while at the prison we at least had to wear the t-shirts and our panties. Of course that never stopped Tori and I from making the most of it, loving each other.

But tonight will be like heaven. We're facing each other in bed and giggle, then shout, "SHOPPING!" We can't wait.

TWELVE

Two days later Tori and I make our way to the main house dressed in our new duds, to start work for Cabot. I figure my job will be to mainly stay near him. Except when I check the grounds once in a while—at least that's what I envision I'll be doing. Tori has a job now, too, she is to help him with his computer, which is good. She and I figure that will give her the access we need to start the work on finding the culprits responsible for this human trafficking operation.

Cabot called us on the intercom this morning during breakfast and said the door to the house would be unlocked, and for us to come on in. It was, and we made our way to the study. We find Cabot sitting in his big chair, but he's not alone in the room. There are two men in there with him this morning.

Looking at them I immediately think—goons. This is the first Tori or I have seen of them. One is over by the window, the other is in the corner behind Cabot by the bookcase. They're wearing what I call goon attire, which are polo shirts, slacks and those damn wingtip shoes. Each man has a hand gun holstered to his hip, both Beretta.9mm. And like most men they're unshaven and seem to have an aversion to a razor. But not Cabot he is always clean shaven and well groomed.

He looks up, "morning ladies."

There's that word again.

We both speak back. "Have a seat," he says. "Sasha, meet Penn and Cash, the other two security people in my employee." Without looking he points to each one of them and says, "boys, meet Sasha Cain, your new boss.

I look at both of them and they nod, I nod back. I didn't know about this part of the job. But then again going from being held captive just two days ago, to being a head of security making half a million a year. I'll take it.

"Tori," he says. "The other day when we agreed for you to do this computer stuff for me, you told me you could rip them apart and build them. What I want you to do, is not only make the thing run right, but I will leave you in charge of putting all the files on it."

"Oh yeah," she says. "I will do that. And I can show you how to access them when I'm not around. Like I said the other day I can build them, program them—whatever you want done."

"Good, I was hoping you'd say that, because as I indicated to you when you were in here the other day, I know absolutely nothing about these ancient, electronic monsters. So I will give you that desk in the next room and we'll move this thing over there so you can have your own work space. That way you can do what you need to do to get this system up to snuff. There's a cabinet full of files in there that I want you to input into it as soon as you have it ready."

"You bet, Mr. Cabot. I will set this thing up for you, then you can tell me what files you want on it first." She looks at me and we smile slightly and shake our heads.

He looks at her and nods approval at her comments. Learning quickly, like I am all of a sudden, that there's way more to my Tori than I even knew.

"As for you Sasha, you and these two guys can go outside and discuss the security of the place. I want you to know right up front, that I know someone is trying to take over some of my business ventures. And the only way that can happen is for them to kill me. So I want you to know that your job as head of security here has way more to do with things other than Westerville."

"Gotcha. Any idea who they are?"

"I do know who it is, and for now I want to see how they react to my latest actions toward them. I'll tell you who they are at the appropriate time, until then I want you, Penn and Cash to be on your toes, extra sharp. Got that?"

"I do."

He pauses and looks at me, "you are in complete charge of this entire place, as to keeping it secure. Just keep me informed as to your movements and decisions."

I shake my head that I would do that.

Then he looks at Tori and says to her, "So Tori—ready to get to work?"

She shakes her head yes. I look at Penn and Cash and motion for them to follow me outside, where we can talk.

Seconds later the three of us stand in the driveway, and I say, "So I guess the routine is to just walk the grounds and keep our eyes open." I'm trying to start a conversation with them. It has been my experience that goons are all a bit dull witted. Both of them are handsome guys and a bit older that me—late twenties/early thirties, I'm thinking.

Then Penn says, "yeah that's the way we been handling it. Just prowl around and try to remain visible.

"I didn't see you guys the other day when Tori and I arrived."

"We were around. Mr. C told us about hiring you."

"So what's that house over there for? Tori and I noticed it the day before yesterday when we got here.'

"That's Mr. C's stable—his house of concubines,"Cash says.

I shake my head when I hear this, and I question, "so let me get this straight, he keeps his own girls here to satisfy him, right?"

"Yeah," Cash responds

"He owns those girls."

"Yep, he bought them all at auction. He buys ems and then he sells em when he gets tired of em, and doesn't have any fun bangin' em anymore."

"How many girls are over there?"

"Four, right now," Cash says. "They've all been here a longtime, ain't they Penn?"

Penn shakes his head, "ya they have." He says, lighting up a smoke.

"So, when is the next auction happening?"

"They happen here every two weeks, so the next one will be the weekend after this. They always happen on the weekend. It's easier to transport the girls out here from Westerville. There's usually a crowd of people here. So you can plan on that," Penn explains. Taking a puff off his cigarette.

I say nothing and just look at them.

Cash asks me, "Mr. C says you ain't to keen on what he does here. So why'd you take this job and are protecting him?"

I don't immediately answer, I nod, indifferently, then say, "well it got me an Tori out of that damn Westerville, and it's a job, and a job that uses my skills, and pays me very well. So Tori and I figured what the hell. It's better to be here and be free— making money rather than to be stuck in that awful place."

"So how'd the two of you end up not being sold? I mean I'm pretty sure why they didn't sell you, but Tori...," says Penn.

"Well they'd planned on selling both of us. But if you are assuming why they didn't sell me, you're right. I wouldn't have been good to sell. As for Tori, she's my girlfriend and Behar left her alone until just before we came here. But they didn't sell her because they didn't want me to go ballistic and kill all of them. The problem was with us being held there, we were in solitary confinement about all the time. So I couldn't do much."

Penn asks, "why was that?"

"My run-ins with Behar. I tried to kill her, by stabbing her with a fork a few weeks before this. I did it to get revenge on her. She and her two bitch babes gang raped Tori."

They just look at me and shake their heads in an understanding way.

"We heard about you, Sasha," Cash says.

Yeah, what did you hear about me?"

"That you're one tough cookie. We're glad you're on our

THE ALLEY OF EVIL

side," Penn says. "They call you the enforcer. Right?"

"That's right."

Then I look at them and tell them that goes both ways. I'm glad they're on my team. To which they both smiled hearing me say that. Then we spend some time talking about how to best protect the estate. They tell me that they make rounds of the property every fifteen or so minutes. I told them there is no use in changing that routine, and they agreed.

"I'll be spending a lot of my time inside with Cabot, but I want you two guys to know that I'll from time to time come out here and make rounds with you. And if you need anything or need me in a hurry, get to me right away and I will come immediately." They understood, and said they would do that.

They leave and go off to do their rounds, and I have a new found respect for them. I find that they're not dull witted as I first assumed, as a matter of fact they seem like pretty cool guys. So much for Sasha Cain's first impressions of people.

After meeting with Penn and Cash, I decide to have a look at the house where the girls are being kept. I walk in that direction keeping in mind what my real purpose is for being here.

If Tori and I are going to get to the bottom of who is running this trafficking operation, then part of it will be doing some old fashioned detective work. That means asking questions when we can, and doing some snooping, like Tori will be doing on the computer. In the meantime I want to talk to the girls in this house and ask some of those questions, too see if they can give me anything fresh to go on.

The house is similar to the one Tori and I are staying in. It's a modest frame house, with white vinyl siding and green shutters on the windows, and a small front porch with porch furniture for setting on. It has what looks like three or four bedrooms. The blinds in the windows are drawn shut in all the rooms.

I walk up to the front door and knock. After a couple of seconds a young woman that can't be more that nineteen opens the door."Yes," she says, in a quiet voice. She's blonde and about five-six or so.

I said to her, "Hi, I'm Sasha Cain, the new head of security here, and I just came over to make myself known. Can I come in and talk to you for just a sec?"

She shrugged indifferently and opened the door wider, letting me enter. Then she turned her back and walked away and into the kitchen, where she sat down at the kitchen table. She obviously doesn't care whether I'm there or not. And why should she?

I follow her in and ask, "can I sit down?"

She looked at me and shrugged again, "suit yourself."

I sat down in the chair across from her, she's drinking coffee. She's blonde and has her hair in a ponytail. She has on a plain pink tank top and denim shorts that are very short—she's barefooted. I study her for just a second, but not so long as to make her uncomfortable with me. I figure she may already be since I told her I was head of security.

"Look," I began, "I know you're probably not comfortable with me, but Penn and Cash told me there are four of you that live here. Is that right?"

"Yeah there are, four of us," she responds, quietly.

"So what's your name? Don't be afraid, I just want to talk to you and the others if they're around."

"They are, and I'm Shelly." She says, quietly, not wanting to talk to me, and I can't blame her. She is after all being held captive by a sick man, who uses her and the others who live here purely for sex.

I was about to ask her another question when I heard voices coming toward the kitchen. Soon the other four women appeared in the doorway, who live here with Shelly. One is about my age, and is black, and the other like Shelly is about nineteen. The third girl is young, only about fourteen years old, and Hispanic. All of them are dressed in similar attire like Shelly is, and are well taken care of. It makes for better sales, I figure.

They continue into the room, and look at me with suspicion. The black girl immediately asks me using a poignant tone, "who're you?"

"Sasha Cain, I'm the new head of security here, and I just came down to make myself known."

"Yeah, well you've done that, so leave," she snaps. Not at all pleased with my presence. Why would she be?

"Look, I know your situation here isn't pleasant, but I just want to talk with all of you for just a few minutes. Okay?"

"Why?" She snaps at me sharply.

"Okay. Let's start over here, I told you my name, now you tell me yours. And then I'm going to tell you that I can and want to help you all with your situation here. If you'll let me?"

"How can you help us? Cabot keeps us locked up in here 24/7. He only releases the locks from the main house during the day. When Penn and Cash can see what we're doing. And why would you do it in the first place? You're working for Cabot." The black girl says.

"Name?"

"Wendy. She's Patti, and that's Maria. So how can you help us? We're sex slaves, girl." She retorts.

"I know that," I say to her.

Then Patti says, "I think she can help us Wendy. I was at Westerville when she and Tori were there. This gal is tough as nails."

Wendy asks, "You were at Westerville?"

"Yeah, Tori and I both were there until just the day before yesterday. Cabot came to the prison and got us out because he wanted me to be his personal bodyguard and head of security."

"Who's Tori?"

"She's my girlfriend and is up at the main house doing Cabot's computer work for him."

"So how do you think you, and this Tori can help us?" Wendy says, sarcasm still filling her voice.

"Well, Tori and myself, we want to get to whoever is behind this human trafficking. I know I'm the head of security here, but my main purpose of being here is to find the culprits that run this. Is it Cabot?"

"No, it ain't Cabot, he ain't nothin' but a mule," Patti says.

"A mule."

"Yeah, he just lives here like we do, but gets paid a lot of money by this big syndicate that's the actual owner."

"Syndicate. How did you guys learn about that?"

"It was common knowledge at Westerville," Patti said. "You and Tori spent most of your time in solitary and away from the rest of the prison population, so it doesn't surprise me that you don't know about it."

"So, what your telling me is that we were, maybe, purposely, kept in solitary for long periods of time. Because someone didn't want us to know about what it is you're telling me."

"Probably," Patti says.

"You just said that Cabot is a mule for this syndicate, he told us he was the owner of Westerville and this place."

"I wouldn't have put it past him, but Cabot doesn't own squat. What we do know is that he does run all the rest of his illegal crime businesses from here."

"Like?"

"Drugs, money laundering. You name it, he's into it."

I shake my head listening to this, though none of it surprises me, and it makes sense because he told us he has enemies in his other business ventures.

"So, Sasha, keep your head up," Wendy says. Her attitude toward me changing quickly.

"Why were you sent there to Westerville in the first place," Patti asks"

"I was railroaded by my client that I did a job for, his name is Colin Lampoor. It was his intent to have me sold like all of you are."

"Why didn't that happen," Asks Wendy?

"Well, I'm a very violent girl, and Cabot got wind of me being there and stopped it I guess."

"How long were you guys there?"

"Four months."

"So he let you and this Tori rot in that hell hole for four months?" Wendy asks me, astonished.

"Yeah, crazy as it seems that's what he did. But from what he told us he had been trying to get us out for some time, but my nemesis Lampoor was blocking him." I paused and looked at all of them. "Here's what I can do for you ladies. I can protect you from being sold to anyone, but for a while you're going to have to play along with Cabot. Tori and I are going to be doing all we can to get at the information that we're looking for. I'll keep you abreast of what we're doing as best as I can. But I don't want Cabot to find out what Tori and I are up too. But if he tries to hurt you in any way, I will kill him and be done with it. I will protect you if anything goes awry. Right now though he's more useful to us alive, than dead."

They shook their heads, that they understood. Up to this time Shelly and Maria had not said anything. I'm standing to leave when Shelly says to me, "so Sasha how are you and Tori going to get at whoever is doing this."

"Don't know yet. Tori is on Cabot's computer and she's a genius with them, so it's important what she finds out. It'll take some time though. Oh, and one more thing. Do any of you know if you're going to be auctioned off next week? Just wondering."

They all shook their head and responded, they had no idea.

"Well, to put your minds at ease. I won't let it happen, so you're not going anywhere and I'll kill anybody who tries to take any of you away. Trust me on that."

"I heard you called the enforcer, when I was at Westerville," Patti says.

"Yeah, that's what they call me."

Before I got out the door the fourteen year old, named Maria, asked me, "those guns you're wearing?

"Yeah."

"You know how to shoot em good?"

"Yeah I do?" I look at her wondering about where she's going with this.

"Would you teach me to shoot, too, so I can kill the bastards that have kidnapped me and sold me like they have?"

"I will, Maria. I won't only teach you to shoot. I'll help you kill them. How's that sound?"

She shook her head and gave me a wry smile, like she wanted to believe me.

I leave that house with the realization that those girls while they live in constant fear, are used to what has happened to them, and have given up hope of any kind that they will be rescued. I can only hope that I quelled some of that fear for them today.

From the house where the girls are I made my way back to the estate house. I look around for Penn and Cash but don't see them. I go inside and head for the study, as I'm sure that is where I'll find Cabot. On the way I pass by the room adjacent to his office, where Tori is. She is hard at work on the computer.

I walk in and she looks up, and greets me, "hey."

I say hey back and I walk over and bend down and kiss her on the cheek. She smiles and takes hold of my hand and squeezes it.

"So, I see, Cabot has you busy."

"Yeah, whoever had this thing though, really screwed it up."

"How so?"

"Ah, it's like most of these things, while the machine itself isn't that old, the technology is. Most people who get hold of computers these days don't know anything about them in the first place. That's why they sell them to guys like Cabot. I told him about it, and said I'd have to fix all the issues and bugs it has before I can even start doing what he wants."

"What did he say?"

"Just do it. So where have you been?"

"Out scouting around looking at the lay of the place." Then I put my fingers over my mouth, bend down and get close. "Is he in there?"

Tori shrugs and shakes her head, that she doesn't know.

I go out of the room and walk gingerly toward the study door, getting to a place where I can peek in and not be seen. I look and he's not in there, so I go back to where Tori is. I stand in the doorway to talk to her, so I can see Cabot if he returns to his study.

"I was just down to the other house and talked to the girls that are being held here against their will. They told me that a syndicate is running all of this."

"A syndicate? But we thought Cabot was…"

"Nope, he's not."

"Did they give you a name for that syndicate?" She says quietly.

"No. But one of the girls, named Patti, told me that this syndicate is common knowledge at Westerville. She was there for a time while we were."

"We never knew about this."

"We weren't supposed, too, that's part of the reason we were kept in solitary. It wasn't just about my violent behavior toward Behar why they kept us in there and away from the other girls. They didn't want us to find out the stuff I was just told."

"Yeah they didn't want us to know about what the other girls knew for this reason."

"Which I haven't figured out yet, but it doesn't matter since we're out of there.

"True."

"They told me that Cabot is nothing but a mule and works for this syndicate."

"So he lied to us."

"Yeah he did," I laugh. "They told me he runs a bunch of other criminal endeavors out of here, so trafficking is just one of his hobbies. Which we know from our conversations with him."

"Well here's what I can do, once I get this thing up and running right. I can find out what all he's into."

"Great. So how long do you think it will take you to do that?"

"All of today at least. Like I said, this things is a mess."

"When you get to where you're inputting information into

it, let me know what it is, so I can decide what I might be able to do here."

"You got an idea?"

"No not yet, that's why it's important for you to relay what you find out to me."

"Well, I already have one thing for you."

"What's that?"

"The guest list for next week's auction. There are a couple of people on the list that you'll be interested in knowing that will be here. I made this copy so you can see the names on the list. I highlighted the names that are the most interesting to you and there's one on there that interests me."

She hands the piece of paper to me and I scan the sheet. I see Colin Lampoor, Commander Par of the Rottendamn cops, which doesn't surprise me. It says the merchandise will be provided by Warden Cynthia Behar, of the Westerville facility.

"Warden Cynthia Behar, my ass," I say. Shaking my head with a grin. Causing Tori to break out laughing.

Tori then points out the name of the store owner that had her put in Westerville.

"That shouldn't surprise you," I said. She smiled at me wryly.

Then I saw a name that was on there that she hadn't underlined. It was at the end, and said the auctioneer for the event would be Tyler Baines.

"That's interesting."

"What is?"

"The auctioneer's name, Tyler Baines. He was in the cell

adjacent to mine in Rottendamn when Lampoor double-crossed me. He made a point to tell me who he was, and he knew all about me. My snitch Cooch told me his name before that. He said that Baines was working with the Seventh Streeters in Rottendamn. Seems they wanted to get rid of me for being on their turf. But Cooch told me he wasn't sure that this Baines guy had anything to do with that. And Baines confirmed to me himself that he wasn't out to get me, when I saw him in that jail cell."

"So you think he might be in on this trafficking, too? Maybe?"

"I don't know for sure Tori. Yeah, he might be. We'll find out."

NANCY HOWARD

THIRTEEN

As the week progressed Tori got the computer fixed and began to input the information that Cabot wanted into it. She also kept me abreast of what it was she was doing, and what data she was putting into the machine.

From time to time she would take me into what has now become her office, and she'd show me what she was doing. She's created a big spreadsheet with numbers on it. Each number corresponds to the picture of a girl who was being held in captivity, and is to be auctioned off. Those who don't get sold remain in holding prisons like Westerville, getting returned until the next auction. She also showed me how she was preparing to hook all of this information up to a gigantic television screen, like what was once called a jumbotron.

She said that the people who are coming here on Saturday are not the only bidders, that she has put together a string of internet connections, so that people from all over the world can have access to the auction here.

Today Cabot is playing golf, and I sent Penn with him. Tori and I are going over what she has compiled. I told him that's why I sent Penn with him, I wanted to go over the guest list with her to make sure everyone was legit. I figure that at least will make him think that I know what I'm doing here. It doesn't hurt one bit, because it will help him build trust in my ability to protect him. Which is what I'm wanting to do, build trust. Because it will give Tori and I time to put together some sort of plan to get to get to the bottom of all this. It gives us snooping time, allowing us to find out who the syndicate is and where they might be located.

"Remember you and I wondered when we first got here about what our Mr. Raymond Cabot is into other than human trafficking? And what else you might be protecting him from."

I shake my head.

"Well I know it all now, and what the girls down at the other house told you is true. Seems as though our so called rich esteemed employer is into all kinds of rackets, that prays on people's pain. He launders money from many businesses both in Roxy and in New Rotterdam. He has cops and attorneys, anyone you can think of on his dole. When they do his dirty work for him, he gives them cash under the table, and plenty of it. He has a crooked judge on his payroll in Rotterdam, who he pays to have his enemies disappear. And that's not all. He runs a meth lab upstate, in the mountains, and he sells that shit worldwide. Not to mention prostitution, which goes great along with this trafficking scheme."

"So if he has all of this other stuff going on, then those girls are right saying that he's just a mule for this syndicate. Whoever they are."

"Right and it's not just him, but Behar, Lampoor, all of them."

I shake my head and smile at her and kiss her cheek and say, "you are such a genius, Tori Nicks."

Now that Tori and I have a feel for what's really going on around here. I have more confidence in my ability to do what I have to do, for what may or may not happen on Saturday.

I do have one guest on my mind though, and for now I'll keep my thoughts to myself about him. That guest is Tyler Baines, the Auctioneer for the event. I wonder if he's a trafficker, too, and gets some sort of kickback out of this. What is his angle? And was he put in that jail cell next to mine in Rotterdam that night on purpose? If he was, who had him put there?

While I have these questions, I am in the position here that I can ask them, and get the answers I want. Plus on Saturday I can keep an eye on all those involved who harmed Tori and I.

I now know one thing for sure, that I'm not really here to protect him from the syndicate, whoever they are. But I'm here to protect him from all those enemies in his other business endeavors.

******

It's Saturday and the day of the auction. Cabot had some men come from Roxy to set up the lawn in the back of the house. I have to admit that this is a pretty setting, with the Catskill Mountains as a backdrop. It's July and they are draped in the fine lush greenery of summer. It is a serene image that belies the fact that there's an auction taking place here today. An auction to sell human beings to other human beings for sexual pleasure. It's repulsive.

The back of the estate house is just as stunning as the front. There's a huge concrete patio that spans the entire back of the house. It is covered by a flat roof that is supported by decorative columns. The patio has different levels that leads down to the lawn and pool area. There's a food table and open bar, both in the shade and out of the sun, up next to the house. The huge swimming pool has bath houses in the rear for guests to change. And the south side of the lawn is where chairs have been set up by the house and kitchen crew, who Tori and I barely know. In front of it is the big jumbotron like television screen, that's where Tori is setting up the computer feed for the auction—it's to begin at noon.

As I walk toward her she doesn't even see me approaching her, she's busy getting everything set up right. She also working with the two guys who set the jumbotron up. She seems almost frantic in her work pace, as I walk up to her.

"Hey," she says to me, without looking up.

"Hey to you. You okay? I can see you're busy as hell, but I just thought I'd stop by to see if I can get you anything."

"I'm good. But if you could get me another set of computer hands that would be nice." She says standing straight up and taking a drink from her water bottle.

"Troubles?"

"No, not so much trouble, it's just that this technology is so damned old that getting it put together to do what he wants done is a challenge in itself."

"It needs an upgrade. Right?" I say lightheartedly. Hoping

to ease some of her tension.

"A serious one," she responds. "I'm just about to get this all connected. The internet is so fragmented—not like it was in the old days when it was virtually worldwide, with the exception of the countries that censored it."

"You got some time, it's only ten."

"Yeah—I got it," she shrieks happily. We high five each other.

I wasn't sure what she got, so I asked her.

"I got all the damn connections right; that's what," she says, happily.

We pause and I notice her watching me look around.

She says, "how are you doing with all this. I know how much it must be tearing you up inside, because it's doing the same to me."

I shake my head at her, "yeah it is. At least we're here and can do something about it, and we're not rotting away in that damn jail cell. I'm just trying to keep this whole thing in perspective, Tori. You know? I'm trying to stay the course as to how we can eventually stop this from happening. It's been two weeks since Cabot got us out of Westerville, and so many times I think about how lucky we are now. But Tori I just can't get those poor girls that are still stuck in that hell place out of my mind. I've thought about them a lot since we got here."

"Me, too. I think about them, but something to be thankful for Sasha is we're not at Westerville. We are fee now. Eventually we will help those poor girls still trapped inside there."

I sigh, and shake my head.

"Don't loose hope, we got to do what you told me while we were there. Stay strong."

"Yeah, for sure." I pause, knowing she's right. "Listen, I know, you're going to be front and center today because you're in charge of the computer and the internet feed when the auction starts. If you need anything at all, motion to me, and I be right there."

"I am in charge, trust me. And I will," she says with a grin.

I shake my head at her and smile.

The guests began arriving at about eleven thirty. I have Penn and Cash out at the gate checking everyone's credentials as they drive through. It's going to be interesting to see who shows up. While the guest list was over two hundred, Cabot says that there are always a few no shows. He also took the time to tell me about the range of guests that would be here. Some he says are the dregs of society, which is laughable to me coming out of someone who's a career criminal himself. Some he says are the cream of the crop, if there is such a thing this day in age.

Other than that he and I say little to each other—meaning, we like, rarely talk—about anything. Even when I'm in his office with him which is rare. He works with or is in Tori's office. She actually talks to him way more than I do. When I am with him I usually set and read one of the many books that he has on his shelves. All classics and all very interesting to someone like me, who, as I told Tori in Westerville, I'd not read much, and really never cared for going to school. I'm learning that I do indeed like to read. So lately I've become a voracious reader.

I'm not reading today, I'm earning my keep. Doing what

Cabot has hired me to do—be his head of security. While Tori is busy with her computers, earning her keep, setting up the auction. I have the responsibility of making sure this crowd of people stays safe and out of mischief. Cabot told me there are factions that will be here that don't like each other. He informed me who to look out for, and he also told me that he's got the word out that he's hired me as his head of security. He says that alone should quell anyone from getting out of line.

I look out toward the gate and see an old school bus come onto the property. It's not a regular size school bus, but one of those bigger ones, and it is painted dark green. It has the words Westerville Prison painted on the sides of it in white letters.

It comes into the circle and stops, and sits for a minute before the doors open. One of the guards gets out, who I immediately recognize. He's the one that gut punched the hell out of me when I stabbed Behar with the fork. I decided not to go over to greet him. Two more guards come out—Behar's bitches. I want to hurl. Then the girls begin to exit. I watch until the last one is off.

Then Behar comes off last, and goes over to the girls, who number about forty, and are huddled in a group with the three guards near them. Behar hasn't seen me yet, as she goes about the business of herding the girls toward the other house. Barking orders at them as she goes. Each girl is dressed in a white tight fitting t-shirt, with a number over their left breast and very short denim shorts, and white sneakers. These are different from the drab tan prison uniforms that they usually wear. I'm sure what they're wearing today is to accentuate any fine physical qualities that the girl has.

The thing is some of them are just kids, no more than twelve or fourteen—hardly what you would consider a fully developed woman. But then again that's what these creeps want—young and virgin.

Those numbers on the shirts I now know now correspond with the numbers that Tori has been inputting into the computer. She also found our two numbers in the database, and she removed them immediately. Which didn't matter because no one will ever put us in that system again, because if they try—I'll kill them.

I thought I'd seen everyone arrive, but then again I haven't been outside all the time. I was inside in the study, retrieving a file for Tori, when I heard a big motorcycle arrive. I came out to see who it was and it turned out to be Tyler Baines. I watched him get off his big Harley-Davidson, remove his helmut, and walk around to the back of the house.

I went through the house and out the back, because after seeing him arrive I definitely want to talk to him. I exit the big patio doors and immediately see him over next to Tori, talking to her. I walk over to him, he hasn't seen me yet and I say, "Mr. Baines, we meet again."

He turns around to see who spoke, and sees it's me, "Sasha. Yes we do. Only this time under very different circumstances."

"Yeah, you know when I saw your name on the guest list, I couldn't help myself to wonder why you do this?"

"I need a job. And likewise, I was equally surprised to see that you took this job. You're head of security here."

"I am." I smile at him and he smiles back, our looks lingering on each other. I hope Tori doesn't notice.

He's very easy on the eyes, quite handsome in fact, even ruggedly so. He has a full head of thick brown hair, and broad shoulders, with strong muscular arms that are accentuated today by the polo shirt he's wearing. He's about six-one and even though I love Tori to death, a romp with him between the sheets I think, as I look at him, could spell nothing but fun.

"Listen," he says. Grinning at me. "After the auction could you and I talk, Tori, too. I have something I'd like to discuss with both of you, if you don't mind."

"Sure," I say. She's listening and agrees.

With well over a hundred people here, it is past noon. The bar is open and the booze is flowing. Many are in the pool. The auction begins. I've spied my old nemesis Colin Lampoor, and Tori pointed out to me the merchant that had her arrested. He has said nothing to her, and he should refrain from doing so.

Lampoor keeps his distance from me and so does Behar and Par, all of them, ignoring me. It's a good thing they're doing so—I have guns on now.

Cabot, too has been here all along and has the girl Wendy seated next to him along with the teenager, Maria, indicating that they are not up for auction today. They are to the left of Tori, who is running this, along with Baines. The other girls Patti and Shelly are not part of this at all, indicating they're not up for sale either. I saw them on the porch of the house earlier.

Each time a girl is sold Tori just looks at me and I at her, then she bows her head closing her eyes. I asked her later about doing that. She told me she was saying a prayer for the person that was sold. Even though like me, she has never been religious in anyway—she hopes someone will watch over them.

And she's right. Once auctioned off they're often put in a cage along with other people to be shipped off to wherever. It's very inhumane. Sometimes they are put in large containers by themselves with little food or water to survive a long trip to somewhere else on the planet for several days. And if they arrive dead—then so what? No one cares and no one will miss them anyway. Not the person who bought and paid for them and certainly not whoever is in control of this.

Even their families won't miss them—most of these kids are runaways. Meaning they left a bad situation in the first place. But running away like they did made them easy marks—vulnerable to bad people who pray on them, promising them the moon. And by the time they, the victim realizes what has happened to them, it's too late.

But Tori and I do care, that's why we're here, to stop this atrocity. These are human beings, not commodities that are being auctioned off and sold just for the hell of it. That is why we're so determined to find out whoever is in charge of this evil charade.

Which brings me to this. What does Baines want to talk to Tori and I about? Is it something about this? I wonder.

The day went on as kids as young as twelve got sold to the highest bidder. It made me sick to my stomach to watch, no matter what I tried to do. I've tried looking away—tried to do what Tori did. Pray for them—it's just not in me. I can't turn my back on this. I must do something about it. And I can only do one thing and that's kill whoever this syndicate is.

I was so caught up in watching what was going on that I even forgot Behar, and Lampoor were in attendance. I never went near them while they were here. They left without approaching me, which was good—I could have done anything to them I wanted to today, given the circumstances. They would have been so easy to kill.

After everyone was gone, and it was nearing eight o'clock in the evening, Tori has found me and we look around for Baines. He's over at the bar by himself having a drink. Penn and Cash are at a table having a beer, and Cabot went off into the house but without Wendy and Maria. He sent them back to the house, which I thought was odd. He certainly was not in a party mood. I wonder why? Though I noticed he wasn't in a good mood at all, and hasn't been for a couple of days.

Tori and I walk over to Baines, he looks up. "Ladies. Can I buy you a drink?"

We both looked at the bartender, who is wrapping things up. I got a beer and Tori ordered ice water.

We make some small talk until our drinks arrive, they soon do and I ask him, "so what is it that you want to talk to Tori and me about?"

"Well before I get to that. I want you to know," he says, looking at her. "You are a genius on those damn computers. Where did you learn all that stuff?"

"I was just exposed to them that's all, and I had a guy who taught me all that stuff. He was a geek and made me into one."

"Really. Where's he at?"

"Dead. He used to beat me, and he got murdered on his way home one night. Just broke my heart when I found out he was killed," she says, with sarcasm."You know it happens to a lot of people in Rottendamn, as Sasha refers to it."

"I know. I'm sorry he beat you like that. You didn't deserve it, Tori." He says looking at her compassionately. Then after a brief pause he says, "I was wondering if the two of you have anytime away from here?

"Why," I ask?

"Well, what I really, really, need to talk about has to be discussed with you girls away from here."

"We get tomorrow off," Tori blurts out.

"We do?" I say. Surprised.

"Yep. Cabot stopped by and told me to tell you that."

I shake my head, "okay."

"That's good because I was wondering if the two of you could meet with me tomorrow in Roxboro, at a coffee shop called Hannibal's. You know where it is?"

"Yeah," I said. Looking at him, and lingering, causing him to grin. "Can you tell us the reason why you want to meet us there?"

"I think the two of you, and I are looking for the same thing if I'm not mistaken."

"And what might that be?"

"The syndicate."

"You know Tyler before that fucker Lampoor double-crossed me, my snitch said that you were working for the

Seventh Streeters in Rottendamn. Were you trying to take me down?"

He looked down at his drink and shook his head no, before he answered me.

"No, Sasha, I wasn't trying to do that, at all. I'm an investigative reporter and I used that cover to gain their confidence. You see, I'd heard about you and the reputation you have as the enforcer, as they call you. I never had any intention of doing any harm to you. I've learned over the years that in order to get to know someone, often the best way to do that is to spend some time with their enemies."

"And what did you find out from them?"

"That they fear you, but at the same time have a great deal of respect for you and what you do. I think it's because you're a woman."

"So why were you doing an investigative report on me?"

"Like I said, I'd heard about you and wanted to do a story about you, and people like yourself—how you survive on the streets. What you do. I wanted first to get their angle of what you're like. Eventually, I was intending to approach you, and maybe get you to let me spend some time with you. You know, following you around."

"That wouldn't have been very exciting," I say.

"Well maybe not for you, but for me I think it would have been. Even today ladies, people like to read about someone like you, Sasha. A woman who lives her life, dangerously—on the edge. You know a lot of people will never have the chance to experience the things you have. So there you have it."

I shake my head listening to him telling us this. I had no idea.

"You were in that jail cell next to me when Lampoor had me put in there."

"Yes that's true, I was. I had been arrested that day for getting too drunk and punching a bouncer. So that's how I was in there at the same time as you. It was purely a coincidence. I saw you in that jail cell that night and wondered how you got there."

Then Tori asks, "how long have you known Cabot?"

"About a year, I guess. I started doing these auctions, to get closer to what I wanted to find. It's the same thing you two are doing now."

"So how can we trust you?" I say.

He looks at me for a second—nodding before he answers. "I guess you'll have to go with your gut feeling on that, Sasha. Just like I will have to with you. I have no quarrel with you, and I'm sure as hell no match for you with a gun."

"Have you killed before?"

"Yes I have." He says standing up, readying to leave. "And I will tell you that it was for my own self defense." He says and pauses briefly, looking back and forth at each of us. "Listen to me, both of you. I want to bring this down just like the two of you, but doing it by myself I have found to be nearly impossible. I need your help, both you, so meet me tomorrow at noon and we can discuss this in more detail."

"Why are you doing this? What meaning does it have for

you," Tori asks?

"It's very personal, and I will enlighten you both about that tomorrow, when we meet."

I look at Tori and we agree to meet with him.

"Then I shall see you tomorrow, ladies." He says and leaves.

THE ALLEY OF EVIL

FOURTEEN

That next day being Sunday and with Tori and I having the day off, I make sure Penn and Cash have my phone number to get in touch with me if they need me. Tori and I hop in the Mustang, and head into Roxboro, to meet with Tyler at Hannibal's.

Before leaving, I noticed that Cabot was not around. I had seen him earlier in the morning as I walked the grounds. He was on his phone arguing loudly with someone. I couldn't make out the entire conversation, because I didn't want him to know I was doing a little eavesdropping. Could this be the reason he didn't take the two girls to bed after the auction yesterday. He seems preoccupied by something and Tori and I have not been able to figure it out. It's been going on for a few days now.

I figure it has to do with what he told me the first day we started to work here. That someone was trying to take over his business enterprises, and wants to kill him. So I can bet it has something to do with that.

Roxboro is a small town in the Catskill Mountains, that time has forgotten, really. It is still surprisingly intact from the early twenty-first century. It still has some class. Like neighborhoods, and stores, and shops, and a real local government that is elected. Roxboro is one of the few places left in the country that's still like this, it has in somehow bucked the trend of privatized government. Which is a refreshing change from the banana republic mentality that has gripped the rest of the country for three decades now.

I'm driving, Tori let's me do that now and then, she's such a fantastic driver I almost feel selfish when I do drive. This is the second time that she and I have made a trip to Roxy as everyone calls it. So on this beautiful summer day with the windows down, we cruise down the old highway at sixty-five miles per hour, having the time of our lives. Both realizing that just a scant two weeks ago we were still locked up in a six foot by twelve foot jail cell, being held prisoner by the very system we work for, but intend to bring down.

"You know Tori, I remember hearing that there were still places like this, where the sun shines bright and the air is cleaner than in Rottendamn. Girl, I think we've found it."

"Yeah, I do, too. Isn't this great. I wonder what Behar is doing?"

I look at her and we both break into an evil laugh.

Then I ask her, "how are you doing with the rape these days?"

She doesn't answer right away, then says, "you know, it comes and goes."

"I do know, Tori, and I'm here for you, you know that, just like you've been here for me with then nightmares."

"I know. All I ask, is when I need you to hold me, do it,

because I'm dealing with that shit. I have to know that you'll always be there for me, Sasha."

"I will be, Tori. I promise."

Arriving in town I park the car across the street from Hannibal's. I don't have my guns on, sometimes it's best not to wear them in plain sight, especially when visiting a town like Roxy. I don't want to draw unwanted attention to myself or Tori, so I pack my small, thirty-eight caliber, pistol under my shirt. Today Tori and I just want to look like two girls on a shopping spree, like we were a couple of weeks ago when we came here to buy clothes.

Approaching Hannibal's we see Tyler setting at a small square table off to the right of the front entrance. He is in a spot where we are in the shade and are far enough away from other customers that we can discuss what we need to privately.

He looks up and sees us. "Ladies, nice to see you again so soon. Thanks for coming. Can I buy you some coffee?"

We looked at each other and shook our heads yes. He called a waitress over and ordered coffee for each of us.

Tyler intrigues me like now other man I've ever met and I'm not sure why. He seems like a good honest guy with a genuine interest in the three of us tracking down whoever is behind all of this human trafficking. But what intrigues me most about him is he's just so damn beautiful.

"So we've heard that this whole thing is being run by a huge syndicate someplace. That true."

He shakes his head.

"It has tentacles all over the world. I'm not even sure how

far it reaches. But I do know that Cabot is just a small part of it. You both should know that by now. Especially you Tori with all that time you've spent on the computer before the auction."

"I do, but like you I felt like I was just finding the tip of the iceberg," she says.

I say, "So where do we begin if it's that big? How long has it been in business?"

He shakes his head. "I don't know the answer to that, Sasha, all I know is that all of my research hits dead ends. Every time I go snooping around for this syndicate. It seems to not exist."

"Like a ghost corporation."

"Precisely. And that's where the two of you can help, especially you Tori. You have access to Cabot's computer and the internet, which most people have no idea how to use anymore because of access to it.

"Look," he says, getting in closer to us, to make the conversation more private and to get his point across. "I watched you string together all those intricate connections yesterday. I told you that you're a genius girl, and you are. You really know what the hell you're doing, and if this is a way we can get to the bottom of this syndicate. Then we should do it."

"With Tori's computer skills," I said. Looking at her and smiling.

"That's right. But we have to be discreet. You two especially. You don't want Cabot to suspect that you're snooping around into this. We don't want him to get pissed off and send you back to Westerville."

"Trust me even if he would find out—that will never happen. Cabot is a non denominator in this. Besides he already trusts Tori on the computer, or he wouldn't give her access to it. He as much as admitted that he knows nothing about them, that's why she's doing what she is."

Then Tori says, "you're both right in your assessment of his trust in me. I have complete access to every thing he does. He knows this and it doesn't seem to bother him at all."

"It's like he knows you'll find out anyway."

"Right," she says.

"Speaking of Cabot did either of you see him this morning before you left?"

"I did. He was on the front portico drinking coffee in what sounded like a heated argument with someone on the phone. I didn't talk to him, but his conversation with whoever it was seemed very contentious."

"Any idea what it was about?"

We shook our heads, and I made mention of what he told us the first day we got here. But told him I wasn't for sure what it was.

Tori says, "he's been preoccupied with something big on his mind the past few days, but has chosen not to tell Sasha or me about it."

"Interesting."

"So yesterday before you left, you indicated that you have a personal stake in all this, and you told us you would elaborate on it today."

He looks at us pausing briefly, like he's rethinking telling us what he said yesterday.

Then he begins, almost blurting it out, "I was at work, at what is left of the news business these days. I lived in New London...Connecticut. I got a call at about three in the afternoon from the only local law officer that could be trusted. He told me I needed to come home as fast as I could get there. I asked him why and he said he couldn't talk about it over the phone.

"I rushed home as fast as I could. My wife, Lea and our then seventeen year old daughter, Janet, I knew were there, when I left that morning. To make a long story short. I arrived to find that my wife had been killed." He stops, and turns his head, not speaking for a few seconds. He swallows hard, clearing his throat, before speaking, "Her, uh...throat had been slit. And Janet, our beautiful Janet was missing, gone, nowhere to be found. I was dead inside and furious as to what had happened. There was no clue, no note, no nothing, that told me anything about who had killed my wife and taken my daughter. The police had no leads either."

"So after my wife's funeral I quit my job and decided to do everything I could to find her. In the meantime I started drinking and went broke, taking one odd job after another just to survive.

"So I started digging, and digging. And each time while I got a little further gathering information, as I told you I hit dead end, after dead end. Eventually my search brought me here to Cabot's auctions. I decided to take a job with him as an auctioneer, I had done that years ago when I was a young guy to put myself through school. I felt like once I was closer to them, that it could possibly lead me to Janet's whereabouts. I figure now that it's too late, and that she's in all likelihood been sold—many times."

"How long has it been," I asked?

"Four years. She'd be twenty-one now."

"So you've been searching for her all those years," I said.

"Yes," he says. Looking down at his coffee, blankly, suddenly not interested in drinking it. He looks up, and says, "That's why I decided to try and hook up with you and Tori when I saw you here at the auction yesterday. And in doing so, I've learned, thanks to your lovely girlfriend, more information than I gained on my own in four years."

"Yeah, she's pretty cool, not to mention what you called her."

"A genius," he says.

"You guys are embarrassing me," she says. We laughed at her comment, as she blushes.

There was a brief pause, as I looked away and shook my head.

"So what's our next move," Tori asks? Her embarrassment quickly gone.

"You, the two of you go back and learn all you can over the next few days. I have to fly out to London tomorrow, and while I'm there I'll see if I can find out anything on that end. We can meet when I get back."

"When will that be," I ask?

"Thursday. So we should plan to meet at the estate then to compare notes. I'll just come by if that's okay? We need to keep this below Cabot's radar."

We shook our heads at him in agreement.

******

On the way back Tori and I talked about Tyler. She's doing the driving this time. I don't want to hog all the fun driving the Mustang.

"What a sad story he told us, Sasha."

"Yeah, yeah it was. I can't begin to imagine what he's been through."

"Me neither. Did you see the empty look on his face as he told it and the anger that remains in his voice."

Yes, yes I did."

"So I gather you trust him?'

"Affirmative on that, too. He said we'd have to go with our gut feeling about him, and mine says he's okay. He's loosing hope in finding his daughter, Tori. I hope we can eventually help him with that."

"Yeah, that' why he wants to hook up with us. He want's to find Janet."

"Yeah, he does."

We pause.

"He likes you Sasha. I see the way he looks at you."

I look at her, "I know he does. But he calls you a genius, so I think he likes you, too." I said, giving her a big thumbs up.

"Yeah, he does like me, but he likes you differently."

I pause and look out the window and say, "the fact that he

likes me that way. Does that worry you?"

She doesn't respond right away, "kinda."

"Well don't," I say. "I love you. I would never hurt you like that Tori, but when you said he likes me, I had to ask. I want you to know you have absolutely nothing to worry about there."

"I know," she says. "But he is very handsome."

"Hum, you noticed that, too."

"Well, yeah."

We laugh as I reach for her free hand and she takes mine.

"So tomorrow, when Cabot's not looking I'll go on a syndicate hunting expedition on the computer."

"Just be careful. I know you can pull it off, but if he finds out, things could get messy."

"I will.

"I know that, I'm just protecting you, because if he catches on and tries anything with you, I will have to kill him. We know he's just a mule for this syndicate, and when it comes right down to it, he's not important at all."

We pull into the driveway at the house where we live and the place seems very quiet. Almost too quiet. After I get out of the car, I look around, and see Penn and Cash walking the grounds. Putting my mind at ease. I decide that it's going to be okay for Tori and I to spend a nice quiet Sunday evening relaxing.

Five minutes after we got home, the front doorbell rings and I answer. It's Cash."

"Anything special for us to do tonight boss?"

"No nothing, just make sure everything is secure. Where's

Cabot?"

"In his study—been in there all day. Something big is on his mind, he's been on the phone all day. Me and Penn have heard him shouting during the conversation, several times."

Cash's comment made me think about the phone conversation I overheard parts of before we left that morning.

"Did he mention anything to you? I saw him doing that this morning before Tori and I left."

"Na. He doesn't tell me and Penn nothin'. He doesn't think we're smart."

I shake my head, "that's crazy."

Yeah, that's what we think, too. So see ya tomorrow, boss." He says walking away.

"Have a good evening Cash, call me if you need me."

He salutes me and I close the door.

"Who was that?"

"Cash." I smile.

"You know Sasha, him and that Penn they're not the brightest dollars in the bunch but their good guys."

"I know that."

"And they really like you."

"They do?"

"Yes...they do. They talk about what a good boss you are all the time." She sits down beside me on the couch, in the family room, and says, "you know for a girl who says she's not a good girl, you sure make a good impression on people."

"I'm not really a good girl, Tori, I...kill people."

"But you do it because you're threatened."

"And to protect you."

"I know," she says. Then she lays her head on my shoulder, something I love for her to do.

"He said Cabot has been in his study all day long, and he heard him shouting on phone calls. He gets the same drift that we do, that he has something big on his mind. Though he never told them, and according to Cash, he doesn't ever tell him and Penn anything."

"Really? Why?"

"He says that Cabot doesn't think they're smart."

We chuckle.

"Anyway I thought about this morning before we left. Like I told you and Tyler today, I walked by the front portico and Mr. C was in a very tense, really heated phone conversation with someone."

"Any idea, who?"

"As you know he told me he'd let me know eventually, and he hasn't yet. You and I both know that he's into a lot of other crap, other than the trafficking gig."

"Well, he hired you to protect him."

"Yeah you're right, just as I'm sure that whoever he's having these phone conversations with has nothing to do with the syndicate, but something entirely different."

******

The next couple of days went by and all was quiet. Nothing big happening at all, which can't be at all bad. One thing has occurred that takes me back to the phone conversation that I heard Cabot having on Sunday. Something has truly upset him. He's quieter than usual. He wants me close by at all times during the day, and has had me rotate Penn and Cash's schedule so they can stand guard outside his bedroom at night. He wants me to make sure that all the electronic security devices are working properly, and that the windows and doors are secure at night before I leave to go home.

Something's sure rattled his cage, but he doesn't talk to me about it. So what is it that has him so bugged that he has suddenly become overly cautious? Maybe as his head of security I should ask him what the hell's going on, so I can be better prepared if danger does come to his doorstep.

"Question," I say, setting down in an office chair. "What's going on? The last few days you've been edgy as hell. So do you care to impart to me what it is? I am your head of security. Just wondering, too, is Tori doing okay?"

"Tori is doing a fantastic job—her IQ is off the charts. And to answer your question as best as I can, it's just business, and I should inform you that things can be this way around here from time to time. That's why I hired you, Sasha. So just be extra vigilant for now."

"Does it have to do with what you told me the first day we got here?"

"Yes it does, it's just taking some time to unfold. I will let you know when the time comes that something may happen. That could be soon, okay."

Realizing he's not going to tell me everything right now, I

nodded to him and got up out of the chair to leave. Turning around I see Tori standing in the doorway, she smiled and I winked at her as I walked past her and out of the office.

NANCY HOWARD

FIFTEEN

Who are those people? Why are they chasing me? Where...where am I? I got to get away from them. The alley it's so dark in front of me...and that light that's behind them...it's so bright. I've got to run away or they're going to catch me. I don't want to go into the alley. Help me! Help! Help! I wake up, dazed, screaming for help. I've broke out in a sweat, and I woke Tori.

"Sasha, Sasha!" She says, shaking me trying to get me to wake up completely.

I set straight up, I look at her and realize I was having one of my bad nightmares. I lay back down, and put my head on her shoulder.

"You were having a nightmare again."

"Yeah," I said. Still not able to shake the images from the dream.

"Was it the same one you had in Westerville?"

"Yeah it was, it's always the same one, except it varies here and there."

"What's happening in the dream? You've never told me."

"I...I'm in this alley and there's these people Tori... and they're chasing me."

"Do they catch you?"

"No, but they seem to be getting closer and closer, and I can't seem to run away from them. It's like my legs are frozen in place."

"Can you see their faces?"

"No, no, it's too dark. They don't have faces. I can only see their shadows, and the light behind them is bright, very bright. It blinds me when I try to look at them,"

"And the alley, you say it's dark, too."

"Yeah, it's…like, it has no end—it scares me more than the shadows."

"Well, it was just a nightmare, and it's not real."

"It scares the hell out of me, Tori. I've killed a lot of people."

"I know that, but dreams are symbolic manifestations of our subconscious, and our conscious minds having a discussion. A battle. And the images that occur are in symbolic form."

"I know." I said. I pause for a few seconds then ask her, "Do you believe in God, Tori?"

"I don't think so. How can there be a God when we live in a world that's become even more violent and chaotic than it was a hundred years ago? And it was bad back then." She asks me, "do you? Do you believe there's a God and that there's a life after this. There are people who do still believe that you know."

"Yeah I know. But as for me? The enforcer. No, and if there is a place we go after we die, then I am one hundred percent sure that where I'll be going won't be a nice place."

"Does that scare you?"

"Yeah it really does, especially if I think about it."

"Well try not to think too much about it now, and curl up next to me and try to get back to sleep."

I did that, but the dream stayed with me for a longtime, causing me to not get back to sleep right away, even though I was next to Tori.

******

The next day is Wednesday and Cabot's jitters haven't gotten any better. If anything they've gotten worse, and instead of preparing for another auction in a week and half. He's now completely absorbed by the problem that has been front and center in his mind since Sunday. He has heated phone conversations with someone, possibly the same someone. Each time whenever that someone calls, he shoos me out of the office and tells me to close the door behind me. That he'll call me back in when he's finished.

I can hear him talking with the office door closed. He lowers his voice, to the point it's not inaudible—making impossible for me to hear exactly what he's saying.

So I go next door and say to Tori, "something big is about to happen."

"Yeah, I know, he's been nuts. He doesn't seem at all interested in setting up another auction. It's like all of a sudden that's not at all important to him. You got any idea what's going down?"

"No. He's not said a word to me, I need to ask him again once he gets off the phone. I need to convince him that whatever may happen he needs to bring me in on it. Soon. He did indicate yesterday when I talked to him, that it has something to do with what he told us when we first arrived here."

Just then we hear his office door open and he calls out, "Sasha."

"Be right there," I reply, and walk next door and into the study.

"Have a seat," he says. Motioning me into one of the chairs in front of him.

He looks at me for a second then gets straight to the point. "I have a business deal that has gone way south on me and since you are my head of security I feel like it's time to tell you who it is. The reason I haven't let you in on more of this sooner, is I haven't been sure of the intentions of these people. You see, some time back I sold a bunch of products to the Russian mob in New Rotterdam.

"I told them how much it would be, and that I wanted a substantial cut from their sales on the street. They of course balked at that idea, and did not pay me that share. I of course have been demanding payment from them for sometime, and they refused to pay. Which led to me having to make a decision. One that caused things to get out of hand and ugly.

"I have connections to associates who I contract out to do my bidding in these situations, in Rotterdam, and last week I did just that. I had them pay a visit to the Russians to collect. The associates I sent there collected my money per my instructions. And a gunfight ensued and several of the Russians mobsters were killed. I have since then of course received the usual threats of retaliation from them, if I don't give them the money back.

"That is what the heated phone discussions you've been hearing are about. So here is what I want you to do each evening. I want you to go through the entire house before you leave to go home at days end, and check every electronic security connection, and door lock in the place. Just as you've been doing all along. Be on your toes. Got that."

"I will. So you think they'll hit us."

"Yes, I do, and soon."

"Do Penn and Cash know about this?"

"No, I haven't told them but you should do so immediately, as soon as you leave here."

I did as he directed me to do, and told Penn and Cash what was up. They're already standing watch over Cabot's bedroom at night. I told them that we could split the time in thirds and all three take turns. They said no to that idea. They had it covered and had done this type of thing before, and not to worry, so I left it at that.

The remainder of the day was quiet, nothing happened. So I checked and double checked the house security at days end, and told Cabot everything was tight. Then Tori and I were off to our house for hopefully a good night's sleep. But knowing that it could be interrupted at any time by a hit from the Russian mob.

That night at dinner I told Tori about the Russians and that Cabot had them hit last week in Rotterdam. He explained the whole thing to me I told her. I said that we could expect retaliation from them at anytime.

"Sasha, this frightens me," she said.

THE ALLEY OF EVIL

I took her hand and said, "It does me, too. Did I ever mentioned to you that whenever I went into a situation that I always scared."

"No, I didn't think you, of all people, would be scared of anything."

"Well, I was always scared, and it's what's kept me alive. Anyone who is not afraid of danger is stupid and setting themselves up to be killed. Being scared makes you alert, it helps keep you alive, in dangerous situations."

"I didn't think you cared about any of that back then."

"Oh, yes, Tori, I wanted very much to stay alive. I just didn't care about anyone or anything else, until I met you. Now I have someone to care about, and protect—you. So if and when the Russians come, I will be frightened by the situation for sure—even though I may not show it. But what I will do is make sure I do protect you."

That night it's off to bed about ten. But I don't get to sleep quickly and really don't seem to sleep well when I do drift off. Suddenly, I set straight up in bed, it's two a. m. Awakened—not from a nightmare this time, but from gunfire. I hear constant shooting from an automatic rifle, and a semi with a bump stock. There they go again.

Tori is awake and frightened. "Sasha! What's going one?" She says fearfully.

"It's the Russians paying us a visit."

I'm up fast and pulling on a tank top, boxers, then sandals. I grab for my guns and put them on as quickly as I can, as I hear more gunfire erupt. This time from a different weapon, a .9mm meaning Penn has responded to whoever is shooting at him.

Cabot is yelling into the squawk box for my help, "Sasha, Sasha, come quickly."

I say to Tori, tell him I'm on my way." Before I leave I hand her my little thirty-eight caliber revolver, and tell her to lock up after I leave and hunker down. To not let anyone in, except me, Penn, or Cash. To kill anyone else.

"Can you do that?"

"I can. Sasha," she says, Calling out to me with trepidation in her voice.

"I'll be okay." I assure her, "Stay put." Then I head out the door, right hand weapon drawn, I quicken my pace, crouching as I go toward the main house. Trying not to be seen by the assailants. My tank top is dark blue and my shorts are denim, which will make me difficult to be seen.

The alarm system is blaring loudly all over the grounds having been triggered by a break in. I look over to the house where the four girls are and the lights are on. I don't know at this point if anyone but them is inside the house. Right now my main focus is the gun battle going on inside the main residence. I have to protect Cabot first.

Gunfire is erupting everywhere both inside and out. As Cash has joined in and is shooting, too. I see two assailants go around the north side of the house and I pursue them. They haven't seen me yet, then they stop just as I come around the corner. Then one turns and gets a glimpse at me as the damn security light comes on bringing me into their view. I jump behind the wall for cover. He fires his weapon at me and misses.

I pop out and I pull the trigger, he goes down. The second man also turns to fire, I take him out.

I proceed on around to the back of the house pointing my weapon at the two of them to make sure they're down for good. I round the back of the house, making my way to the patio doors and see Cash approaching. The patio doors are wide open, broken into, which set off the alarm. He and I enter. We split up as he checks the lower floor and I go up the stairs, where I hear most of the gunfire coming from.

I hear Cash's gun go off several times below me. He's encountered one of them, and it seems to be coming from the study. I slowly but surely make my way up the steps, one at time, gun pointed up at the landing above. I hear more gunfire from above me and below, telling me that my security men are doing their jobs efficiently. I reach the landing and see two men crouched in the hallway in front of me. They're shooting at Penn who is returning their fire from Cabot's bedroom.

I see the bedroom door at the end of hall suddenly open. Claus! He has a hand gun and is shooting it at the intruders. They return his fire with their superior weapons. Causing him to retreat quickly for cover back into his room, as bullets go through the door and walls. Then one of them turns and sees me behind them—he fires at me with the automatic weapon. I take cover behind the wall just outside the hallway, as bullets whiz by me and into the walls on the other side. He has me pinned down, too, as the other man continues to engage Penn and Claus.

I hear someone coming up the stairs, I turn and point my

gun and it's Cash coming up. The man with the bump stock, has finally stopped shooting, possibly to reload. I pop out from behind the wall, he sees me but it's too late, as I fire two rounds hitting him—he goes down. The other man turns and points his automatic weapon at me and I kill him, too. Then it's quiet, I look at Cash.

He says, "I think that's all of em boss."

I shake my head and yell out. "Penn you guys okay?" I hit the lights.

"We're good boss"

Claus comes out of his room, "thanks for the help," I said.

"Don't mention it."

Cabot emerges from his bedroom and has put on his robe. He walks out and into the hallway.

"Nice work, all of you." Then he says to me. "You earned all earned your keep tonight, Sasha."

I shake my head and give him a half grin as he returns to his bedroom and shuts the door.

About that time we hear someone come into the house. We turn and go out onto the landing.

"Sasha." It's Tori, she standing at the bottom of the stairs. "Sasha." she says again.

"I'm up here, babe."

"Is it safe to come up," she asks?

"Yes it's safe, the shooting's over."

She runs up the stairs and when she gets to me we hug tightly and then we hold each other at arm's length.

"You're okay."

"I'm good. Not a scratch on me," I said. Smiling at her.

"Thank God! I heard so much gunfire. I was scared to death for you."

"And I told you to stay put. Remember?"

"I know you did, Sasha, but... I was so worried for you."

I hug her again, "I know."

Cabot had told the men to get rid of the dead Russians before he went back into his bedroom. The men have begun doing that, and Tori and I leave and go back down the stairs. I tell her to follow me.

"Where we going?"

"To see if Wendy and the other girls are okay.

We walk across the lawn and approach them they're all standing out on the porch.

Wendy asks. What happened? We been hearin' all the shootin'."

"Apparently we got hit by the Russian mob. Anyway they're all dead and we came out to see if you guys are alright."

"Did you get them all," Patti asks?

"Yeah, we got these, I don't think there are more with this bunch. So you can relax."

They shook their heads. Then Maria says cynically, "Cabot. Is he dead?"

I shook my head no.

"Dammit!" She exclaims angrily.

I said to them, "listen this may be hard, but all of you need to try to go back to bed and get some sleep." I tried not to linger on Maria wanting Cabot dead, which I understood.

They shook their heads in agreement though I doubt they'll be able to sleep, after all this commotion. I know I don't feel like going back to bed, and I'm sure Tori doesn't either.

We get back to our house and ready to lay down, but neither of us wants to sleep. So I get up and go into the kitchen and make coffee. Tori follows me and sits down at the table—it's three thirty in the morning. I sit down across from her, while the coffee brews and we start to talk about the events that just happened.

"So now that we have had an encounter with his enemies, makes you wonder what's next."

I laugh. "Yeah, like, how many more enemies does he have like this."

"I'm sure he has many."

"Yeah," I agree, then I say, "is there anything new he wants you to put into the computer about his other businesses?"

"No, not at all. Most of what he wants in the computer is about the auction. He doesn't talk to me at all about his other endeavors. He's very tight lipped about all of that. These past few days like I said he's hasn't cared about the auction, or what I'm doing. He seems to just let me do as I please."

She pauses for a second then asks, "did you hear the bitterness in Maria's voice when you told her that Cabot was still alive?"

"Yeah, I did." I sigh. "That poor little girl has been kidnapped and she's only fourteen years old. You can't blame her for how she feels. Even when I went out to talk to them after we first got here, I told her I could protect her. I'm not sure she believes me, Tori."

"It's so sad, Sasha. Has she told you anything else about herself?"

"No. I only have been out to talk to them that one day. We've been so busy and all. I wish I could help her more, but I'm not sure what or if I can do for her right now."

Finally it gets to be seven o'clock and after a quick bite of breakfast, we got dressed and walked as usual up to the house to go to work.

Penn and Cash come out to meet us right away, and Cash says, "Boss you gotta see what Mr. C is doin'."

"Yeah, what's up?"

"Follow us."

We shook our heads and motioned to them to lead the way. We follow out to the far back of the property and the big garage where the limo is. It's parked outside and running. Claus passes us carrying bags out of the back of the house, and loads them into the limo.

"What's going on," I ask?

"Cabot will tell you."

Just then we're joined by Wendy and the other girls. Along with the kitchen and house crew who are arriving for work. They ask me what's going on, and I tell them I don't know, that Cash just told me what Raymond was doing.

Cabot comes out of the back of the house, and crosses the lawn, carrying a large bag and a satchel. I ask him, "going someplace?"

"I'm going away," he says.

"Away? So for how long?"

"For good. That's how long. And if all of you have any sense you'll get the hell out of here, too." He hands me the satchel, "that's full payment for your services, that I promised both of you."

I open it and look inside—it's full of money. I hand it to Tori.

"Why are you leaving and what about the auction, next week?"

"I don't care about the auctions anymore, and you shouldn't either."

I decided to change the subject. "So before you leave what can you tell us about the syndicate that's running these auctions."

He seemed surprised that I asked that question and says, "nothing."

"Now, come on Raymond, can't you just let us in on a little something?"

"All I know is that for the past three years they, whoever they are, have paid me a very generous salary and told me to live here as the owner. I took the job because it was a convenient way for me to run my other businesses. I would get calls about the auctions and would contact a computer firm to run them. But when she got here I no longer needed them, because she's so damn good with computers."

Tori asks, "so you have no idea who they are?"

"No" Then he stops loading the car with Claus, turns to us and says, "just curious. Why do the two of you want to know this anyway?"

"Well, it's like this, let's say that me and Tori, we have our own agenda with this."

He looks at me and asks, "what might that agenda be? Sasha."

"Well for one thing, you know I don't have a damn bit of use for your auctions, you knew that when you hired me. But Tori and I have it in mind to get to the bottom of this and find out who this syndicate is, and put an end to them, and their slave trade."

"You're crazy—both of you, to even think you can do something like that. It's a really stupid idea, Sasha, they are way to big for you to go after. You're biting off more than you can chew."

"Maybe, maybe not. One more thing, since you're leaving and no longer my boss and we are well aware of the truth. Why did you wait so long to get Tori and I out of that hell hole Westerville?"

"I had needed a personal bodyguard and head of security for sometime, Sasha. And as it happened you fit that bill. Yes I knew you were at Westerville, I tried to get you out—several times, but Colin kept blocking it. He was hell bent on selling you, and Cynthia kept telling him that it wasn't possible. I finally convinced him that you were to dangerous to be auctioned off, and after a lot of conversation he gave in and let me get you out of there. He's afraid of you Sasha, now that you're out."

"He should be."

Then he says, "Listen, I don't usually say this kind of thing to anyone, but I like both of you girls. That's why I'm warning you and all of them to leave. It's not safe here, anymore, even with you Sasha. If the Russians send more soldiers then you might not survive."

"You think they will, send more soldiers," I ask?

"I don't know for sure. That's why I'm getting the hell out of here." Then he shakes his head at me and gets into the limo. Claus closes the door and goes and gets in the drivers side. He backs it out, turns it around and they drive away.

Everyone is quiet, for a few seconds, flabbergasted at Cabot leaving like this. No one says a word, as we watch the limo pass through the gates.

Then Cash says, "what do we do now boss? Where are we all gonna go?"

I shrug and look at him, then I look at the rest of them, as they look to me for answers.

"I don't really know guys. I can't make your decisions for you, any of you. Tori and me we don't have anywhere else to go —so we stay. The rest of you can do as you want." I look at the girls. "You ladies are no longer part of the human trafficking and haven't been since I got here. You all can do as you please."

Wendy looks at the other three, and says, "we might as well stay, too, Sasha, since we ain't got no place else to go neither."

"That's fine with me and Tori," I say

Then Cash says, "we'll stay too, Sasha. You'll need help in case them Russians come back. Sides I'm like them I ain't got no place else to live and neither does Penn."

"What about us?" The housekeeper speaks up. "We do have

places to live, but that bastard left here just now and owes all of us a week's wages."

I look at Tori, my eyes widened at her, and she says, "tell us how much he owes each of you and we'll pay you."

"But that's not your..." The housekeeper says.

"Hush," she says, not letting her finish. "It's the fair thing to do. And you're all welcome to stay on and work for us."

That's my Tori.

They looked at each otherr and decided to do that. Then they and all the others walked away talking and shaking their heads at Cabot leaving so suddenly like he did.

Tori looks at me, and says, "now what?"

"Well for one thing we keep digging. And with Cabot out of our hair, you won't have to be indiscreet in nosing around. You can just do it. Dig."

SIXTEEN

That whole day was quiet and there were no more attacks by the Russian mob. This Thursday morning finds Tori in the house and in the study, she's sitting in the big chair at the desk as I walk in. I tell her she looks great seated there—like she belongs.

She smiles at my comment and shakes her head. She's found a second computer, a laptop that she got up and running last week. She's using it instead of the big one. She's also located what is called a tablet.

"Find anything new." I ask?

"Oh, yeah. Pull up a chair and let me show you. You're gonna be interested in this."

I pulled a chair around behind the desk and she began to show me what she's found.

"Here it is. This house and this property are owned by this syndicate as we already know. We know that they own Westerville as well. And what I've been able to find out as he told us, he was on the payroll of this large corporation called WASP."

"The syndicates name."

"Right."

THE ALLEY OF EVIL

"You know what's that stand for?"

"Not sure yet. It may be an acronym or it may be the title of the organization. Who knows."

"You got any idea where they're located?"

"No. And every time I look, I hit a dead end, just like Ty did. I will tell you that I have found a list of properties all over the country and world that is owned by WASP. They bought this property and had this estate and the houses built in 2096. Apparently Cabot was one of the many, owners, that was employed to stay here and do their dirty work for them."

"It was a perfect job and cover for a career criminal like Cabot."

"Right," I look at her, "good job."

"Well, it'll be a good job when I find out more, I'll keep digging."

I shake my head in agreement. And I start to look around the room at the bookcases, and all the volumes that are on the shelves that give it the feeling of a library. I get up from my chair and begin to look around at the shelves.

She notices and asks, "what are you doing?"

"You know, Tori I was just wondering what secrets this room holds. It looks like just an office and study, but I bet..."

I begin to nose around, looking at some of the little statues on the shelves that act as bookends. I pick each of them up and look behind them, and see nothing. Then I pick up one that is directly behind where Tori is setting, a nymph, I take it off the shelf and look at it. Embedded in its belly button is another button. I look at her and she at me, raising her eyebrows.

"I wonder what happens if I do this?" I push the button and the bookcase directly behind her slides open. Surprised, she gets up. The opening of the bookcase reveals a stairway leading down. I reach for the light switch on the wall and flip it on motioning for Tori to follow me, which I don't have to, she's already next to me.

I take her hand and we slowly make our way down the steps. I have my right hand on my gun, just in case. But as we reach the bottom I see that there is no need for that. What we are standing in is a huge basement that spans the entire underside of the house. I walk around and begin to pull on all the lights in the place so we can see. Along the walls are lines of metal shelves that reach all the way to the ceiling. All of the shelving has metal storage boxes that look to be a foot long and about eight inches high. Each pad locked, like they've not been touched in years.

Tori says, "I wonder what's in them?"

"Well there is only one way to find out."

She blurts out, "keys. I wonder where Cabot hid them?"

"Don't know for sure. If I could just find some tools."

"Tools?"

"Yeah, to see if I can find a pair of channel locks to cut those pad locks with. I don't want to shoot them because if I don't hit the lock just right, and miss, the bullet could go anywhere."

She says lightheartedly, "you miss? Not a chance," She pauses and then says, "you know Sasha there could be some tools in that closet."

She's pointing to the one underneath the stairway.

I walk over to it and turn the door knob, it's unlocked so I open it. Inside in the back I see a big tool box on a shelf that is eye level. I pull it down and open it. I rummage through it for a few seconds, then I find exactly what I need—channel locks. I take them out and we go back over to the box that I intended to open. Tori is right next to me, and she reaches up and pulls the box off the shelf and sets it on a nearby table, and I cut the lock. She opens it. What's inside leaves both of our mouths wide open and gaping.

Inside is money—lots of money. No telling how much, but we both guessed at least ninety or a hundred thousand dollars. All in one hundreds. We looked around and then began to open other boxes and find the same thing. Opening several at random all over the basement. The place is a veritable money room, and we conclude that all this cash must belong to this WASP syndicate.

"Sasha, have you ever heard of a place called Fort Knox?"

"Yeah I have. It was where all the gold reserves were stored long ago."

"Right. And this must be its cousin." We chuckle at her comment.

"Tori there must be millions down here, maybe even billions."

"You know now that Cabot isn't here anymore and once WASP finds that out, they're going to want this money, and this property—since it does belong to them."

"But for right now they don't know he's gone and the more

they don't know, the more time it will give us time to find them."

"Do you think this is what the Russians were after the other night?"

"No, no I don't. They were after Cabot because of the soured meth deal. I'm sure they had no idea that this was even here, just like we didn't until now."

"Why all the separate boxes with money in them and locked up?"

"I can't answer that," I said. "I don't know."

"What do we do if they come here, Sasha, and they send bad people here to try and kill us?"

"Well if that happens, we'll kill back. But I don't think we have that to worry about that right now, because they don't know Cabot is gone. If we can just find out where they are located, then we'll go to them before they come to us."

"So should we keep all this a secret, between you and I?"

"Yeah, for now I think that would be wise."

"And Ty when he gets here?"

"Ah...yeah, we should show him."

With that we close up all the boxes, returning them to the shelves. We turn out the lights and head back up the stairs to the study. I push the button on the little nymph's belly again and the bookcase closes. Tori sets down at the desk again, and I tell her that I'll be outside if she needs me for anything.

Out the front door, I see Penn and Cash comfortably sitting in two chairs on the portico, that they've found to their liking. I greet them and in the distance I hear a motorcycle engine revving up and down as the driver shifts gears, pushing the bike up and down the surrounding hills and around curves. I think, it's got to be Tyler Baines and his big powerful Harley.

I was right as seconds later I see him race through the front gate, quickly reaching the roundabout, stopping in front of the fountain and us.

We all step down off the portico and walk over to him, as he has shuts the bike off. He removes his helmet, and dismounts, greeting Penn and Cash with a hello and handshake. And me with a hello and a lingering smile. There is an inclination for us to hug each other, but we don't. His smile at me is one that I find pleasing, and hard to resist. Every time he looks at me I feel his eyes roam all over me.

I know I love Tori and would never abandon her, but I do find Tyler extremely exciting. I have never really had a man do what he does to me. Look at me like he does. Most men look at me and then look away, not wanting to have anything to do with a girl that wears two Glocks. But Ty does this anyway. He's not at all intimidated by me or any reputation I have. He just likes to looks at me. And I wonder where it could lead if I would let it. I think he wants to sleep with me, he tells me that with his eyes every time he looks at me. And I wonder, too, am I telling him the same as I return his gaze at me?

What the hell do I do? I am beginning to realize that I'm bisexual. I grapple with his looks at me and my love for Tori at the same time. It would be easy for me to fantasize what it would be like to make love to him, and that would serve no other purpose than me being unfaithful to Tori. How do I balance something like that? I don't love Ty, I love Tori, and hurting her is something I could never do.

After a few words with Penn and Cash they leave and head up to the house where the girls are.

"I was wondering when you were going to show up."

"I just got back into the country this morning, and came straight here. So how have things been? Where's Cabot?"

"Well things have changed drastically around here since we talked on Sunday. Come inside to the study and Tori and I will enlighten you, and bring you up to speed on all that has transpired over the past few days."

He looks at me curiously after I said that and follows me inside the house. In the study he greets Tori and she does the same to him. We tell him what has gone on and the reason there is no more Cabot. We spend time telling him about the attack from the Russian mob, and what Tori has found out as she digs deeper into the workings of WASP—aka the syndicate.

We are all three looking at the computer screen and Ty says, "so you haven't been able to locate their whereabouts, yet?"

"No. So far all I've hit are dead ends, like has happened to you. I'm really running out of options as to where else I can look. The internet is so fragmented these days. Some of the old GPS satellites have just quit working or have plummeted back to Earth and burnt up. So it's hard to put together a way to find— say a place in Europe. Even London, Paris and Berlin are hard to get to."

"I've was never able to even do what you've done Tori. You've at least found a name and we can check for that name everywhere we look."

"You know Ty, since this WASP syndicate owns all of this. Tori and I wondered how long it will take them to find out that Cabot is no longer here. Once they do that, do they have soldiers that will come here and attack us to get it back?"

"That's a good question. Since we know so little about them."

"Unless I can get to them first," Tori says. "Even though I'm running out of options to find them. They own a lot of places and there has to be deeds and records on the purchase of those properties. And that's what I was starting to look for when the two of you came in here. So maybe that's the way to find WASP."

"I wonder how they bought all the properties they did? They're so allusive," I said.

"They hired mules like Cabot, Sasha. They told him to tell people that he was rich, and the owner of this huge estate, and people never questioned it."

"Especially if he had falsified deeds that they gave him that showed he was rich and owned this property," Tori says. "It would be easy to do, especially now, since no one checks that stuff anymore."

"Exactly, money talks," he says.

Just then Penn pokes his head in the doorway. "Hey boss, we got company."

The three of us get up and go out following Penn through the house. Outside I see my old nemesis, Colin Lampoor. He's out of the car he's riding in and standing next to it. When he sees us he walks up to me, immediately demanding to see Cabot.

I look at him, then behind him, and see he's brought a

couple of goons for muscle.

    I want to kill him, but instead I answer him, "well Lampoor, I hate to disappoint you, but he's not here and won't be back."

    "The hell you say? You're lying. You killed him didn't you, you little bitch."

    "No I didn't. He left of his own accord—seems he's having trouble with the Russian mob."

    "Well, if he's gone then why the hell are you all still here? This is private property."

    "That's right, we know that," I say, getting closer to him. "You see Lampoor we know all about WASP and that you're one of their pissants, and work for them, too. Right?"

    "I never heard of them. And my name is pronounced pour, not poor. I've told you that a hundred times."

    I say, "you know Colin you're a liar. I don't give a damn how you want your name pronounced. But I do want you and your two buffoons to leave, while you can. You double-crossed me and had me sent to that hell hole, Westerville. I've not forgotten that."

    "Yeah, well you stole money that was rightfully mine, Sasha.

    I'm just inches from his face—fighting my urge to kill him, after he said that. "I didn't steal anything from you fuckhead. That money I took belonged to a dead man and you claimed it as yours for no other reason than to railroad me. Now I ask you to leave. So do it."

    Then he says, "there will be an auction here a week from Saturday and when I come back you all better be gone."

Then Ty says. "Or what Colin? When you come back will you bring WASP soldiers with you to get us off this place? Don't threaten us. Because there's not going to be an auction here next week, not then, not ever. So I suggest you do as Sasha has said, and get out of here."

Ty is right next to me, having approached us as he spoke. Lampoor looked at him and then at me, and smirked, then he turned and motioned to his two goons to get back in the car to leave. Before he got in he looked at us and said, "This is not the end of this."

"Well Lampoor just for your information it is. Don't you and your goons show up here again," I said.

Then they get into the car and drive away, we watch until they're through the gate.

Ty said, "think he'll be back, like he said?"

"No, because he knows that Cabot is gone from here and he has no leverage with us. It doesn't matter anyway, because if he does come back, I'll kill him."

After Lampoor left taking his goons with him, Tori headed back into the study to continue her search for WASP, and to see if she could locate their world headquarters. Ty and I in the meantime decided to walk about the property and discuss our next move.

But that wasn't his conversational intention with me. He is far more interested in pursuing me, and I can feel it by the way he begins talking to me.

"So, Tori and you have been together now since you were at Westerville. How did that happen?"

I told him about how Cynthia Behar was abusing her and was doing it to get at me. That when she struck and kicked Tori, I went to her aid. Then Behar kicked me and a fight ensued, where I embarrassed the bitch in front of all the other kidnapped girls in the room. She had us thrown into solitary together, where we remained for most of our time at Westerville. Then Cabot came that day and got us out of there. I also eluded to him the beatings I received while I was there.

He was quiet and looking at me, then comments, "sad. So, question. Have you always been interested in other women—same-sex relationships, I mean."

"I looked at him, surprised that he'd ask such a question of me. "No." I said.

"So your inclination was always toward men."

"I thought so. I had no idea that I might even have the slightest inclination to be with another woman, until I met Tori."

"And you truly love her, right."

"Of course I do. Why are you asking me all this?" I say to him.

"Sorry, I don't mean to pry, I just wondered do you love her, or does she give Sasha Cain someone to protect? I'm not judging you Sasha, it's okay. I'm just curious, so please don't take offense at my questions."

I pause. "Well to satisfy your curiosity I was always with guys before Tori. When I first met her I wanted to kiss her the second I laid eyes on her, and for the life of me I don't know why. It just happened. Does that answer your question?

"She needed me and I saw that I guess. She's not like me,

and I figure you've noticed that. She would have never survived at Westerville without me, those bastards would have sold her, in a minute if it hadn't been for me."

"So being in a gay relationship hasn't bothered you?"

"I was confused at first about falling in love with her, but no, not now."

We pause momentarily as we walk.

"So let me get this straight, someone knew you were in there and they left you there for what? Four months."

"Yeah, it was all Lampoor's doing. Cabot said that he wanted me sold, but they all knew that wouldn't work. He told me before he left that he had tried to get me/us out of there sooner, but Lampoor was blocking him."

"So they kept you there and left Tori, too, because she was with you."

"Yeah, they did."

He pauses, still looking at me and says, "So you had that chance today. Why didn't you kill him? What kept you from doing that."

"Because he's nothing but a pissant, Ty, and you know that. I will kill him, eventually, but I'm after bigger fish. We are after bigger fish." He shakes his head in agreement.

We stand for a second quiet, then he turns. He's directly in front of me as we face each other—just inches away from me. I feel the urge to kiss him and I want him to kiss me.

He puts his hands on my arms running his hands up and down them. Looking deeply into my eyes, he asks, "you do know what you do to me, don't you?"

"Yeah, and you do the same to me, too. I could very easily make love to you, Ty. But I can't do it, I will not be unfaithful to Tori."

We're close, and I'm looking up and into his eyes and I want him to kiss me so bad."

"I could love you, Sasha Cain. Forever."

"Even knowing what I've done and how many people I've killed? Ty I'm a violent girl."

"Yes I do know, and like your Tori, I don't care about any of that."

"Why do you find me, of all girls, desirable? I don't get it. I mean..."

"You want to know the answer to that? Well here it is. You're so beautiful in your own right, I saw it that night in that jail cell. You're strong, independent, and untamable. And that's what drives me to want you every time I look at you."

Then he takes me into his arms, pulls up me close to him, our lips meet and we kiss long and deep. Probing each other mouths, tonging each other. Kissing then breaking several times, as he arouses me, causing a fire to erupt inside me like I've never felt before. When he stops and holds me at arms length, and looks at me, deep into my eyes. I want more from him.

He senses that and kisses me long and deep again, like before only this time his hands were up and down my back, squeezing my buttocks. Then we break again. I want him, I think, but then remember my Tori.

He's still holding me, looking into my eyes, and softly brushing a whisp of hair out of my face. He says, "Sasha. I will always desire you, call it chemistry, call it whatever you want, too. I know you love Tori, and I would never want to be the one who destroyed that wonderful relationship.

"But for just these few minutes I got the chance to do something that I've wanted to do to you since I first saw you in that jail cell that night. Kiss you and hug you to the point it aroused you and me."

I'm biting my lower lip, as he says this to me.

"Will you do something for me?"

"What's that?" I said quietly, wanting him to kiss me again. I want to make love to him.

"Don't you ever sell yourself short, Sasha. You are one beautiful girl."

Then he turned and began walking toward the house. I just stand there stunned, like a dummy at what he just said, wanting him to kiss me again. He stops and turns around and says, "coming?"

I shake my head running to catch up to him.

******

He and I return to the main house and go inside and we sit down in the study, with me in the chair next to Tori. Ty sits down on the other side of the desk. I sit there next to her with the freshness in my mind of what just happened between us. Then I look at her, so pretty, so busy. I feel safe with her somehow. I can't explain it, but that's how I feel. Safe.

"So Sasha, what about the Russian mob, you think they

might be back," He asks. Bringing me back to our task at hand, and at the same time relieving the sexual tension that still remained between us.

"I don't think so, because it that was about Cabot and his soured meth deal. Anyway, we need to go to Westerville tomorrow."

"Why?"

"Because Tori and I plan on shutting the fucking place down for good. Don't we?"

She smiles and shakes her head not looking up from her computer. I wonder if she's suspicious as to what just happened between Ty and me. I can only hope not. But she probably is, she's as smart as they come and she also know how much he likes me, because she mentioned it.

He asks, "do you think that's possible, given the fact that they have all those guards there?"

"Yes we do."

"I know this is crazy asking the two of you this. But do you have a plan? The front gate will be locked so how do you plan on getting in?"

"That's where Tori comes in."

"I'll take care of the locks at the front gate," she says. She stops what she's doing and holds up the electronic device called a tablet. "I'll take this with us. I can not only get us into the prison, but I can unlock all the doors to the place and the cells. Plus I can disarm their security system and shut down all their cameras. When it's all said and done, I will have complete control of everything in the building that's electronic. I will have disarmed every device in the building."

"And in the meantime you and I can take care of the guards, and Behar. I want to get there at noon when all the girls are in the chow hall. Most of the guards and Behar will be in there, too, so you and I will make our way up to the PA room. Where I will get on the it and make the startling announcement to all of them that Westerville is closed. I'll tell the girls they're free to go, and if the guards try to stop them. We'll kill them."

"But it's Behar you really want."

"Yes, and Tori and I have that all planned out, too. Don't we babe?"

She looks at me out of the corner of her eye and gives a devious smile.

I pause for a second, then I get up and go to the bookcase behind her and pick up the little nymph statue.

Tori turns to see what I'm doing.

"I think it's time we show him this. Agree?"

"Yeah, I do."

"Show me what," he asked?

"Watch this." I push the button on its belly, and the bookcase slides open revealing the darkness to the basement below. I turn on the lights and say, "Ty come with us, you won't believe what we're about to show you."

He gets up and we all go downstairs. Once at the bottom I walk around turning on the overhead lights in order for him to see all the shelves that are full of metal boxes stuffed with cash. We tell him that we found this place by accident earlier today.

Then we proceeded to open the boxes that we did before,

showing him the cash. He was in awe at what he was looking at.

"So all of these boxes are filled with money?"

"That's what Tori and I believe to be true, yes, because we opened several of them at random."

"So this has got to be WASP's money."

"We figure it is," Tori says. "But we want to keep this between the three of us, no one else is to know."

"Gotcha, that will not be a problem," he says. "So if we find WASP and get rid of them what happens to all this money?"

"I guess we keep it and start a revolution," I said. Causing them to laugh.

That evening at dinner Tori tells me about an idea she's got cooking inside her magnificent brain, that could help us find WASP. She said, that she thinks that she can put together a fake auction on her computer and make it look real.

I asked how it could find WASP and she tells me that once the auction is over and customers don't receive their merchandise, they would get upset. She wants to what she calls a virtual auction, and have the upset customer contact WASP with their complaint. She tells me that she's in the process of setting the whole idea up on her computer.

I think it's a great idea, and tell her keep at it.

That night after sleeping for about two hours. Tori wakes me. Crying. "Hold me," she says.

I do and say, "what's going on? My God baby you're trembling."

"I haven't been able to sleep." She say's getting close to me. "I was okay until you turned out the lights. Then I began to relive the rape and what Behar and her bitches did to me."

"You want to talk about it?"

"No. I just want you to hold me. I just want to feel you near. I want to feel safe in your arms."

"I'm here Tori, and you're safe, you're with me. Just try to relax and let it go."

"They hurt me, Sasha."

"I know they did, and I haven't forgotten. Are you still sure you want to take care of them the way we discussed? Because if not—I'll just kill them and be done with it."

"No I still want to do it that way."

I held her for a longtime. After a while she settled down and feel asleep.

NANCY HOWARD

SEVENTEEN

Before Tori, Ty, and myself head out for Westerville, I leave Penn and Cash instructions to shoot to kill if there is trouble, especially from the Russians. They assured me they would, and tell me not to worry. That they had something to show us before we leave, that will put our minds at complete ease. Penn said that they've wanted to show this to us for sometime but the time never seemed right. He said he and Cash knew that Tori and I were busy working on the WASP stuff, so what they were about to show us would have to wait.

They motioned for us to follow them—we did off of the grounds and into the woods behind the estate. We first walk up a steep incline that flattens out for a short distance before rising up another hill. We follow along a narrow path for another twenty-five yards to an old cave, that is tucked deep into the side of a hill. The place looks old and deserted, like it hasn't been used in years. Then Penn and Cash began to move the brush and downed tree limbs from in front of it, which gave it perfect seclusion. This reveals a big heavy reinforced timber door, that's made of logs. Penn takes out some keys and unlocks the door and we all go inside. They immediately show us how the door can be locked from the inside, so no one can gain entrance. The place is cavernous, and is stocked full of food and provisions—enough to last for several weeks, even months.

After looking around, I ask them, "where's the water?"

"Come on we'll show you,"Cash says.

They lead us further back into the cave and we enter a room with a pond and water coming up and flowing out an opening in the rocks like a mouth on the other side of the cave.

"Here's the water supply," Penn says. "It's an Artesian well, been pouring out water for thousands of years.

Cash says, "so not to worry, the girls in the house know about this place and how to get into it if trouble comes. And Wendy has a set of these keys, so if we're busy she can get her and the other girls to safety."

We shook our heads agreeing with him. We left the cave, locked it, and headed back down to our place and to get the Mustang to head for Westerville. Barring unforeseen incidents, we'll get there right at lunchtime.

******

The drive to Westerville takes about an hour. With Tori driving and me riding shotgun. Ty was in the back, and less than ten minutes into the trip he's sound asleep, even snoring a couple of times, causing Tori and I to giggle.

She's quiet for a longtime. I notice, and ask her, "you're quiet, everything okay?"

She thinks, then answers, 'That depends, Sasha."

Awe oh, she knows.

"Depends?" I ask dumbly knowing that it's stupid to try and trip her up like that. She's too smart for that kind of crap.

"It depends Sasha, on where we are with each other. I saw you and him walking and talking yesterday. Want to share with me what that was about?"

I respond to her, trying to keep guilt out of my voice.

"Yeah. He asked me how we met. I told him. It seems to surprise him that you and I are together."

"That you're in a same-sex relationship."

"Right. I told him in so many words that it was that way for me, too, but when I first met you I couldn't resist the urge to kiss you and love you."

"But he wants you, Sasha. I know that, I'm not dumb."

"I know you're not. And yeah, he does, I won't lie about that, but he gets it, that you and I love each other."

She looks at me. "Remember our conversation from the other day about my concern."

"Yeah, and I told you not to worry. Didn't I?"

"Yes you did. But I see the way he looks at you, and you at him. I've seen it since the first auction at the estate."

"I know that, and you're right I have looked at him. But, he gets it. He really does."

She pauses for several seconds and says, "did he kiss you?"

I looked at her and didn't answer her right away, then murmured, "yeah he did."

"Did you kiss him back?" She asks sharply.

I looked at her then blurted out, "yes."

"Did you like it?" There's indigence in her voice now.

"Yes, I did," I said. Realizing she's hurt and very pissed. "Tori...I'm sorry. It just...you know, it happened."

"Did you want him to kiss you?"

"Yes, I did, so there." I replied sharply, not meaning, too. "Does this mean you're going to break up with me and hate me?"

"No, I'm not going to break up with you, or hate you, Sasha," she says. "But, yeah it occurs to me now. A lot."

"Well don't. I'm truly sorry, Tori."

She's still not ready to accept my apology and glances over at me. She asks, "how did it make you feel when he kissed you? He's hot."

"I know he is."

"So you never answered my question."

What's that?"

"How did you feel inside when he kissed you?"

"It made me feel...like a fire was exploding inside me."

"That's how it would make me feel if he kissed me."

"It would?"

"Yes it would. I would want him to kiss me, too, if he looked at me the way he looks at you."

"But I've told you have nothing to worry about. I...I felt, so guilty, afterwords. I was...being unfaithful to you when I kissed him. I know that. All the confusion I dealt with when I first met you and fell in love with you, returned for just those few minutes. It won't happen again, I promise." Pleading with her now.

"I'm not trying to make you feel guilty. It doesn't surprise me that you kissed him. I've known all along that you're bisexual. I've always worried that I could satisfy your craving for a man, just as much as you crave me.

"You know when we first met, because of what you said when we were in that cell together and you first realized that you were falling in love with me, I saw the confusion. It made you uncomfortable—not with me. but with yourself."

"Yeah, that's right. But that's not true now."

"Evidently it is Sasha. There still must be confusion or you wouldn't find him desirable. So am I going to have to fight for you and for your love, Sasha? Or should we end this? Tell me."

"No. You're not, and we shouldn't end our relationship over my stupidity. You're not going to have to fight for my love for you. I love you...and only you Tori Nicks. Got it? I'm sorry I did it —kissed him."

Dammit! I shouldn't have kissed him. It's my fault that she's feeling this way and she has every right, too. I can't blame her for that.

"I'm sure you are and I got it, I know you love me. I hope you continue to love me, Sasha," she says. "Because I love you." I see a tear making its way down her cheek.

"Hey, hey, hey," I say. Reaching up and wiping the tears away. "I know you love me, and I will always love you, I promise."

I looked at her and reach for her free hand and she took it. But not tightly like she usually does, and there is no return look or smile. She shook her head as I said that, I thinks she believes what I said, but... This is the closest I've ever been to loosing her.

I was stupid, I don't ever want to do this again. I would not know what to do without my Tori in my life.

We hold hands and I look out the window, and realize that for the first time in my life I love someone so much, that if I were to loose Tori it would devastate me. Me, the enforcer, actually does have the ability to love someone, and she loves me.

"So are you okay with him," I ask?

She looks at me and glances at him in the rearview mirro, he's still asleep. She says, "I am. I just have to put what happened between the two of you out of my mind as best as I can. It's gonna take time to deal with it, and get over what you did, Sasha. You have to realize that."

"I know." I say, quietly. What I did was unfaithful to our relationship when I kissed Ty. This is something I never wanted to do, hurt Tori by being unfaithful to her. But I gave into my carnal desires and now I've caused her to question her trust in me. And more importantly my love for her. I only hope she doesn't stay mad at me for very long.

We are quiet for a few seconds, before I say, "he's a good guy, Tori."

"Yes, you're right he is, I know that. You know when we get back maybe I can help him find his daughter. WASP keeps records to track all of their sales for some reason that I haven't been able to figure out. So I'll search for her and try to help him."

"You'd do that, even after..."

"Yes. I will." She says to me with sharpness still in her voice.

"That's a great idea," I say, quietly. But I know I've hurt her. The poor girl got raped by that bitch Behar because she got tangled up with me. I thought so many times before I don't deserve her. It makes me realize how fragile our relationship really is.

******

An hour later we find ourselves at the front gate of Westerville and of course it is locked like we knew it would be. Some of the conversation between Tori and I still lingers in my mind, and I'm sure it does hers, too. It's not something that you just shake off. I just hope I put her mind at ease that I love only her, and she starts to trust me again.

Ty is awake and apologizes for drifting off. We told him not to do that, apologize for getting much needed sleep. He told us he has not had much of a chance to get a good night's sleep, because of the ever gnawing feeling he will never find Janet.

As he said that, I thought to myself that it must be the most horrible feeling in the world as a parent, to loose a child. No matter what the circumstances are that surround that loss.

Then Tori mentions that she will see what she can do to find the girl. Which makes Ty set up and lean forward. "You think you can do that?" He asks her with hope in his voice.

"Well, I can sure try. I can't promise you anything, but now that I have access to WASP's files on the computer. I'll give it my best shot."

"Thank you, Tori," he says. "Thank you."

"Don't thank me now, do it if and when I locate her."

Half a minute later Tori stops the Mustang in front of the

gates and then picks up her tablet and begins to punch in the codes she needs to hack into the prison's computer system.

Just coming back here gives me a sick feeling in my stomach. It's the same feeling I had watching that snitch of mine, Cooch, puke in the alley at Kegs in Rottendamn that morning.

"You guys okay with this," Ty asks? After what the two of you went through here."

"I'm good," I say.

"Me, too," Tori says. Working on her tablet and not looking up.

"What about the security cameras," I ask?

"Already taken care of. I just shut everything electronic in the place down." She replies coldly, not looking at me. She's really pissed a me.

Tori drives up in front of the place and we all exit the Mustang in unison. Ty climbs out of the back seat on my side. He and I are both armed. He asks Tori to open the trunk. He retrieves a semi automatic rifle to take in just in case. I check my weapons and re-holster them, then the three of us walk toward the doors. I tell Tori to stay behind us because she's not armed.

As we enter, I draw my right hand gun. I put it up in front of me in a defensive position and look over at Ty who is doing the same. We move slowly and deliberately through the prison hallway, that will lead us to the elevator.

The hallway is long, but empty as we make our way—the elevators are clear at the end. Reaching it Ty and I keep watch as Tori touches the up button. The doors open and we get in, she pushes three. The doors slowly close and the old car ambles up taking us slowly to the third floor.

We get out—Tori and I remember where the PA room is. She points to her right and we go that way before making a left turn. We walk another fifty feet and find it. To our surprise, it's empty and we go in. The place has another door that leads out onto the catwalk, and the stairs that lead down to the chow hall.

I walk over and stand next to Tori who is already looking down on the tables filled with girls who have been kidnapped. I'm looking at them, too, but I am searching for one person in particular, Cynthia Behar. Bingo! I see her and her little group of rapist bitches setting at their usual table on our left. I also count the guards that I can see. And I count six, meaning there are at least six more below me, that I can't see from my vantage point.

"Ty," I say, speaking in a low voice. "Go back out and make your way around to the other side to those windows across from us. There's an office of some sort over there. I don't know if it's occupied or not but go in it. That way you can cover the guards that are underneath me that I can't see. Give me a signal when you get there. I'll wait for that."

He goes out of the PA room and heads around to the other side of the building. After a few minutes I see him and he gives me a thumbs up from the other side. He's in place to watch the guards I mentioned.

The PA room I'm in is a very secure place. The doors are made of steel with electronic combination locks on them that have been rendered useless by Tori. The glass in front of us that looks down on the chow hall is bulletproof. The room has only a long desk that's more of a table, a file cabinet that looks to be a hundred years old, and an equally old mic, that I am about to use.

I look at Tori, "Ready?" She shakes her head yes. Then she leaves and heads back downstairs to meet the girls as they come down to get their belongings on the first floor.

"I click on the mic—but before I talk, I get a better idea. I walk over and open the door and walk out onto the catwalk and stand there, the mic in my left hand, I put my left foot on the railing. My gun is cocked and ready in my right hand. No one has looked up and seen me yet.

"Well, good afternoon ladies and gents." Now they're looking. "My name is Sasha Cain. Yeah, remember me? The enforcer. Well like I promised when me and my Tori got out of here, I along with her and another friend, have returned to shut this fucking wretched facility down. And to free all of you ladies that have been kidnapped and are being kept here against your will. So, that said, you, all of you are free to go." I sweep the room with my armed right hand. "Oh, and if any of the guards try to stop you I will simply kill them for you.

"And guards you should pay close attention to what I just said and lay down your weapons. Don't even think about shooting me, because I will shoot back, and kill you if don't do as I say."

Not one of the ladies seated has moved yet. Behar and her two bitch guards that helped her rape Tori are now up standing below me. She's glowering up at me, and so are Violet and Wanda. I just smile back at them.

"How the hell did you get in here, you little whore. You can't kill all of us alone."

"Don't have to, Cynthia, I brought help." I pointed at Ty across from me his semi pointed down at them.

"The auctioneer?" She cracks, breaking into an evil laugh.

Then she orders her guards to shoot me. None moved to carry out the order. Again, she orders them, this time raising her voice, and they still don't do what she says.

Maybe they're a bit timid about taking me on, though they haven't laid down their weapons, and the girls were all still seated telling me this might be tougher than I thought. So I reiterated my demand. "Guards put you guns down. Now." And again all you ladies seated at the tables—you can leave. You're free to go. They won't stop you, I promise."

"You have no authority to tell anybody leave here." Behar growls at me.

I look down at her and yell, "Is that right? Cynthia. Well, you have no fucking right to keep these women here as prisoners against their will, only to be sold into slavery."

She looks around the room. Some of the girls are standing up, readying to leave. Cynthia yells at them to set back down. Some do, but most are looking up at me.

I say again. "Go ladies—you can leave. I mean it and they won't stop you I promise. When you leave, go down to the big locker room and get your belongings, that's where they are. Tori is there waiting and will let you in. If the guards try to stop you from leaving this room, I will kill them."

With that they got up and started leaving. First one by one, then all of them got up and headed for the exits. The guards moved to block the doorways.

"I point my gun at them. Get out of their way and let them pass, or I will start shooting along with my colleague. Do as I say. All of you know me as the enforcer, and I will enforce." They then put their weapons down and left the hall, too. I guess they don't want to get shot today.

The room cleared out quickly as the women ran for the exits, the stairs, and elevator that would take them down to the first floor and the locker room.

As the last girl left I descend the stairs and come down to the chow hall floor. Ty stayed where he was. All but two of the guards are gone, both of them Cynthia's buddies.

"Put your guns down, if you want to live to see another day," I said. They do that and I looked up at Ty, motioning for him to come down.

Seconds later he walks up to me and says, "you've got this, so I'm going to go check out the security room,"

I nod, as Tori returns to the chow hall, and comes up and stands close to me. Her arms folded in front of her, her stance widened. I notice a look of menace on her face, I've never seen before from her.

"Did you get the girls taken care of?"

"I did," she says. Her stare never leaving Behar.

"So Tori, I think it's a good time to do to these three "ladies" what we planned. Don't you? I smile at her with a devious grin on my face.

"Yeah I think so, too, Sasha," she says, firmly. She's not

smiling.

Behar isn't done verbally bashing us and says, "you two little bitches will pay for whatever it is your planning on doing."

"Shut up, Cynthia, you have no right to order us," I say. Then I tell them, "Now take your fucking cloths off, all three of you."

"You want them off, you take them off," Behar hisses.

I'm standing very close to her when she says this and without thinking I use my free hand and hit her with a left hook right in her mouth, which draws blood. She staggers back. I shift my gun to my left hand and I hit her hard again with my right—the blow landing squarely on the side of her head. She falls down.

I go stand over her and get down in her face and say using a very harsh tone, "hurts. Doesn't it Cynthia?"

I let her lay there a few seconds, then I tell her to stand up with the other two, and say again. "I said get naked."

Her two buddies take off their clothes, I look at Tori who is looking at them her stance still widened—arms folded in front of her. She hasn't changed her position or look at them, concentrating on Behar. Who is taking her clothes off.

They're standing in front of us naked as jaybirds. Now, all three of them are not by any stretch of the imagination. How shall I put it? Trim or attractive. These women are all in their early fifties, obese, and out of shape in every sense of the word. So the sight of them all standing front of Tori and I in their birthday suits is laughable.

But what Behar, Wanda, and Violet did to Tori was not

funny. They gang raped her. Forcing themselves and their grotesque bodies on her. Making her preform sex acts with them that were so awful she's never told me about all of them. They hurt her, they damaged her, as they tried to turn her against me. She held strong. She stood by me. They could not break her so they punished her, by gang raping her.

I want to kill them all so very badly, but Tori and I talked about how we should do this. And we decided that she should be the one to dish out the revenge on them.

About that time Ty came back into the chow hall and stops, abruptly.

"Whoa." He says, covering his eyes.

"You don't have to watch this if you don't want to, and we'll understand. But it's payback time."

"Gotcha. And you're right I don't want to watch. I'll go down to the locker room and check to see if all the girls are gone or need help. Then I'll do a roundabout and check to see if anyone is left in the place."

During this time I was talking to Ty, Tori has handcuffed Behar and her buddies, hands behind their backs. Then she shoved each of them over to a space in the wall where there are no tables, backside toward us.

I nodded to her and I saw a look on her face that I had never seen out of her before. It wasn't the look of the sweet little girl that I have grown to love and cherish. She has a look of cold hate and calculation. She pulls her broad leather belt out of her jeans, wrapping the buckle end around her right hand, securing her grasp on it. Then without taking her eyes off of them and without any hesitation whatsoever. She stepped closer behind the three of them, drew the belt back and began flailing it into their buttocks.

Again and again, she drew the belt back, lashing each one of them with all the force her one hundred twenty pound body could gather. Each time, she hit them she let out a primal scream of revenge that echoed through the now empty hall. It was a scream of satisfaction, as the belt cracked against their flabby skin, singing out through the place and not dying until she hit them again. They're screaming in pain, begging her to stop.

Several minutes later, she's done—exhausted, from the physical exertion, and Adrenaline rush, Tori backed slowly away from them, gasping, and out of breath, slumping like a distance runner. But with a satisfaction on her face that I again had never seen from her. It was the look of the victor—she had won.

I walked over to her, and put my hand on her shoulder, "you okay?"

"I'm good."

"Damn, girl, you're a warrior. Remind me never to piss you off."

She looks up at me with a half grin, and shakes her head at my comment.

The bitches, Violet and Wanda are crying out loud, each of them with big red marks on their butts from Tori's relentless punishment. I walked over and uncuffed each of them and they all fell over onto their sides on the floor. Looking up at me.

"Now I want you all to get the hell up and get out of here."

They laid there, each of them for a few minutes and then finally began to drag themselves up.

When Behar gets up she looks at me and squints through her pain, "I'll get you two back for this. Both of you."

I swung at her again, hitting her in her left cheek, she stumbles back against the wall grabbing her face, I got close to her and said, "Cynthia you're lucky to be alive. You all brought this on yourselves, you gang raped her, and she had every right to avenge that with you. The only reason you're not dead is because Tori is the one who needed revenge today. If it hadn't been for that I would have killed you and them, without thinking about. Now, I said for the three of you to get out."

Then they go toward their clothes.

"No, no, no. You leave just like that."

"Naked?" They protest loudly.

"Yeah, you heard me—naked."

They leave reluctantly, but with no choice—staggering out of the building and not look back at us.

Tori says, "God that felt so good, Sasha."

I put my arm around her and hug, she hugs me back. Indicating she may not be as mad at me as I think.

Ty comes back into the chow hall and says that he has been through the entire building and has found no one left except us.

"Well, mission accomplished right, Tori."

"Yep," she says with a smile at me. We high five each other. The look of coldness and hate I saw earlier when she was whipping Behar and her buddies, is long gone. Back is the sweetness that I see in her face all the time, that is my Tori.

"Are you two okay with what you did to them," Ty asks?

Tori says, "Yeah, I wanted to do that to them for a longtime."

"Yeah Ty, I found out something new about, Tori."

"What's that," he asks?

"That she's one hell of a warrior.

"That right."

"She is." We all laugh.

"Now we need to get back to the estate, so you can put together an auction that is a scam you told me about."

"Scam auction," Ty asks?

"Yeah I figured out a way to do an auction from my computer that is fake. I told Sasha about how I would do it last evening. We'll fill you in on the details on the way home."

With that I put my arm around Tori and the three of us left Westerville empty of kidnapped women, and a few sissy boys for the first time in forever. It's a good feeling to shut the place down, but all we did here today is win a battle. The war is still to be won and we won't be able to do that until we can locate the headquarters of WASP. That's where Tori's computer genius will come in handy. Not only will she be putting together a scam auction, but that auction may help her electronically find where this is all coming from. Which could possibly lead us to bringing down this syndicate organization—WASP.

THE ALLEY OF EVIL

EIGHTEEN

After our return things around the estate have grown very quiet. No Russians attacking, and no Cabot to contend with as we further investigate WASP. Especially Tori, she's front and center in finding out all she can about them.

During this time, Tori and I have made up, we're back on the same page. I'm glad, because I didn't like being in her doghouse one bit. She didn't stay mad at me for long, which I'm thankful for. She a very forgiving person, which I already knew anyway. I promised her I would never do something that stupid again, and I won't.

People call here for Cabot wanting information on the next auction, and all Tori and I tell them is that he's out of town on business. We just don't tell them that he's not coming back. They say that he doesn't answer his cell phone when they call him directly. We just answer saying we're sorry and don't know what the reason for that is, or what else we can tell them. They usually hang up disgusted with our answer, which causes us to giggle.

But we do inform the caller that their will be an auction on Saturday, because we want them to see the fake auction that

Tori is going to run from her computer. We want them to bid on people so they'll contact WASP when their merchandise doesn't arrive.

"Look what I got a hold of," she says.

"What is it?"

"This is a list of names and pictures from Westerville."

"How did you get your hands on that?"

"It's all right here in that file cabinet in the next room. Actually there are boxes of these files. All the names of people that have been auctioned off from there, and other prisons everywhere. Here let me show you."

She's carrying an arm load of files, each that are inches thick and lays them on the desk. She opened the most recent one and it had two or three hundred names, some with pictures and some like ours that were in there, that just had vitals on us.

"Cabot kept all his files in this manner because he only got this computer a few weeks before we arrived here. And as he told us he was technologically inept, and this was one of the things that he wanted me to do. Input all the information from these files into the database on this terminal."

"Was it a database for just Westerville?"

"No, because WASP does things like this all over the world. But look at all of this, Sasha, all of these files are full of people that were kidnapped and sold. It makes me sick."

I'm thumbing through one of the folders, and comment, "I does me too, Tori. Can you believe this?"

"Yeah, and to think we almost became a part of it."

I shake my head in agreement and then ask her, "But we

didn't. So what else did you want to show me?"

"Well, here's what I plan on doing, I can scan the pictures with my phone and put them on here to match the person's written file. I've already uploaded a bunch of these files, so I'll be able to run them and what I all ready added for the scam auction. When Ty starts the bidding all they will be doing is bidding on a picture, with a few vitals.

"I'm only going to use pictures of the girls from Westerville, because we freed them and they won't so up. They're all in this file I just showed you."

"Won't they know," I ask?

"Nope, they'll have no idea. Once the auction takes place it'll take a few days for the client not to get what he/she paid for. I'll leave specific instructions for them to contact WASP, not us. I will run the auction from this laptop and then track the client activity. In other words, I'll hack them."

"You can do that?" I smile at her, knowing she can.

"I can, it's to protect us from unwanted visitors. Once the customers start sending emails from their computers to WASP, and they respond back, I hope, I can locate their signal and IP address. That is if they have one, which so far I have not been able to find, based on my searches so far."

"They still have those? IP addresses"

"Yeah, but nowadays, they're erratic. Hard to locate. And WASP they're allusive. That makes it even harder."

Ty has come into the study and has been standing behind me listening to Tori. He says, "I still wonder if they have soldiers to do their dirty work for them, or is this just a bunch of rich people on the hunt for these poor souls, because they have too much time on their hands and nothing else productive to do. It sickens me."

I look at him and say, "well, it sickens us, too. But you know Ty I'm beginning to think that you're right on one point. They're just running this thing. I don't think WASP has any soldiers, I don't think they're in this for blood. But come Saturday maybe, just maybe we will be a little closer to answering all those questions."

Tori says, "and they still don't know that Cabot has disappeared, or at least that is what I think. There has been no change in anything from what I can see."

******

"**Ty would you come into** the study, please, I have something that I want to show you. You, too, Sasha," Tori says from the doorway.

Ty and I enter the house and walk back to the study, and Tori motions for him to set in the chair next to her.

"What's up," he asks?

"This is. I want you to take a look at this." She says handing him a picture and a file.

He takes a long look at the picture and says, "my God, it's Janet. How did you find her?"

"I've been looking at these old files, and inputting them for the auction. I was looking for Janet based on your description of her. I found that description and it looked like the description you gave me, which I kept in mind. I just came upon it and decided that it was close enough to what you had said she looked like, so I called you in here. But that's not all that helped me. In each of these files are notations of where the girl was sold from. And like I've said before this WASP keeps good records on that, but they also take the girls to one of their holding prisons near where they lived. That's where you said you lived right?"

"Yes, yes. New London...Connecticut. Have you been able to locate where she is." I ask?

"Well that's another story. She's been sold a couple of times according to these records, and I was able to trace her last time to be auctioned to this address in Rotterdam."

"Rotterdam," he exclaims!

"Yeah." She hands me the address, "Sasha, do you know where this is? I don't. I checked what I could from aerial photos that still exist and it appears to be some sort of bar or strip club."

I take it from her and say, "yeah, you know, I do know this place. I think it's a strip joint called *The Regulars*."

She shakes her head at me as we look at Ty.

He's quiet and holding the old tattered picture of Janet in his hands. He's just staring down at it with an empty look on his face, then he looks at Tori and says to her, "thank you, thank you for taking the time to do this for me."

"Remember the other day when we shut Westerville down, I said I'd look for her and that's what I've been doing since we got back, along with putting this scam auction together. I wanted to see if I could find her for you and I think I have."

He then reaches over and gives her a hug and kisses her on

the cheek, causing us both to smile.

"Well this means we will be taking another trip. This time to Rottendamn," I said.

"Yeah, and while we're there we can kill two birds with one stone," Tori says. "Sasha I need to locate and find my brother Davy. And if we can do that, I want to try and convince him to come back here and live with us."

I shake my head in agreement, "And we can kill a third bird."

They look at me curiously.

"I need to go and get something of value that I left there."

"What's that," Ty asks me?

"I'll show you when we get there. It's a secret."

"So what are we waiting for? Let's go," Ty says.

"What about this fake auction that you're doing," I ask?

"Oh, that's no problem."

We both look at her, curiously this time.

"Back in the old days when the whole world was connected with this technology," she says pointing at the computer. "They had these cell phones that we still use all the time, and this laptop computer, and it's much more powerful than that old desktop computer that Cabot bought. I can take it with me, and if I can find an internet connection somewhere that works, I can run the entire auction from wherever we are. We don't have to be here for me to put on a show."

"Enough to fool WASP," I ask?

"You got it, They won't know the difference. Anyway it's all a scam and none of it will be real any way. It's just to try to locate their headquarters."

"This is true."

Ty looks at Tori, "girl, I've said this before about you, you're a genius."

"She is at that," I say, and smile at her. "So what are we waiting for? Let's go to Rottendamn."

******

The trip to the city takes about an hour and half, barring unforeseen incidents and if the roads we take are passable, and the bridges aren't out. We decide that the best way is to go toward Westerville and then onto the city. I told Ty and Tori that I thought that would be the best way. That I was sure now, that's how I was brought to the prison.

Tori is driving the Mustang as usual. I'm doing shotgun duty, again, and I don't mind at all. While I'm a good driver, Tori is a fantastic one, she loves to drive. She has amazing control of the vehicle, it's like she was born to be behind a steering wheel.

After several minutes of chatter and laughs, we grew quiet as the wheels on the road began to put Ty and myself to sleep. Sleep for all of us has been a precious commodity lately. As Tori does her computer work and Ty and I along with Penn and Cash continue to be on the lookout for any kind of trouble that might approach the estate. When we left though we were secure in the thought that Penn and Cash would again take good care of everything in our absence. We know about the special hiding place that they and the girls can retreat to it if danger approaches them.

About an hour into the ride, I'm half out of it, when I think I feel the car slow down and come to a stop.

Tori says, "Sasha, wake up." She's jiggling my shoulder. "Sasha."

"Hump," I jerk and say, groggily. 'Why...what are we stopping for?"

She nods for me to look out the windshield. "Road rats," she says. I look out through drowsy eyes and see three men and three women. The men are armed and they've placed three motorcycles on the road in front of us to keep people from getting by.

I look at her, and murmur, disgustedly, "Awe, fuck! Okay, I'll handle this." My comment cause her to laugh out loud.

I open the door to the car standing behind it for cover. I shout to them, trying to be non-threatening, "hey bud, could you move the bikes so we can get by?"

The girls they're with are off to the side of the road sitting under some shade trees. One is staring relentlessly at me, making me uncomfortable. Then the one guy, who seems to be the leader walks a little closer and says, "well lady, we ain't gonna move the bikes cause we want your car and your money. So hand em over."

"That so. Well, I can't let you do that, because we need the car to get to Rotterdam."

He didn't respond right away because the girl who has been staring at me all this time, has gotten up and has walked over to him.

"I wonder what that's about," Tori asks? "She's been fixated on you ever since she saw you."

"Not sure. May be she's your new competition."

"Ha, that'll be the day. I don't think so."

I laugh.

"By the way if this gets ugly in a hurry, and I start shooting, get down as fast as you can. Okay?"

Ty is now awake and is watching this too. They both concur that they would get down if I started shooting, which it will in all likelihood I will.

The girl and the guy are looking at me and talking about me. Then they look back at each other like they're arguing about me. I hear her say, she's sure. Then she walks away from him and goes back to where the other girls are. She's still staring at me and it's beginning to creep me out.

Then the guy says, "she just told me, she thinks you're Sasha Cain. Is that who you are?"

"That's right. Who are you?"

"They call me, Bear."

"Well Bear, I ask you to move the bikes so we could get by, and you still ain't done it."

"And if we don't?"

"Just do it. Will you? Dammit!" I say, becoming more irritated at this guys stupid arrogance.

Then he get even more stupid if that's possible, and points his gun directly at me.

"Ah, Bear, now what the hell did you go and do that for?"

I hear Tori chuckle inside the car.

"Because, Sasha Cain, you ain't in no position to be orderin' me to do nothin, cause I got the drop on you. So throw your guns down. Cause if you don't, and you don't give us your fucking car and money, then I'm gonna start shootin' and kill you and your two friends. So hand it over. I ain't gonna say it no more."

His tone is aggressive at me. I can see this is going to end badly, but I want to try one more time to get him to cooperate before I kill him.

"You don't hear so good do you, Bear? So I'll repeat myself." I said, "I can't let you do that. You can't take our car. So, will you and your two buddies please put your guns down, and move the goddamn bikes." I'm shouting now. My right hand is on my Glock.

"Fuck you, I'm done talkin' to you, Sasha Cain."

I hear Ty say, "does that idiot have any idea who he's fucking with?"

"Apparently not," Tori says.

Then Bear makes the last stupid move he'll ever make, and prepares to shoot me.

I see him do this and quickly draw my right hand weapon, at the same time. I fire at him, before he gets off a shot. My sudden quick move surely surprised him as he died. Then just as quickly his two buddies get in on the act, and start shooting at me. I duck behind the car door for cover. They miss me. I then crawl to the front of the car and pop up, and in the same move I fire four quick rounds at them and kill them both. It is over in an instant, The three girls begin to wail and scream in horror at what I'd just done, and begin running frantically toward the three dead men I had just gunned down.

I get out from behind the car and walk cautiously toward the girls, gun pointed at the one next to Bear. She's hovering over him, then I see her reach for his gun.

"Ah, ah, ah. I wouldn't do that," I warn her. "I've never killed a girl and I don't want to start now." She quickly draws her hands away from the gun and puts them in the air. Smart move.

Ty and Tori are now out of the car and he walks by me to go move the motorcycles off the road.

The girl who was by Bear, looks up at me and says, "you killed him! You rotten bitch! What are we gonna do?"

I didn't immediately answer her, as I watch Ty get the bikes off the road. He walks back by me and hands me the keys to them. Then I look back down at the girl. She's not crying, but she's angry as hell at me. Looking up at me defiantly from time to time. I'm sure she wants to kill me, but is unwilling to try, because she knows who I am.

"You know how to drive a bike," I ask? Looking down at her.

She shouts at me, hatefully, "NO!"

"Well it's time to learn," I sat. Then I toss the bike keys on the ground in front of her and I walk away.

Soon we're back in the car and on our way to Rotterdam again. We are all quiet.

I break the silence, "I didn't want that to go down like that, guys" I said. "Dammit!"

"Sasha, don't be so hard on yourself." Ty said, putting his

hand on my shoulder. "He didn't leave you any choice. He was going to steal from us then kill us. He had no intention of letting us go anywhere after he robbed us."

"I know that. But I just kill. It's so easy for me. I knew it when I was standing there trying to talk to him, I was going to kill him. I was thinking of ways to do it without him killing me first, because he had the drop on me."

Tori looks at me and reaches for my hand and I take it. She squeezes it and says, "Ty's right, Sasha, he left you no choice. He was stupid, and arrogant, to try that with you, and it cost him his life."

"Yeah I know, but you know about my nightmares, too, and this is what causes them."

"You haven't had one in a while," she says.

"Nightmares," Ty questions?

Yeah, I have these awful nightmares where I'm in this dark alley that frightens the hell out of me, and the only light is the one that is behind these shadowy figures of people that are chasing me. I can't see their faces, they're just shadows, and they're running toward me. I'm trying to get away from them, but my legs won't move, they seem frozen in place."

"Do they catch you," Ty asks? "And is it the same dream?"

"No, they don't. And yes, it is."

"What about the alley?"

"It's dark and scares me, I don't want to go into it, even if I could. I wake up screaming and in a cold sweat. Ask Tori she's seen me have them."

"Do you have them a lot?"

"That's just it, she hasn't had one in several nights now," Tori says.

"But you were raped," I said. "By Behar and her two bitches, Wanda, and Violet. They did it to her to get back at me."

"Damn, Tori," he says. "Are you okay?"

"For the most part. I don't really want to talk about it. Her dream is more serious."

"How do you figure that," I say.

"I don't want to talk about it," she declares.

I look at her, and she's shaking her head no.

I pause looking at her realizing that she's not going to open up about the rape, especially in front of Ty. I say, "Anyway it scares me. And the dream will stay with me for a longtime."

"It's just a dream, Sasha."

"I'm not sure about that, and what it's trying to say to me?"

"She believes that it's some sort of omen that she's going to go to a bad place after she dies."

"Yes I do, and you, you're still dealing with what that fucking bitch Behar did to you."

She looks at me and says softly, "I know. I got them back though."

"I know that," I say to her, gently, with compassion.

"Do you believe that, Sasha? That there is a place we go after this life is over," Ty asks?

"I don't know for sure. Tori and I have talked a lot about that very thing. I just don't know, but if it's true, then I for sure will end up in a bad place."

"Hell," he says.

"Yeah, hell," I say, turning to look at him. "I've told Tori this, and I'm not lying. I'm not a good girl, Ty. You both just witnessed my ability to kill. That's what I'm good at."

He looked at me and grew quiet the rest of the trip, as Tori drove. I looked out my window at the scenery and wondered about what we just talked about. It does scare me if I spend too much time dwelling on the dream and my killing.

I think back to that girl who was leaning over Bear, I felt no remorse for her. I was pretty mean to her, I just threw the keys at her, and she didn't know how to drive a motorcycle. And I didn't care about that either. It seems as though I have a Jekyll and Hyde personality. One minute I can be loving and caring with Tori, then a vicious killer the next. I never cared about think of things like this before I met her. I just didn't care. But now I do—I love Tori.

I look at her, her eyes on the road and touch her leg, causing her to break out in a broad smile. She glances at me and I think again, I don't deserve her. She's so sweet and kind. And the only time I saw her get even close to being vicious is when she lashed Behar and her two butch thugs, Wanda and Violet, with that belt. She truly enjoyed that. But I've not seen her exhibit that type of behavior since that day.

She has since returned to being just the same sweet girl I have now been with for over seven months. A person that I know I can trust and can never be without. I love her, and I can't imagine life without her. I don't even question my love for her anymore, like I did when we met. Gone is the confusion of loving another woman, leaving me with a joy that I never knew could exist before I met Tori. And as for my kissing Tyler that day—never again. She seems to have gotten over my doing that, I nearly lost her, I never want to loose her.

Many times we've expressed our love for each other. Both in conversation and in the act of making physical love, knowing that it is something that we both want. Something we want never to end and both want to last forever.

Today she is dressed in this little pink sundress that I enjoy seeing her wear. It makes me just want to grab her. She has a lot of these, but this one accentuates her soft curves so very much, which makes me even more hungry for her.

I want to ask her to marry me and I plan on doing just that when we get back from this trip to Rotterdam. After we return I'm going into Roxboro and get her an engagement ring, and surprise her. They have an old style jewelry store there, and I'm sure they'll have exactly what I'm looking for. I'm excited about doing it for her, she deserves it so much.

I only hope she will say yes. I'm sure she will. In fact she may be wondering why I haven't asked her already. But she would never say anything to me, because she's that kind of person. The best.

In wanting the best for her, I would like for her to open up to someone about the rape. I know she got her revenge, but she still needs to talk about it. She won't tell me everything and I don't push it, because I'm just to close to her to do that.

NANCY HOWARD

NINETEEN

As we approach the city, things around us begin to change. The sky has completely changed. Gone are the blue skies we are used to seeing in the Catskills, having been replaced by the dingy yellowish haze and polluted air of the city. We are on the outskirts now as we speed toward the place where we believe Janet to be. Everywhere we look now we see humans and their dilapidated dwellings that line the narrow streets everywhere. And the closer we get to where we think the girl is, the worse the city becomes. It makes me sick to think that we've come back here, but it's necessary because we need to find Janet and Davy. Then I want to go and get my eighty grand I buried at the base of that memorial in the cemetery that night.

Tori says. "It's Friday, and tomorrow I have to find a place that has an internet connection, so I can feed the auction out to all the sick moguls looking for a cute little girl to abuse with their perverted minds."

"I say, "we will. I know a place where we can go to do that, and I think it still has internet capability."

After several minutes of driving and my directions, Tori turned the corner, and we saw the place where we believe Janet might be. The place is an old dump titty bar that sits mid block, on fiftieth called *The Regulars.* Tori parks about fifty feet from it and to the south. The windows to the place are all darkened so no one can see in from the outside. The building that it's in is an old one story brick building, with an alley on it's north side. The one thing that never seems to change no matter the decade is strip clubs, they're the same now as they've ever been.

I have been in here before, looking for people for my clients. I know the place but not all that well. Looking around the streets are quiet, very few people are out. It's about four in the afternoon in late August—it's hot and muggy as usual. We can hear rumbles of thunder in the distance, indicating rain.

"Once we get in there we need to start asking questions right away," I said. "To make sure we have the right place."

"Yeah we need to make sure someone has seen her,"Tori says.

"Let's go in and check it out," Ty said.

We exit the car. Ty arms himself giving me extra help, Tori grabs her laptop out of the back seat and we walk up to the front and go inside.

The place isn't busy, it's to early, so we seat ourselves. It's just as dark and dingy as it looks from the outside. It reeks of old age, the smell of liquor and cigarette smoke, which makes me sick to my stomach every time I smell it. The lights in the place are dim like all bars. There is one stripper doing a pole dance, to the delight of two or three men sitting at tables near the stage, tipping her. She's dancing to that damn nauseating, boom, boom, music that I just hate. It's rhythmic sound drives me to distractions.

After sitting for a few seconds a scantily clad waitress in tight shorts and an equally tight t-shirt, with too much makeup on, comes over to our table. She asks us what we're having, and we all ordered a large draft beer, plus a pitcher of it. Though I don't have much like for beer, today it sounds good, because it's so hot and humid outside.

Ty is setting across from us, Tori is next to the wall and I'm to her right. She's opened her computer and turned it on to see if the bar has an internet connection. It doesn't, but she has Janet's picture in a file on the desktop and she opens her picture up from that.

The waitress comes back and gives us our beer and Tori shows her Janet's photo on the computer. She asks her, "You know this girl? Does she perform here? Her name is Janet Baines."

The girl looked at us and asked, "you guys cops or something?"

"No," I say. "I'm Sasha Cain, this is Tori Nicks, that's Ty Baines. The girl in that picture is his daughter. We want to know if you know her, because she was kidnapped by someone and we have good reason to believe that she's here. Do you know anything about that?"

The waitress' eyes grew wide and she shook her head no, as if in shock to learn about kidnapping.

"Were you kidnapped," Tori asks?

"Me? No. Hell no," she exclaims! I don't know nothin' about that shit. But I've seen that girl in here."

"When?" Ty questions anxiously, getting closer to the girl.

"She comes in every night with the owner and his entourage."

"Then she's not a stripper." I say.

"No, when that girl that comes in here, she's dressed to the nines, I mean she always looks like a million. I guess for the owner."

"Do you perhaps know the owner's name?" I ask her.

"Yeah I do…let me see…oh yeah, Colin Lampoor."

Lampoor, owns this dump? I never knew.

I looked at Ty and could see the anger building in him after she said Lampoor's name.

"Any thing else folks?"

"No," I said, "Just keep our tab running. We're gonna to be here a while. Oh, and thanks for the information."

"Don't mention it," she says, and walks away.

Ty looks at me and exclaims, "that rotten little son-of-a-bitch! He has my daughter, and has bought her from someone."

"You know Ty, he may not know she's your daughter," Tori says.

"How so?" He questions, sharply.

"Well, as I was looking through those files building a database so we could locate more of these girls, I noticed something. That all of their real names had been wiped out. WASP apparently has the names changed to make it harder for people looking for the girls to track them down. As a matter of fact I would not have been able to locate Janet if I hadn't read the dossier on her. This WASP, whoever they are does a great job of covering their tracks."

"But you found her."

Yeah, only because I read her back story, and the description of her you gave me matched. I knew there was a good chance she might be your daughter, which is why I had you come in and look at the picture of her."

I say, "Ty, I know it pisses you off to find out that it's Lampoor that has her, it would me. What Tori is saying is right, because these girls are held captive and are in all likelihood told to keep their mouths shut. At all costs."

"Meaning?"

"Meaning, they're not only told to do that, but they're scared out of their wits that if they don't do as they're told, they'll be punished, even killed. Something as simple as giving out their real name could get them killed. I know, I'd be scared, too. Right Tori." I looked at Tori and she's shaking her head in agreement at what I just said.

The late afternoon slowly became early evening. It's pouring rain outside as the thunderstorm we heard earlier has made it to the part of Rotterdam we are in. We waited and even went so far as to order something to eat in order to soak up the beer in our stomach. Tori ordered water instead of drinking her beer. So Ty and I drank our full glasses of beer, and most of the pitcher, and we waited. Assuming that sooner or later Lampoor would show up, we hope with Janet.

During our waiting we talked and from time to time I noticed Ty watching me, he's always looking at me. But this time he's watching me scan the room over and over again. "You do that a lot I notice."

"Do what," I ask him?

"Look around you. I see you from time to time studying the place. Looking at it like a worker would look at a project before he begins to toil and grind out his solution to his problem."

I shake my head, "I like to keep an eye on things. Where I am—the coming and going of people. I want to look around at the layout of a room to see what would best suit the situation if trouble comes. It's always good to look for more than one way out. So yeah, you're right, I do study a room it is part of my work to study things around me. It's kept me alive all these years."

"So those men you killed this afternoon it's all part of the job."

"Yeah, it goes with the territory."

"You seemed upset after you shot them, Sasha."

"Yeah, like I said earlier, I'd like for stuff to happen where I didn't have to resort to killing, like I do."

"But, like Tori and I said, that guy, Bear didn't leave you much wriggle room. He was planning on killing us no matter what you did. You did the right thing, girl."

"But Ty, I just do it, no remorse, no feelings. I…"

"It sounds like you're beginning to have those thoughts and feelings of remorse."

"I don't know, maybe I am."

"Well be careful with that, because you're going against your gut instincts. It's who you are. Feelings like that could get you killed. I'm sure this little lady sitting next to you would not want that to happen."

We both looked at Tori still busy on her computer, she's

been listening to our conversation and she's shaking her head no at Ty's comment.

The late afternoon drags on and finally became evening. Seven thirty approaches and there are now three girls pole dancing, to that damn boom, boom music. The place is starting to pick up in business, as I look at the tables in front of the stage, now filled with horny old men. Each of them fantasizing what it would be like to bed down with one of the dancers.

I wonder, too, if those girls work here or have they been kidnapped. I mention this to Ty and Tori and they say they've thought the same thing.

As we grow more wary of seeing Lampoor this evening, suddenly our desire gets full filled. He comes in and lo and behold as part of his little group we see Behar, Wanda, and Violet, along with none other than Commander Par. Lampoor is accompanied by a beautiful young woman, and his two goons follow close behind them.

Even though the place is dimly lit, the girl is, as the waitress said, decked out. She's a knockout, and has on a thigh length cocktail dress that appears to be silver from my vantage point. The dress has glitter, and a plunging V-neck that shows plenty of cleavage. She's wearing four inch strappy heels that accentuate her long legs. Her long hair is beautiful and doesn't have a hair out of place. It is draped perfectly over her shoulders and lays half way down her back. She's adorned with lots of jewelry that compliments her outfit perfectly.

Lampoor is his usual scruffy self, though he is wearing a jacket, slacks and an open collared shirt.

THE ALLEY OF EVIL

As I watch the girl's movements she is looking around the room—nervous, as well as anxious about her situation. It's like she's saying come and rescue me—someone, please. Or maybe she's not. Maybe it's just me studying her too much, but that is what I feel as I watch her. I'm usually not wrong about things like this—studying people is part of my job, too.

Ty is leaning forward doing his best to get a better look at the girl. As a waitress seats all six of them at a table across the room from us. They haven't seen us yet, and in all likelihood would have to strain to do so, because it's so dark in the place.

Behar and her two bitches sit opposite Lampoor. They and Par all have on pantsuits as their evening attire. Makes me wonder why Behar is here? Of course she's not a warden anymore, Tori and I took care of that job for her.

I say, Ty is that Janet?"

"Yes, yes it is. I'm one-hundred percent sure of it." He says, recognizing his daughter immediately.

"Well, since that's the case, I think it's time to go and spoil the party before it gets started. Don't you?"

They agree, Tori shuts down her laptop, and we all get up and saunter slowly across the room toward their table. As we proceed I take note of where the goons are and the two bouncers out in the vestibule, who are looking in on the main room. All four men are armed with .9mm Beretta and are watching us as we walk toward Lampoor's table.

Right now my main concern is if this should get ugly and I'm sure it will, is for Tori. My main responsibility is to protect her, as I know Ty will protect Janet.

"Well, well, if it isn't Cynthia Behar the former criminal who was running that place...Westerville, pretending to be a...warden! And Commander Par, how nice to see you again." I smart off at them with plenty of sarcasm in my voice. They look up, surprised to see me. "Surprise, surprise," I sound off again.

Lampoor sees me and asks gruffly, "what the hell are you doing here, Cain?"

"Well Colin, you see I'm here to collect."

"Collect? For what?" He snaps at me.

"Not for what, for him," I say, nodding at Ty.

"Well I have nothing of his, now get the hell out or I'll have you thrown out."

"Well Colin, you see that girl that you have sitting next to you happens to be his daughter, and we've come here to take her with us."

"You're lying, Sasha."

"No, I'm not. You're Janet Baines aren't you sweetie," I ask?

She looks at me and shakes her head yes.

"Then get up and get away from him." Ty makes a move and takes Janet's arm pulling her toward him and away from Lampoor.

One of the goons makes a move to try and stop her, and I say, "I wouldn't." He backs off.

"You, can't, fucking do that." Lampoor protests loudly. "I paid good money for that little bitch."

With that remark Ty has heard all he can take. He's standing next to Colin, and draws back and hits him hard with a right hook, sending him flying backwards and off of his chair and onto the floor. Bloodying his nose.

I notice the boom, boom, music has stopped. Then one of the goons makes a stupid move and pulls his gun and starts to shoot Ty. I see him and draw my gun at the same time. I fire at him and he goes down. Then other goon and the bouncers draw their guns and start shooting. Bullets are flying everywhere. In all this chaos I hear yelling and screaming as people try to get away from the gunfire.

I fire at a goon and miss. "Shit." Then he and fires at me and misses as I go down on top of Tori, knocking her down to protect her. The bouncers are shooting at Ty. The goon shoots at me again. His bullet hits the edge of the table ricocheting off of it and into the room. I roll over and shoot, killing him. Tori and I get up off the floor and scramble to a nearby booth for better cover, as one of the bouncers continues to shoot at me and Ty. I tell her to get down and I return the bouncers fire, and kill one as Ty takes the other one down.

I get out from behind the booth, and see Lampoor standing up, nose bloody, and rage filling his eyes. He quickly pulls a revolver from his jacket and points it at me, to shoot me. Without even blinking, I shoot, and I hit him right between his eyes. I shoot him two, three more times. Before Ty takes hold of my arm and says, "he's dead, Sasha. You killed him."

"I told that slimy little fucker I'd kill him one day. That's for double-crossing me, and having Charley Bill killed."

Then I turn my attention to the four women. All of them are cowering behind a half wall, where they took cover from the gunfire. I stand up. Helping Tori as I do. Then I shout at them,

"Get up!"

They drag themselves up as I point my gun at them, readying to kill them.

"Go ahead kill us," Cynthia chides, using a fearful tone at me. "We're not armed."

Then I feel two hands softly touching my arm. Tori.

I'm fighting the urge to kill them, when I hear her say, "don't do it, Sasha. Please. Don't kill them. Do it for me, but more importantly do it for yourself."

I listen to her—teeth clenched, face contorted with anger, and say raising my voice. "She raped you. They raped you."

"I know they did, and I got them back for it, remember." Her voice speaking to me calmly.

"I remember, but I've always wanted to kill her, you know that," I said, loudly.

"I know, but right now ask yourself what purpose it would serve, to kill them? Look at them. Even though she dared you to shoot her—look at her, and the four of them they're scared shitless of you death of you. They just saw you gun down four armed men. I saw you kill three more earlier today. So Sasha, do this for you. Don't kill them."

I looked at her, her soft brown eyes looking at me, melting my heart and her words making sense to me like they always do. I lower my gun.

Then I hear Ty say, "she's right, Sasha, let em go." I looked over at him with his arm around Janet, still not sure if I would listen or not.

I look at Tori and she's shaking her head. Then I turn my

gun on them again—fighting the urge to kill them. I look at them as they cower in front of me—my eyes filled with hate for each of them. For a split second I wanted to pull the trigger again. But I don't, I lower my gun.

I look at Cynthia and say quietly, "this is the second time I've let you live, Cynthia Behar. Consider yourself very, very lucky today, that Tori stopped me from killing you. I've always wanted to kill you, ever since that first day, when you humiliated my Tori. So, you, and your two bitches get up off of your asses—you, too, Commander Par. I ought to kill you for what you did to Charley Bill." I pause and then say raising my voice, "get the hell out of my sight, all four of you. Before I give in to my primal instinct and change my mind, and kill you anyway."

As they left I said, "one more thing, Cynthia." She turned around and looked at me. "Don't you ever let me see you again. You will not live if I do."

She shook her head at me like she got the message this time—she better have. All four of them left in a hurry. Running out of the building like the rats they are, and not looking back.

The Regulars is in a shambles with dead men all over the floor, as people left—running out of the place for their lives. The bartender walks up to us and says that after we've all gone he would call the cops. For us not to worry, he would be long gone by the time they got there. He would tell them nothing.

Then Ty says, "let's get out of here. We got what we came for."

On the way to the car Ty and Janet walk, arms around each other, hugging each other as Ty kisses his daughter. Tori looks at me, and puts her arm around me and hugs me, too, as we walk, she says, "I am so proud of you."

"Really?"

"Yes, I am, you showed so much strength in there by not killing those women, no matter how much you wanted, too."

"Me, Tori. I showed strength? You're the one who did that. You talked me out of not killing them. No one has ever dared to try and do that. But you, you know me so well now that you felt comfortable and confident doing it. I am so proud of you, babe. Talk about strength."

We all get into the Mustang. Tori gives Ty the keys to drive. We are all quiet. I set in the backseat with Tori.

"Where to," Ty asks? "You want to go find Davy now?"

"No not tonight," Tori says. "Let's look for a place to spend the night. That okay with you?" She looks down at me.

I shake my head yes.

"Sasha, this is your old stomping ground so, where should we look," Ty asks?

"You know there's an old hotel over on Seventieth Avenue we could go to. It's not far, and I think it still has the internet, though I'm not sure."

Twenty minutes later he pulls up in front of the old hotel on east Seventieth Avenue and stops. Ty and I get out of the car and go inside, we get two rooms for the night and the next day, because Tori has to have time to work on the fake auction with Ty.

TWENTY

Tori is the computer master today as she is everyday. She's set up the scam auction of girls on her laptop making it look legit. It's what she called a virtual auction. She's running it for the entire world to see from her laptop in a rundown hotel in Rottendamn. And it being all electronic it takes her and Ty less than two hours to get it done. By one in the afternoon it is over, freeing us to go and look for her brother Davy.

"That was quick." I said to her, referring to the time of the auction.

"Yes and much simpler, too. Before Cabot left I was trying to convince him that this would work much better than the way he was doing it. The only difference is, this one was a scam."

"Why couldn't you convince him that this was better?"

"He was old-fashioned, you know, and he didn't have the slightest idea on how these things worked. Plus I think he liked having a party at the estate every two weeks, even though he knew it was a slave auction."

"In other words he liked the company," I said.

"Exactly."

"But aren't there are still girls in captivity," Ty asks?

"Yeah, unfortunately, and they won't be freed like the ones

at Westerville until we find out where WASP is," Tori says.

Janet Baines has been standing by listening to our conversation, and tells us she was in a prison in Ontario and there were at least two hundred girls in that facility.

Ty puts his arm around his daughter, hugs her, and says, "that will never happen to you again, sweetie. Trust me."

Tori and I watch and smile, as he protects her like any father would.

"So do you know where we can start looking for your brother," I ask?

"A good place to start is my Uncle's house, maybe he's there or he's seen him."

"What's your uncles name, you've never mentioned it to me."

"Gabe."

The noonday sky is again dark and foreboding as a huge storm brews to our west. Indicating it is going to pour any minute, as we make the twenty minute drive to Gabe's. He lives in an old neighborhood of rundown houses that are at least a hundred and fifty years old. At one time this was a pretty tree lined area of homes with families that were called middle class, because of the income they earned. Then the calamity hit and that middle class that was the backbone of the country completely disappeared.

Gabe's house sits in the middle of the block on an old street filled with potholes, broken curbs and missing sidewalks, with very few trees. The houses along the way are unkempt, with yards barren of grass and overgrown with weeds. Gabe's house is an aging tri-level that is in very sad condition, like the street it sits on. The concrete on the stoop at the door is breaking off and crumbling badly from being old. The aluminum siding is completely gone in some places revealing the construction of the house. The lawn like the others we see has a couple of trees and is overgrown with weeds that are knee high.

The front door is open and only the screen door is closed. Tori knocks on it, as we wait having not gone up the steps yet.

After a few seconds a man in his sixties appears. He doesn't open the door for her to enter.

"Uncle Gabe it's me, Tori."

"I know who you are. What is it you want?" He asks her in a tone, meant to tell her he's not really happy to see her.

"Can we come in for a minute? I want to ask you about Davy."

He scratches his head and mumbles, "suit yourself." Then he turns away from the door, still not opening it for her.

She opens it herself, and turns to look at us with raised eyebrows. We go up the steps and follow her in, and not to soon either, as it starts to pour down rain in windblown sheets.

The house on the inside is worse than on the outside, if one could believe that. It's dirty, and hasn't been cleaned in years, like before I was born. Junk and stacks of old magazines and boxes fill the house with clutter everywhere you look, it reminds me of Lampoor's apartment.

Gabe is a scraggly man, he's thin, and balding and has on a pair of old tattered tan Bermuda shorts, and a skivvy shirt—he's barefooted. He sits in an old worn out recliner chair, with an end table next to it. The table has several empty beer bottles on it, an ashtray, a pack of smokes, and a lighter. He's watching an old television, that is as old as he is.

'Uncle Gabe, this is Sasha, Ty, and Janet," she says. Introducing us.

That really brought him to life, he didn't even look up at us.

"Have you seen Davy recently?"

He doesn't answer her right away, and sighs, like it pains him to answer her. Then says, "Yeah he hangs his hat here most of the time. I ain't seen him in a couple of days though. But he usually doesn't come home until after I've gone to bed, and he gets up early, too."

"You know where he is during the day?"

He looks at all of us, then says, "I ain't sure about this, but I think he hangs around that old pool hall over on tenth. *Sharkey's*. For all I know he may work there."

She looks at me, "you know where he's talking about?"

I shake my head yes.

Then he looks at me," she called you Sasha. You, Sasha Cain?"

"I am."

He looks at Tori and says, "interesting company you're keepin' these days girl."

Tori looks at me and gives me a half grin. Then she thanks Gabe for the information and we go out the door. He doesn't return her gesture, he just sits there.

"Is he always that friendly?" I say once we're outside as we run to get to the car, because of the rain.

"Don't know for sure, I've never spent much time with him, except with the go-carts. He wasn't so bad back then, but soon after my aunt passed away he just changed. He was my dad's younger brother and they were never very close."

"Was your dad like that?"

"No, he wasn't." Was her replay.

We all get back in the car, Ty is driving and I'm riding shotgun. We make the ten minute trip to the pool hall called *Sharkey's*, where Tori's uncle Gabe said we could find Davy. Ty parks the car across the street. The rain has completely let up.

"So how do you want to handle this," he asks?

"Well, you and Janet can stay out here if you want. I'm sure you two would like the time alone. Tori and I will go into this place, to see if Davy is here."

"Look, Sasha I know you go into these kinds of situations all the time, but do you think you might need some back up. It looks like there's quite a few people hanging out over there."

"Thanks for the offer, but, no, We'll be okay. Places like this usually are not like the bars and clubs, like *The Regulars*. These are mostly young people just killing time because they don't have anything else to do, and nowhere to go." I turn and look at Tori, "ready?"

She says. "let's do this."

We get out of the car and walk across the street, there are ten or twelve people hanging around out front of *Sharkey's* as Tori and I approach. I see only three women, each seems to be with one of the guys. All of these people are mostly younger than twenty-five, and drinking beer. A couple of them are smoking. I don't see any one who is armed.

I'm an attention getter wherever I go, especially from the men who see right away that I'm armed. A couple of these guys immediately begin to jeer at us. Tori hears it and I tell her to ignore them and keep walking, that it is something I hear all the time. I told her none of them have weapons that I can see, so I doubt they would cause us real trouble.

We walked past the jeers, and I opened the door for Tori to go in ahead of me. Then I heard one of the men say something I almost couldn't ignore, "fags." he says. Then all the rest of them laughed out loud at his rude comment. I ignored it, too, and went inside.

Immediately, people stopped what they're doing to look at us, especially me. I could already hear my name being uttered in the room.

This place *Sharkey's* has a bar with stools, and eight pool tables, all busy with several people playing. The floor is old with brown tile and the walls are the same color, and are paneled. The place has lighting over all the tables and just a few overhead lights elsewhere.

"You see him anywhere," I ask?

"Not yet. If he works here he may be someplace else. Let's ask the bartender." she says.

We walk over to the bar, and I call the girl tending bar over. She's about our age with blonde hair and wearing a t-shirt and jeans.

"What can I get you ladies," she says.

Tori says, "Well I'm wondering if you have a David Nicks

working here, or have you seen him in here? I'm his sister, Tori."

"Yeah he works here, he's in the back, I'll get him for you." She comes out from behind the bar and goes over to two double doors next to it and opens them, and yells in, "hey Nicks, there's a girl out here who says she's your sister. Would you come and talk to her?"

She comes out followed a few seconds later by a young man, who is Davy. As he approaches I knew right away that he's Tori's bother. Not just because of the family resemblance but because of his native skin and black hair, like Tori. He's a couple of inches shy of six feet, fit, and trim, somewhat muscular. Handsome fits him.

He walks over to us, and glancing at me briefly. He says, "what are you doing here, Tori?"

"I'm looking for you," she says.

"Why?"

He's obviously not happy to see his sister either.

"I just wanted to see if you're okay, that's all."

"Yeah, well you found me, and I'm okay, so leave, I'm working."

He starts to leave and she takes his arm and he yanks it away.

I am beginning to think that Uncle Gabe is wearing off on Davy.

"Look Davy, I, we, were in town on business and I just wanted to find you and see if you'd like to come and live with us up in the Catskills. I've been worried about you."

I could see that her comment about worrying didn't go over

well with him, and he motions for us to follow him. We do and go out the back door of the pool hall and into the alley behind it, where Davy gets close to Tori. His body language since he came out to talk to us inside has been condescending—not happy to see her.

"You were worried about me, you say?" You left me. I damn near starved to death because of you, big sister. Like what the hell happened to you?"

"Davy, look, just give me a minute to explain."

"Well make it quick. And who is she?"

"This is Sasha."

"Sasha Cain, I thought so," he says. Curtly.

"Davy, I'm sorry. I was kidnapped and put into Westerville, for taking food from that butcher guy so you and I wouldn't starve. He turned me into the cops for being a thief. Westerville was a prison for keeping girls to be sold into slavery. It was all part of a human trafficking scheme, which Sasha, me, and another friend are trying to sort out. So I didn't leave you on purpose. You weren't home when they came to get me. So you see, I never meant to leave you to fend for yourself."

He looks at us, then says, "how'd you get out? You ain't in there now."

"That's a whole other story, and to make a long story short as to how we got out. We had help. And we, she, and I shut Westeville down for good last week."

"So you still ain't answered my original question. What do you want with me?"

"Like I said, I would just like for you to come with us to live on this estate in the Catskills. Davy it's so much better than this. I'm sure living with Uncle Gabe is not fun at all. So what do you say?"

I've been standing right beside her listening, and say to him, bluntly, "you know, your sister has done nothing but worry about you for months. Ever since I've known her really. Now I don't profess to know you at all. But I do know Tori and all she wants is for you two to be a family, and for you to be safe. And if that means you coming to live with us, then she's right. She always is. She loves you, and all that she just told you is true. I can attest to that."

I see his anger at her has relented and disappeared.

"That true, what she says?"

"Yes Davy, it is. She wouldn't lie, she has no reason, too," she says, quietly.

He pauses for several seconds thinking about what she and I said. He looks at us then away. "Do I have time to go to Gabe's and get my stuff?"

"We'll make time. Right now," Tori says.

"Okay, I'll go."

Gee, that was a tough sell.

With that settled, we go back inside and walk through the pool hall—Davy is with us. I again hear my name being said, only louder this time. Adjectives, some of them pretty ugly, were being used to describe me. It's nothing that I haven't heard before. Outside we again hear the same remark from what sounded like the same guy. Again the word fags came out of his mouth, and laughter from the others. I was about to turn around and say something to him, but before I could Davy intervened and walked briskly over to him.

"You fucking dumbass," he said to him. Getting into his face. "You know who she is?"

The guy shrugs and then says, "I don't know some fag broad with guns on."

"You're stupid, bud. She's Sasha Cain. She could kill you, all of you." He says looking at the others. "In the blink of an eye."

With that the smirks went away and there were no more jeers, as the man cowered up bashfully and said no more.

We went back to the car and made the trip back to Uncle Gabes to get Davy's few belongings. With five people, we're all packed into the little mustang like sardines. We have to make better seating arrangements I think.

Uncle Gabe never even said hello or even good-bye to his nephew and again ignored Tori altogether.

After we left Gabe's I told Ty to drive over to the Vet Cemetery. He wasn't sure of the way so I told him where to go.

"Cemetery?" He says, in a curious tone. "What on earth do you want to go to the Vet Cemetery for?"

"It's…well, what I told you I need to get. I left it there before I got slammed into Westerville."

"Tori, you know what it is," he asks?

"Not a clue." Was her response.

Ten minutes later Ty drove the Mustang into the Vet. The old graveyard for soldiers who died many years ago fighting senseless wars that still rage on today. Where young men still die senselessly.

THE ALLEY OF EVIL

Driving in I notice right away that the Vet looks very different in the daylight and the summer. I tell everyone to look for a very large grave maker with the name Carter on it. After a few seconds Janet spies it on the left. Ty parks the car and we all get out and walk toward this big old grave marker. I say, "we need something to dig with."

"I got a little shovel in my stuff," Davy says. "But it's in the trunk of your car."

"Let's go get it," Ty says. They go back to the car to retrieve Davy's shovel while we wait. When they get back they hand it to me and I decide on the right place to start digging. If my memory serves me right, I buried it about midway in back of the grave marker.

"You got any idea what she's doing Tori?" Ty asks her again.

"She's said nothing to me about any of this. Only what we heard before we left."

I look up at all of them, grinning, and say "I bet right now you're all probably thinking that old Sasha has gone and lost it all. Right?"

"Ty says, "it's crossing our minds, yes."

They all laugh, and shake their heads. Tori says she's anxious to see what I'm looking for.

They all watch as I begin to dig, and after a few minutes I hit something, "it's still here," I say to them.

"What is," Tori asks?

I'm squatting down and reaching into the hole and pull out a bag. The container is still inside just like I left it that night. I pulled it out of the bag and opened it up, as they all gathered around me, curious to see what is in it.

"This." I say opening the can.

"Money," Tori says.

"Yes, money. The eighty-eight thousand dollars I took from Diego Sanchez after me and Charley Bill killed him and his gang. He owed Lampoor ten grand. I took that money to him, but he got wind from his snitch hookers who got away that day, that I took this money too. I gave him the money Sanchez owed him, but he said that since I was working for him that this money belonged to him, too. He demanded that I give it to him, which I didn't do as you can see. I buried it out here the night before he had his crooked cops pick me up."

"She never told you about this," Ty says. Looking at Tori and smiling.

"No." She says, pretending to be upset and haughtily surprised.

"Sorry, babe, I just didn't think about it until the other day when we knew we were coming here to get Janet and Davy."

She smiles at me, shaking her head that it doesn't matter. "I'm messing with you. Anyway no need to feel guilty, I'm just glad it was still here."

I place the money back in the bag and we all go back to the car. I put it in the trunk as everybody starts to get into the car. Before they do, I tell everybody to stop. They all look at me.

"Before we go back we've got to make different seating arrangements in this car."

"What do you suggest," Ty asks?

"Well how about this for starters. You two guys set up

front, and we girls in the back since we're smaller. Having one of you guys back there makes it very uncomfortable for him and us."

"Gotcha," Okay, Davy you ride shotgun," Ty said.

The trip was both uneventful as well as more comfortable going home. No road rats to contend with this time, and better seating arrangement made for a nicer trip. Ty and Davy seemed to male bond on the way back, and we stopped and got something to eat along the way. We were all starved. When we got back to the estate the place was quiet. Soon Cash appeared and greeted us and told us everything was a. o. k.

Janet and Davy were amazed at the place, as she and her dad went into the main house to get her settled. Davy followed us into where we live, and we gave him one of the other bedrooms and told him to make himself at home. It was late past ten thirty, and we all just went our separate ways and off to bed. Tori and I curling up against each other kissing and giggling, and touching, before falling off fast asleep. I was looking forward to a good night's sleep in our own bed, then all of a sudden.

NANCY HOWARD

TWENTY ONE

I rare straight up not fully awake, my tank top that I sleep in is soaked in sweat that's running down between my boobs. I'm out of breath as I shriek out, screaming, waking Tori up.

She sets up alarmed, "Sasha, Sasha. Are you okay?" She puts her arms around me, holding me.

I look at her with my head on her shoulder. My eyes dazed, as I slowly but surely begin to fully wake up from another nightmare.

"H...hold me," I say in a small quivering voice. I'm shaking, shivering—suddenly cold.

Just then I glance out of the corner of my eye and see Davy appear in our bedroom doorway.

"She gonna be okay?"

"I think she will be in a few minutes. She has these terrible nightmares from time to time. They've been happening for sometime now."

He comes over and sets down on the edge of our bed and says gently, "can I get you anything, Sasha?"

"You know some water would be good," Tori says. He gets up and goes in the kitchen to get some water for me. Tori and I set up, leaning against headboard of the bed, as my shivering subsides, but the images of the nightmare are still with me.

She looks at me and says, "want to talk about it? That one was pretty bad."

Before I answer her for some reason I look at the clock and it says, two forty-four.

"It's just like the other ones I've been having, Only this time the ones chasing me were about to catch me. My legs…they felt like they had lead in them and I couldn't move them. Like always they were frozen in place. Just as they were about to catch me I woke up."

"By they, you mean the shadows."

I shake my head yes.

Davy comes back into our room with the water and I thanked him. I take a sip, it felt good going down.

He sets on the edge of the bed again and says, "dreams are symbolic you know. If you don't mind me saying, maybe you should go see someone to help you process the dreams. There are still shrinks around you know."

"We don't know who we could go talk to," Tori says.

"Maybe Mr. Baines knows someone. Have you ever asked him? He seems like a really smart guy."

"Your right he is, and he knows about Sasha's nightmares, but we've never talked to him about getting her help, and if he might know someone."

"I would, maybe he can help," Davy says.

******

Ty walks into the study that morning and sets down across from Tori and I. She is diligently watching her computer screen tracking the workings of the auction. Today is Monday and she thinks that it will take a little more time, three, possibly four days for disgruntled auction customers to start pounding WASP, with disappointment. So she's been unable to trace them yet. She says they seem to have no IP address that she can find.

We greet Ty and ask him if Janet is getting settled okay, he tells us that she is.

"So anything yet," he asks?

"No," Tori responds. "Like I've just told Sasha before this is going to take a few days, but I'm sure we may have something by weeks end."

I look at her and she says, "go ahead, ask him."

"Ask me what?"

I say, "well we were wondering if you might know of a shrink close by."

"I might. So why do you want to talk to a shrink?"

"It's for her," Tori says. "She's been having that nightmare again, and it's getting worse." She looks at me eyes widened shaking her head, "it is."

"And you," I say. "She's right they're getting worse." I say in agreement. Tori doesn't look at me, she knows I'm talking about the rape.

"It's just a dream, Sasha. Why do you think you need to see a therapist?"

"Like I told you that day in the car it's reoccurring."

"It causes her to wake up screaming and sweating and gasping for breath during the night. Last night she had the shivers."

"So do you? Know someone."

He pauses, thinking, "I used to, her name is…um…let me see. It's been years since anyone asked me a question like this. It's uh…Ellie, Ellie Yost. She used to have an office above the pharmacy in Roxboro."

"I wonder if she's still there," Tori questions?

"That I would not know. You have the computer see if you have a phone number on her, and give her a call. I don't even know if she's still there and still practicing. Those people are few and far between anymore. And keep in mind if she's still there she may not be able to see or help you, Sasha."

"Symbolism or not, I hope she's still practicing. The damn dream is getting worse."

"Okay, how are they getting worse?"

"The shadows of what appear to be people in the dream are chasing me and are getting closer to me each time it occurs. They've been trying to catch me, or at least that is what seems to be going on, and last night they almost caught me. And I can't run away from them. My legs are like, frozen to the ground, and I can't move them. And like I've said before the alley in front of me scares the hell out of me. So I have nowhere to go in the dream."

He looks at me with concern on his face, and shakes his head.

Tori says, "I have a phone number for a Dr. Eleanor B. Yost

PC. She's the only one I can find."

"Let me try it."

I look at the number on the computer screen and pull out my cell phone and tap in the number, and it rings. Once, twice and on third ring a woman answers.

"Hello, this is Dr. Yosts office, Dr. Yost speaking."

"Yes, Dr. Yost...uh...my name is Sasha Cain. I was wondering if you might have time to talk with me about some dream issues I'm having?"

"Yes I do, and I'd love, too, can you tell me a little about what's going on?"

"I'm having trouble with a reoccurring dream, a nightmare actually, and it's bad. So is that something that you can help me with, because if not I don't want to waste your time."

"No, no, you won't be wasting my time, and I do think I can help you. How did you learn about me?"

"We found out your name from our friend Ty Baines."

"Oh, my gosh. You know Ty?"

"Yeah I do. He's sitting right across from me. Grinning."

"I haven't seen him...in...well years." I smile wondering if Ty's acquaintance with Dr. Yost was more than casual.

"So Sasha, would you like to come in at one this afternoon? I have time then to see you then. I'm in Roxboro and my office is over the pharmacy."

"Yes I can. That would be great. And could I bring my girlfriend with me? I think she should be there, because she's the one I wake up at night when I have the nightmare. And she has some issues that I think she needs to talk to you about."

"And what is that?"

"I'll let her tell you." When I say this she's shaking her head no.

"What's her name?"

"Tori Nicks."

"Tori, great. So I will see you two ladies at one."

"Yes you will."

We disconnect the call.

I put my phone back in my pocket, and said, "we're going to Roxy this afternoon."

"Why did you say that?"

"Because Tori I think she could help you, too."

"I thought we going to see her for your nightmares."

"We are, I just think we could kill to birds with one stone, that's all."

She looks at me shaking her head in near disgust, but not really and asks me, "So does she think she can help you?"

"Yes, at least that's what she told me. That's why I made an appointment."

******

That afternoon we park across from the pharmacy, we didn't have any trouble finding a parking spot.

Roxboro is an anomaly, really. It is a small town stuck in a time. It is how life used to be, and while that was often chaotic, too, it was way better than it is now. It's always refreshing to come here. The people, like the town, are almost normal. Roxy sets in a beautiful valley, surrounded by hills and farms that provide a bounty of fresh food for the town. The air is fresh and the sky is a rare deep azure blue today. Driving into town taking a deep breath you could smell the aroma of the countryside. The sky here can be hazy at times like at the estate, but neither is as bad as Rottendamn. I often wonder what it would have been like to live back then, a century and half ago, where life at least worked for the good of people. Until that one span of time when everything suddenly changed and all went to hell in a handbasket.

We get out of the car and lock it, and walk across the main street to a door north of the pharmacy entrance. Painted on the window in white letters, it says, Dr. Eleanor Yost, Therapist, and gives the phone number. We open it and go up the one flight of stairs to a small landing, and open her office door. We walk into a reception area, but there's no receptionist. So we sit down and wait. There is a desk and desk chair, a computer terminal, and of course the chairs for sitting.

We are a bit early—it's only fifty past the hour, and we know that Dr. Yost is busy with another client. Because a sign on the door to the back says that very thing. After about five minutes the door to the back office opens and first we see a woman come out, followed by a second woman that Tori and I figure is Dr. Yost.

After a few words and instructions, for the lady, she leaves and the doctor turns to greet us, "You must be Sasha, and Tori. Right?"

We shake our heads and say we are.

She offers her hand and we all shake and exchange greetings. "It's so nice to meet the two of you."

We said likewise.

"Follow me ladies." We do and she leads us into a room in the back part of the office. It has two recliner chairs, and a loveseat. The room has brown paneling, and gray carpeting. There is a standing lamp by one of the recliners and one on the end table next to the loveseat.

"Can I get you ladies anything? Coffee, water, soda?"

I'm still hearing that word lady, and more often.

We both said water would be fine, and she said for us to have a seat, while she retrieved our refreshment.

We sit down close to each other on the loveseat, and hold hands. She returns to the room with our refreshment. Dr. Yost, like Ty is in her late thirties or maybe even forty. She's an attractive lady, and is not overweight by any stretch. She has on some makeup but not a lot, a nice print dress, and no jewelry except ear rings. She has shoulder length, brown hair, and is wearing wedges. I would say she's a very pretty lady.

She hands us our water before sitting down in the recliner, then she picks up a clipboard, with paper on it and a pen, and seats herself.

"So, Sasha," she begins. "You were saying on the phone that you're having some trouble processing dreams."

"Yeah, a reoccurring nightmare."

"So before I go any further, I need to get some information on you."

She begins to write. "How old are you?"

"Twenty-four."

"And how long have the nightmares been occurring?"

"I look at Tori, "oh...since long before I met her."

"And how long ago did you two meet."

"Um...seven—eight months now," I say, looking at Tori.

"And where was that?"

I chuckle lightly, and she gives me an odd look, "Westerville."

"Oh my, that God awful prison."

"Yeah."

"Why were the two of you there?"

"We got sent there to be sold, but that didn't happen."

"Sold?" She questions, shockingly.

"Yeah, you see doc that place was not in any way a real prison for incarceration for being bad. But it was a prison used for human trafficking. Girls that had been kidnapped were being sold into slavery from that facility."

Still with shock in her voice she says, "oh my God, I had no idea."

"Neither did Tori and I until we talked to some of the girls that were already there, and they told us. Tori and I knew very little, because the so-called warden kept us locked up together in solitary confinement together."

"How did you both get put in solitary?"

We told her about how I defended Tori, after the so called warden did her best to humiliate her as a means to bait me. I told her about the fight and that is how we got put in there together. I told her that I was beaten more than once, which left her aghast.

She shakes her head in amazement, and asks, "How did you get out?"

We told her about Cabot and why he came to get us. We also told her that Westerville had been shut down. By us.

"How did you do that?" She asks us curiously.

"Well Dr. Yost to make a long story short, I used my persuaders that I usually wear to get the job done. And Tori took care of the warden."

After hearing that she just sat and looked at us, shaking her head in disbelief.

She says, "so Sasha, back to the nightmares you're having. Are they in any way in direct relation to the experiences that you had in Westerville?"

"No, not at all. I think they're happening because something is going on in my mind."

"Tell me all about the nightmares."

I begin, nervously, "I remember the nightmare all the time. It stays with me, and haunts me even during the day when I think about it. And even when I don't have it, it's on my mind it never seems to be far away. Especially the day after it occurs. Doc, I want you to know I've killed a lot of people, and I'm only twenty-four years old. I myself wonder what the dream is about or what it's trying to say to me. I can tell you one thing, it's scaring the holy be-jabbers out of me."

She looks at me and puts the clipboard and pen down. "You know I usually gather information from a client in our first session, but for now I'm going to forgo that part. I can see you need immediate help with this, so I want you to tell me everything that's happening in the dream."

"I...I'm in this alley," I stammer.

"It's okay, take your time."

I look at Tori who's been sitting quietly next to me, with tears in her eyes. Our fingers still entwined tightly, just like when we were in the jail cell.

"You two girls are a couple. Right?"

I shake my head yes, and say, "the truth is doc I wouldn't know what to do without her. She's my rock." I look at her, my eyes watering up. Tori is already crying softly and has big tears rolling down her cheeks. I didn't figure that this would get emotional at all. I'm just here to talk about a silly dream after all. But the opposite has happened, it has become feeling.

Dr. Yost smiles at us, and says, "you girls are so beautiful together. Go on Sasha. What happens in the dream?"

"I'm in this dark alley, and as I look ahead of me it's like the darkness has no end at all. Behind me are five shadowy figures of people, all men, all wearing what appears to be trench coats and fedora hats. And there's a bright light behind them, that blinds me when I look at it. It seems to create deeper shadows on the figures in the dream.

"When I realize they seem to be chasing me I want to run deeper into the alley to get away from them. But I stop. I don't want to run into the alley. Because I feel too scared to do it."

"Why do you feel to scared to run into the alley, Sasha?

"I'm scared of what lies beyond me in that darkness, that it has no end. It feels like whatever lurks in the alley is very, very,

THE ALLEY OF EVIL

bad. That it's the alley of evil"

"Do you know why the alley feels so nefarious to you?"

"No, I only know that if I run into it to try and get away from the shadowy figures, that whatever is in there will consume me, too. Whatever I feel is in that alley is worse than the figures chasing me."

"Does it feel like alley is a way to hell or something of that sort?"

"Yeah, that's it, it's hell," I say. "So I have no place to run. But I can't run away from the figures anyway. I can't move my legs, they're completely frozen in place. Every time I have this nightmare the figures get closer and closer to me, Dr. Yost. I'm afraid I'll die if they catch me, and if I try to go into the alley I know that whatever is in there will surely kill me.

"Last night the shadows were very close to me, and almost caught me. That's when I woke up screaming. I woke Tori and her brother Davy who lives with us. When I woke up I was sweating, then I shivered, and I was gasping for breath."

"So you can't run forward because of you fear of what's in the alley and the figures chasing you, scare you, too. So do you feel trapped?"

"Yeah I do."

She looks at Tori and asks, "what do you do when she has the nightmare and wakes up screaming like this?"

"I just try to comfort her. I hold her until she settles down. That's about all I can do doc. She thinks this is some kind of omen to her, that she's going to go to hell

She shakes her head. "Sasha, tell me what happened the

day before."

I paused and looked at the ceiling. I shake my head. "Doc before I go there, you must know what I'm called."

"I do. You're a bounty hunter, known as the enforcer. I did some research on you this morning, after you called, and told me who you were. I thought I'd heard your name somewhere, though I don't know exactly where. And that led me to do some background on you. Anyway go ahead."

I pause for a couple of seconds, and began. "I lived up to that name, the enforcer, this past weekend. I shot and killed three men known as road rats, who were blocking the road in front of us on our way to Rotterdam. Then later that day I killed four more men, in a gunfight, in bar there. We were looking for Ty's daughter and we found her, with my former client, who railroaded me and had me sent to Westerville. When he refused to turn her over to us, the gunfight happened, and I did a lot of killing. Doc I want you to know that I'm not a good girl."

"You believe that don't you?"

"Yes I do."

"But she just told me that you only kill when you're threatened. That True?" Were the road rats threatening you? And in the bar, did you start that gunfight?"

Then Tori interrupted and said, "Doctor, in both of those situations she did what she could. We were being threatened by the road rats, and they left her no choice, but to defend herself, Ty, and me.

"In that bar, a goon went for his gun to shoot Ty, and Sasha defended him and killed the man. So to answer your questions, yes we were threatened in both of those situations, and if it weren't for her I wouldn't be setting here right now."

"But you have killed for other reasons. Right Sasha?"

"Yeah I have, when I was working in Rotterdam, I was looking for people to collect money from, and they never wanted to pay. It forced my hand to have to take what my clients were owed. And that usually, always ended up badly, with me shooting someone. Doc I did it to stay alive."

"But again, was that in self defense, too?"

"Yeah, most of the time, because they drew down on me and my associate first."

"Leaving you little choice," she says.

I shake my head yes, but nonchalantly.

"Sasha I'm not condoning what you do, that you have killed people, but this nightmare seems to occur when you commit what you must see as a violent act.

"From what you're saying it seems like when you get violent, your subconscious tends to react with this particular nightmare. It seems to want to deal with the deaths that you committed on some level. Does that make sense?"

I shake my head yes.

"And Sasha, this too may be happening because you yourself may be experiencing some sort of moral remorse for what you do."

I look at her, "yeah, I know that I've started to not feel all that great when I do kill someone. But I almost killed four women in that bar Saturday, too."

"And you didn't kill them. Why?"

"She stopped me." I looked at Tori.

"Why did you stop her?"

"It seemed like the right thing to do, that's all," Tori says.

"But why don't you tell her what those bitches did to you?" I say looking at her.

There's a pause as Tori looks at me.

"What happened Tori?"

She's not wanting to open up about this.

"Go on tell her what they did to you Tori. If you don't I will. Talk to her Tori."

Tori paused and looked down, starting to cry again.

"When we were at Westerville, they, the warden and guards, for the most part left me alone. Because I'm her girlfriend. Then one day the guards came and got me out of the cell and took me to Behars office."

"Behar was the warden. Right?"

"Yeah, fake warden. She tried to turn me against Sasha. When I refused, Behar and two other women, named Wanda and Violet, gang raped me."

She looks at both of us, with compassion. And looks at Tori, shaking her head, "my God sweetheart! You were gang raped, by those women?"

Tori looks down shaking her head. She crying deeply as I pull her closer to me.

"You must have terrible post trauma after an experience like that."

"She still does, and she won't talk to me about it."

Tori looks at me then the doc, through her tears, "I got my

revenge with them."

"And what happened with that?"

We told her that during our trip to Westerville to shut it down, that Tori extracted her revenge on Behar, Wanda, and Violet, with a belt."

"Did that help?"

"Some, I guess. I'm better than I was, Sasha will tell you that." Her voice is so small—quivering, as she talks—I hug her tighter.

"You must still have many left over issues from that. Would you like for me to help you process all of that. I can help you, Tori. And I think you need it."

I'm looking at her and shaking my head yes.

"Yeah, I guess it'll be okay." She says, finally relenting to get help for what Behar did to her.

"She needs you doc," I say.

"Do you spend much time comforting her with this issue, Sasha?"

"I do, but about all I can do I hold her, which is what she wants me to do. We don't talk about it."

She shakes her head that she understands, then says, "Are these the same women she stopped you from killing, Sasha?"

"Yeah they are."

"So would you, would you be willing to let me help you Tori?"

Tori shakes her head yes.

"Good, because I want you, both to come back and see me.

"Makes my dream seem insignificant. Doesn't it?"

Dr. Yost shakes her head and says, "in some ways, but you two girls have been through pure hell. So we started with your nightmare, Sasha, lets deal with that first, since that's where we began with. Then we'll deal with these other issues, Okay?"

We agree.

"So back to your dream, Sasha. I think that what I said about the dream is what's happening. I think you, on some level, Sasha, you're growing weary of what you do. Causing you to question why you do what you do.

"But what seems to be happening in the dream is this. The alley represents hell to you. You're afraid of it, but you're frozen in place. And while I'm not one hundred percent sure what the figures represent. They may just be symbols of some sort that your mind has created, and they themselves are running into the alley—into hell so to speak. And you mention that your legs are heavy frozen in place, that you can't get away. What that may mean is, you stuck there trying to make the decision of running back toward the light or continuing down the path you've chosen and into that dark alley. It seems to me like you're at at a crossroads with your life Sasha."

"That's what I think, too, doc. But Ty told me to be careful about thinking like that. He says that I'm going against my basic instincts. That, that kind of thinking could get me killed. What if the figures in the dream catch me and I don't want to run into that alley? That scares me, I'm afraid I will die and not wake up."

"I don't think you have anything to fear in that happening. And if they do catch you you'll just wake up. I'm also thinking that if you go ahead and let that happen, let them catch you, they may just run right past you and into the alley and into what you describe as hell. That may be the last of the nightmare. You may not have it anymore after that. And Tori you're right in what your doing to help her. About all you can do is comfort her, until the dream wears off."

"I do that. I just worry about her. I love her Dr. Yost."

"You worry about me, Tori?" I hate it when I can't comfort you when you're dealing with Behar's abuse."

"I know that," she says. Looking at me with compassion in her eyes.

"Doc, I don't deserve her, she's so much better than me," I say. Looking at Tori.

"I think you sell yourself short Sasha, you are not just a bad girl—a killer. You are capable of loving someone—Tori. And I want you to listen to what I'm saying here. The fact that you have the nightmares and feelings about what you do are all natural. You are human after all with feelings. And maybe, it could be because you love and care about someone so much like you do, Tori. Did you feel this way before you met her?"

"No, no, I didn't, I just did what I do, and collected my money. And if I killed someone it went with the job. I wasn't thankful or did I care about anything but staying alive."

"So there's part of you answer. You care about someone now—Tori."

She looked at the clock and said, "I can see we're about out of time. But I want you both to comeback. I want us to spend the next sessions on you, Tori, and what this horrible woman Behar did too you. It's going to take time. Understand?"

Tori shook her head in agreement.

"I also want to get complete information on both of you next time."

The session came to an end and Tori and I paid Dr. Yost and left. On the way home with Tori driving we started to talk about the session.

"So did she help?"

"Yeah I think so. She at least gave us her diagnosis as to why I'm having the nightmare. As to its ending, I guess we'll just have to wait and see. But you need to let her help you with the rape, Tori."

"I know, and I will." She says not taking her eyes off the road.

"Good I'm glad to hear you say that. I want that for you," I said. "You know I think what is happening with me is that I have someone to care for now, you. And if I get killed you'll be alone. That I think is what scares me most."

THE ALLEY OF EVIL

TWENTY TWO

While we were in Roxboro, I made it a point to see if the little jewelry store is still open and doing business. They are. I have to make a trip back here tomorrow by myself. I have a surprise for Tori and I want to get it done before we have to go someplace else to find WASP.

Tori drives the Mustang through the front gate and onto the estate grounds. All is quiet, as I look around. Not a soul in sight as we pull up to our house, and stop. We get out of the car and look down toward the lake, and we can see Davy and Janet laying on the small beach together. Indicating that they have discovered each other. We see Maria and Shelly down there too —all of them having fun, engaged in a game of volleyball.

We enter the house and leave the car keys on the coffee table in the living room.

Tori says, "let's head up to the main house to see if we have any hits on the computer about WASP. I doubt we do yet, but it's worth a look."

In the main house we walk though it to go to the study and as we walk by the great room we see Ty sitting on the sofa and talking to someone. He sees us and says, "hey girls, you're back."

"Yeah we are." We can see that Ty is talking to Claus as we

walk into the room. We greet him and sit down in two big comfortable chairs over by the windows, with the magnificent view of the mountains.

I say to Claus, "nice to see you. What brings you back?"

"It's nice to see you girls, too, I..."

Ty cuts in and says, "Claus was wondering if it would be possible for him to come back here and stay for a while."

I say, "sure. No problem with that. So what happened to Cabot?"

He pauses before he tells us, shaking his head. "Well after we left here, we headed south and west to St. Louis.

"St. Louis?" Tori asks, with astonishment.

"Yes, Cabot had some business dealings there and we decided to go there. We've been there for all this time. He was still leery and was always watching for the Russian mob to show up, but they hadn't done so. Cabot had begun to feel that it was safe there, and was getting ready to buy a house, when that all quickly changed last week. He sent me on an errand to get some pain medication for his back. While I was gone, apparently the Russian mob or someone else showed up and put an end to Raymond Cabot.

"When I returned, he was on the floor face down, hands tied behind his back. He'd been executed, one shot to the back of his head at close range, it blew his face off," he says. Pausing a few seconds before he continues. "It...was...uh...pretty gruesome. I figured it was most likely his Russian friends who killed him.

"I was scared, and I wasn't sure if they knew me or who I was, and if they were looking for me, too. So I gathered what belongings I could take and got on a bus and came back here, as quickly as I could. Hoping all along that you were all still here, and could put me up for a while."

"Yeah, you know your welcome," I said. Has Ty brought you up to speed on what's been going on around here?"

"Yes, he has."

Tori says, "you know even though he was criminal, Cabot treated me right while we worked together. I think he did the same with Sasha."

"Yes, you're right, Tori, he liked both of you girls. He stated that several times after we left here."

"So how was your session with Dr. Yost?" Ty asks, changing the subject.

"It was good. I told her about the dream and she gave me a diagnosis and told me how to deal with the dream the next time I have it."

"What did she say?"

"To make what she said a short story, she said that it's my subconscious mind reacting to my violent behavior. That those, shadowy figures are symbols for something that it's dealing with, though she doesn't know exactly what. She also thinks that the fact that I have Tori in my life now, and that I care for her is causing me to question my actions, and making the nightmare surface."

"Did she give you any advice on how to handle the dream next time it happens?"

"She said to just let it happen. She said I'm not going to die from it, but to just see what happens. I have another appointment with her in two weeks, she wants to try some hypnosis on me. She thinks that will help give her some answers to the dream.

"But more importantly I finally got her to open up to the doctor about Behar's abuse of her. So she's going to get help with that."

******

The next morning after breakfast with Tori and Davy, of eggs, bacon and toast. I tell Tori that I won't be around that morning that I have to go back and do something in Roxboro.

"What's that?"

"I have to purchase some more ammo at the gun shop there and have the gunsmith check my pistols. I forgot to do it yesterday when we were there. And I really had that session with doc on my mind, so that's where I'll be this morning."

"Okay," she says. Knowing that my guns are the tools of my trade. "I'm going to see how many of the captive girls I can find on the computer, so I will be busy. Plus, today is Tuesday and maybe we will get some hits on WASP."

"That would be cool," I say. I take the car keys and give her a hug and kiss and head out the front door."

She follows me out the door and stands by the car, "be careful."

"For sure." I say backing the car out of the driveway.

One thing about Tori is she trusts me again even after my little fling with Ty. She's trusted me since we met at that horrible

THE ALLEY OF EVIL

place, Westerville. She seems to have gotten over my stupidity, and our relationship is back on track even though I told her about kissing Ty—I regret kissing him of course.

An hour later I park in front of the jewelry store, I'm here to buy an engagement ring for Tori so I can ask her to marry me. Before I left this morning I told her that I would be cooking dinner for the two of us this evening. She asked me what the occasion was, and I told her it was a surprise. And that I wanted her to wear her pink sundress that I love seeing her in so much.

I've been planning to do this for a longtime, and of course I couldn't do it yesterday because she was with me. And the truth is until today I haven't had the time, and it's not because I haven't wanted to. It was always getting pushed back somewhere, because we closed Westerville or had to go to Rotterdam to find Janet and Davy. So today is the day I buy Tori a ring.

Before I go into the store I take off my guns and secure them in the trunk of the car. I don't want to scare the people who work inside, by coming into a jewelry store armed with two semi-automatic pistols. That would be a bad idea.

I open the door to the store and walk in. I immediately get caught up in the place. It is so quaint—an old time jewelry store where time seems to have stood still, like the rest of Roxboro. It's a place that when you walk into it, you swear you're suddenly thrust back to circa 1960's America.

Inside the floor is covered by a white tile, scrubbed clean. The walls are of drywall, painted white, and there's wood stained shelving all around. It's adorned with expensive dinner wear and clocks. Everywhere there are clocks. Real time pieces that actually make a tic-toc sound. There are so many that their sound gives the little store it's very own music. There's a counter that runs along the longer wall and a shorter one in the back. The counters are wood and are encased in glass that are chocked full of every type of jewelry one could imagine. Watches, rings, bracelets, necklaces, everything one would want to wear.

While I love jewelry, I have never given much thought to actually wearing it. Though it may give something of a new aura to me.

There are two people in the store, a woman and a man who look to be in their sixties. The man is in the back and has the strap with a light on it around his head with two desk lamps burning brightly. He's a real jeweler. He's balding and has on overalls, which makes me smile. They strike me as a motherly and fatherly type.

I'm the only one in the store and I walk slowly along the display cases looking down into them. The lady behind the counter looks at me and asks, "can I help you find something Miss?" She has on a print dress and wears glasses, her hair just covers her ears and is gray, with a perm.

"Yes, yes you can," I replied. "I want to buy an engagement ring."

"Do you know his ring size?"

"Oh," I say. "No, it's not for a man, it's for my girlfriend. And I'm guessing that her hands are about the same size as mine, so we'll go with that."

She doesn't say anything and reaches down behind the

counter and pulls out a bunch of rings for sizing and says, "let me see your left hand."

She put one of the sizing rings on my hand and it was a bit big, so she tried another and it was perfect. She notes the size then asks me if I had anything in mind, and at the same time tells me to come to the end of the counter. There I looked down to see all kinds of rings.

"No I don't. You're gonna have to help me out here, because I know absolutely nothing about jewelry, let along engagement rings."

Then she asks, "how much do you want to spend? They can be quite expensive, you know."

"Cost is not the problem, I just want to get her exactly the right one."

I look into the counter and see one that I like.

She opens the counter and reaches in and takes it out, and says, "this one is fifty-five hundred and it's the same size as your finger. It'll fit, that is if her ring finger is the same as yours." She hands the ring to me.

"I'm almost sure it is." I say, referring to Tori's ring size. I take the ring and look at it, she's telling all about it and I think how pretty it will look on Tori's hand. After a few seconds I look back into the display case studying the other rings I see. I decide that the one I have in my hand, is what I will buy for her.

"I'll take it."

I go to the register, pull out the cash, and pay the woman. She says if it doesn't fit to bring it in and they will resize it. Then she asks me the name of the lucky other girl.

"Her name is Tori, Tori Nicks."

"What's your name."

"Sasha Cain."

She gives me an odd smile and a nod as I leave the store. Happy with my purchase.

After I left the jewelry store I had one more shopping stop to make before I left for home. It's a purchase that I know will shock Tori and blow her mind at the same time.

THE ALLEY OF EVIL

TWENTY THREE

It's evening time and Tori comes out of the bedroom wearing her pink sundress. She has showered and washed her hair. I did that first because I wanted to get dinner started. I left specific instructions to all the others staying here that I didn't want us to be disturbed this evening, that I was planning something special for Tori.

She stops as she walks into the room—suddenly shocked just like I knew she would. She covers her mouth with her hand as she enters the dinning room where I'm setting the table. When she last saw me after I showed I was wearing boxer shorts and a t-shirt.

"You, you look…beautiful, Sasha. I am…like, totally shocked. You have a dress on."

"Yeah, you like it," I said. My face flushing. "I bought it and the shoes today in Roxboro at the dress shop."

"So you did something other than have your guns checked."

"Yeah I did."

"No wonder Ty wants to have you. You're hot, Sasha. You better not let him see you dressed like that."

"He won't. But Tori I've never thought of myself as beautiful. I don't have nice curves like you do."

"You know why you don't think you're beautiful? It's because no one has ever told you that, that's why it's so hard for you to believe it about yourself."

"You think?"

"Yes I do."

The dress I bought was like Tori's pink sundress only it's teal colored, with a scarf that I've tied around my waist as a sash. I also purchased a pair of beige wedges that make me even taller.

She walks over to me and hugs me and we kiss, something I've never stopped wanting to do. Kiss Tori.

Finished eating, it's dark now, being late August. Looking at her from across the table the chandelier above us is turned down low to soften the light, causing the soft contours of her face to stand out even more. Which takes me back to what she said earlier about me being beautiful. Maybe that's true and I should start to believe that about myself. My face is not like hers though, with her wide set eyes and little turned up nose. My face, while girl soft has more angular features and my nose is not turned up. Still Tori thinks I'm beautiful and that's all that matters to me.

I say to her, "I'll be right back."

She looks at me curiously, as I get up from the table, and she watches me walk down the hallway. I go into the bedroom and retrieve the ring from a chest drawer that I use, and come back out. I pull up one of the side chairs and sit down next to her.

She cocks her head at me and says, "You know you should wear a dress more often. You are a girl, Sasha."

THE ALLEY OF EVIL

"I know that and I'll think about it." I said, grinning at her.

She notices that I have something in my right hand.

"You know today when I went into Roxboro, it wasn't to have my guns checked or to buy ammo. So I fibbed."

"You fibbed to me? Ah, ah, ah!"

"Yeah and did, I didn't just buy this dress and these shoes either. I bought this." I opened the little box in my hand revealing the ring to her. She looks at me shaking her head, putting her hand over her mouth.

I took the ring out of the box and took her left hand holding the ring, "Tori Nicks," I say, "will you marry me?"

I look at her and she gets up out of her chair and reaches for me and kisses me, then holds my face in her hands and she says, "yes, Sasha Cain, yes I will marry you. It will be my honor to do so, and to be your wife. I love you, Sasha."

"I love you, too, Tori," I put the ring on her finger. As my face broke out into a broad smile, that must have bordered on goofy, and my eyes began to water at the same time. But I don't care, I've never been so happy. We embrace and kiss again, and kiss again several times.

I look at her holding her right hand, she's smiling, she's happy. I say, "you know all those months ago when we were just trying to survive in Westerville. I knew even then, even in those horrible conditions that we were living in, that I loved you. I didn't want to loose you in spite of the confusion that I was having over loving another girl. I just...loved you and only you, Tori." My eyes are tearing up and tears begin to sneak down my cheeks." Something I'm not used too. Maybe the doc is right, the enforcer is human after all.

Tori's crying, too, but its a cry of happiness. She says, "Sasha, you are so much more than what people think. I have grown to know how loving and caring you are. That's the true Sasha, and I want you to know that while we were in that horrible place, I didn't ever want you to let me go. I wanted to keep you, too. I wanted nothing more than to be with you. Remember I told you that day I had wanted you to kiss me since I saw you and that's just as true now."

Then we just hug, kissing now and then, holding not wanting to ever let go. Not talking. After a few minutes we began to gather our emotions. She's looking at her hand with the ring on it and I ask, "does it fit? It went on okay."

"Oh it's perfect. How did you know my ring size?"

"You know I didn't, so I used my own ring finger. I know from holding your hand all these months that our hands are about the same size. So that's what I went by, and I got lucky. Your ring finger and mine are the same size."

We didn't clean the kitchen, I made arrangements for the maids to come down and do it for us. So we spent a nice quiet evening together curled up on the big sofa in the family room in front of the fireplace.

After a while it was off to bed, and I slept very well, no nightmares. I am happier than I've ever been, which made me sleep like a baby. After of course, Tori and I loved and loved each other until well past midnight. Causing me to think that Doc Yost is right, that loving Tori has made me have feelings. Something I have never let show until I met her.

THE ALLEY OF EVIL

TWENTY FOUR

The next day was quite uneventful, as a matter of fact most days at the estate are that way now. I see some things that are changing. I see Penn spending a lot of time with Patti, as a matter of fact I think the two of them are becoming a couple.

There's not much to do, and we really don't worry about the Russians coming back, and the anxiety that was prevalent just after those five came here, has disappeared. So for the most part today, like we will everyday we wait for customers of the auction to become unhappy and agitated with WASP.

Like I said the day was uneventful, we knocked off at four in the afternoon, and went home.

As dinnertime approached, I'm hungry and in the refrigerator looking for something to make, when Tori comes in and asks me, what I'm doing.

"I was getting ready to fix dinner and wondered what you wanted?"

"Well before we decide to do that would you walk with me back up to the house. I left my phone in the office."

"Sure."

On the way as we walked across the big lawn, I said, "this is sure a far cry from just a couple of months ago when we were locked up in that damn prison, with no hope."

"Yeah it is. Are you happy, Sasha?"

"You bet. You?"

"Yes, I am, it's like we were never in that place, and things have changed so much around here. Everybody is so relaxed now."

"You noticed that, too, huh." I said as we reached the front door and I opened it."

"I have," she says.

We walked into the study and she picked up her phone off the desk and then said, "let's go out back before we head home.

I wondered what for, it was dark. We walked through the dining room and she unlocked and opened the big sliding glass doors that lead out onto the patio. I followed her.

Then the lights inside the house and all around the backyard suddenly came on, startling me. I turned and saw everyone who lives here, and they all shouted in unison. "Surprise!" Then they all begin singing happy birthday, to me. Tori is standing directly in front of me and singing with a big smile on her face. I am completely shocked, and surprised by this, and my face has now broken into a big silly smile.

The singing stopped, and Tori said, "happy twenty fifth birthday, babe." And she then gave me a big hug and kiss.

She and I released and I looked at everyone and said, "thank you. I don't know what to say…I…I've never had anyone do this for me."

"It's about time someone did something nice for you for a

change," Ty said. Hugging me and kissing me on the cheek. And as he did this time I felt nothing.

Then everyone got in on the act of giving me a hug, I looked around and said, "You're all too much, so let's get at it and have a good time."

We did, but I had to have a little help from Tori to get all twenty five candles blown out. Then Ty said, "Tori I noticed that ring on your left hand today. Care to let us in on that."

I looked at her smiling face, something she does a lot of now. She says, "yeah, I guess this is as good a time as any to announce our engagement. Last night I was asked by my beautiful Sasha to marry her, and I of course said, yes. So in the near future there will be a wedding here at the estate, and of course you're all invited."

They all applauded and came forward congratulating us, and this time we both got hugs and kisses. The four girls who live here wanted of course to see the ring, and Tori being Tori, she let them see it. As I watched her she saw me looking at her, and she smiled at me. It's something that I don't want to ever end. She and me.

******

The next day it's about noontime, I'm standing on the front portico with Penn, Cash, and Ty discussing the arrangements on the estate. Our conversation involved how much security we now needed to do, since things have calmed down and are normal.

"Sasha, Ty, come in here, quick." I turn around and see Tori standing in the doorway, of the house. She's motioning for me and Ty to come inside. Seconds later all three of us are in the study in front of her computer.

She looks at me and says, "bingo! We got a hit. Actually we got several. I've been tracking the footprints of where the return signals are coming from when WASP responds to their disgruntled customers. I believe they're here." She says, and points to a map of Nevada.

"Nevada," I exclaim! "Why the hell there?"

"Don't know, but yeah, apparently that's where they are, right in this area in the middle of the desert."

"You sure," Ty asks? "Because it looks like they're near that military base that used to be called Area 51."

"Sure as my love is for her," she responds. Looking at me. "And it still is a military base called by that name. Not everything in the country changed all those years ago."

"So how do we get to Nevada? That's what, a four/five day drive from here? That old superhighway system that was built a hundred and fifty years ago is crumpled and in bad shape in places. So what would have been a three day drive is now, four/five at least. And we'll have to drive across New Plains, and I ain't too keen on us doing that."

Then Ty says, "you know we may not have to worry about driving all that way and crossing New Plains. There just might be another way."

We look at him with raised eyebrows waiting for his suggestion.

"A guy I used to know flew a Learjet out of the Syracuse airport. If he's still there and still in business, maybe I can get in touch with him, and we won't have to drive."

"Do you have a phone number on him," Tori asks?

"No, unfortunately I don't anymore. Maybe you could look him up on that thing."

"I can try. That kind of information is hard to find nowadays, it's not like a hundred years ago when this internet was the major way of finding stuff."

"You've been finding stuff out about these girls," I said.

"Yes that's true and it was made somewhat simpler because of WASP. They actually built a network and I latched onto their coattails and followed that trail." She looks at Ty and says, "what's the pilot's name?"

"C. J. Dorn. The name of his company was Dorn Transport. Try that too."

"Give me a few. Businesses can be a challenge, but not like people."

"After a couple of minutes looking at this, and that, she found a listing for Dorn Transport, and told us that it was at least five years old.

"Is there a number," Ty asks?

"Yeah," she says. Then she takes a pen and writes the number on a piece of paper and hands it to him.

He reaches into his back pocket and pulls out his cell phone, and taps in the number. He waits for several seconds for someone to answer. Phones like everything else in New America are a challenge nowadays.

"C. J.," a pause. "Hey buddy this is Ty Baines, remember me?"

"Great, yeah buddy, it has been a longtime. I've got a question for you, are you still flying people all over the place?"

A brief pause.

"That's great, too, because I was wondering if you could fly me and a couple of ladies that are friends of mine, to Nevada anytime soon? That is if you're not booked solid."

After another pause, Ty again asks him if he could do it as soon as possible.

"Where? Let me ask."

He leans over and asks Tori and she already has his answer.

"Reno, C. J. Would Saturday be good for you?" A pause again. "Great that works for us, too, we need to get out there as soon as we can. You're still in Syracuse I presume."

A pause again as C. J. answers him."

We'll be driving there to Syracuse to your airport, yes."

C. J. says something again.

"Fifteen hundred a piece will be fine. C. J. is that to go out there because if it is we'll just pay you nine grand for the round trip. And leaving at six thirty on Saturday morning will work great for us," he says. Looking at us and shaking his head, as we nod back.

Another pause.

Ty says, "Great, see you then." He disconnects the call.

"So he'll fly us out," I ask?

"Yep and we don't have to drive. That could have been an eventful dangerous trip this day in age, even with you along,

Sasha. I'm glad this worked out."

Now I have to explain that while I know that even now flying in an airplane is still a safe way to travel. It's not like it was all those years ago. The airline industry is a shambles like everything is in New America, and I've never been on an airplane before. I'm a girl who's been planted on mother earth and no matter where that is, I like it down here. So I ain't too hot on flying.

But in order to get to Nevada and bring down WASP, getting on an airplane and flying there will be easier and will only take a few hours. It is also better than facing the prospect of driving across the State of New Plains in the middle of the country, that was formed from seven US states after the collapse. It is not a state at all in any sense of the word, it' a giant cult. It is like a hostile foreign country to the rest of New America.

NANCY HOWARD

TWENTY FIVE

That all happened on Thursday, and Saturday morning came quickly. Tori and I packed a few essential things, and for me that meant lots of magazines of ammo that I put in a bag. Ty and I decide to also take along two semi automatic rifles and a lot of ammo for them, too. Penn and Cash showed them to me some time ago, they were located at the far end of the basement where all the money is.

It's mid morning as we pull into the old airport at Syracuse, which is all but deserted now. Very few jets fly in and out of here anymore. I see one at a gate, loading passengers. At one time all the gates would have had planes parked at them or they would be waiting on the arrival of another flight. But not anymore. Flying on a jetliner is way out of the reach financially for everyone these days, as the planes get older and older.

The buildings that used to house a bustling terminal are old and in bad need of repairs, that will never happen. Because we live in a time where our government is now one that only takes care of itself. The plutocrats, who've ruled for over thirty years, long ago abandoned the ideals that once made this country a great republic. It is now a private federation, ruled by those who have all the money and use it to buy their way into office and power.

We park alongside a hanger at the far end of the airfield, and get out. We see a Learjet parked inside the huge building that also houses several other small aircraft.

We get our belongings out and Ty tells us to wait, as he goes in search of C. J. He walks to the back of the hanger and goes into an office, after a couple of minutes we see him emerge with another man, walking toward us, who we assume is C. J.

He's about the same height and build as Ty is, and is about the same age, it appears. He's wearing green camouflage pants and military style boots, and a baseball cap. He has on a white t-shirt and like Ty it reveals his well muscled masculine chest and arms. At a glance he impresses me as an individualist, someone who does his own thing. For some reason as he approaches us the word swashbuckler comes to mind in describing him.

Ty introduces the two of us to him, and he responds by taking off his hat and shaking our hands, "ladies."

"So C. J. how long will it take for you to get us out to Reno," Ty asks?

"Well from here that's a two thousand mile flight, and I have to stop and pick up some cargo in K.C. So not counting that, our time in the air will be about, oh, I say five/six hours in the air give or take."

Great, I get to spend most of the day on that contraption.

Tori is standing next to me, her arms folded in front of her and her right leg straight out, and she asks him, "Which plane is yours?"

"This one." He says walking over to the Learjet in the front.

"I built her myself about seven years ago. I put new engines on her and completely rebuilt her, including the entire cabin and controls. She's like a new airplane, given the fact that she was originally built in 2035. She has a range of twenty seven hundred and fifty miles."

"Did I hear you say 2035? Isn't that kind of old?" I say trying to hide my anxiety about getting on an airplane and flying anywhere—especially one this old.

"Yeah, but not to worry, she's perfectly safe."

That's what you say.

Tori asks, "is she fast?"

"She is. She has a high speed cruise of four hundred sixty-five knots, that's about seven hundred mph. But we'll only be going about three hundred fifty knots—five hundred thirty mph."

I look at Tori and Ty, they're both grinning at me about my apprehension of flying.

"Yeah, as Ty here'll tell you, and I'm sure you both know this, too. We just don't build this stuff anymore. Most of the big airplane companies went broke in the late nineties, when everything collapsed, and now we're left to fly stuff that is, well, just old.'"

"So C. J. when can we get going," Ty says.

"Soon as I get my gear. I already laid out a flight plan, though that's just a formality any more. She's full of fuel and the hatch is open so you all can go ahead and get on board. I'll be right back."

"Oh," I said, and called him back and reached into my

satchel and took out the nine grand for the trip, and gave it to him.

He took it and thanked me and walked away.

Ten minutes later we were in the cabin and strapped into our seats, when C. J. returned.

Before he did, Tori said to me, "are you okay with this? Flying I mean."

"No."

"Just try to relax, Sasha, and enjoy the flight," Ty said.

"You have flown before," I said to him.

"Yes I have, several times, in fact. Most recently to London, as you both know. I was a journalist for a major news outlet in New London and I had to fly to Washington, and the west coast several times."

"Wasn't that kind of dangerous this day in age."

"Yes, but I never really gave that a thought until Lea was murdered and Janet got kidnapped." Then he looked at Tori and said, "you seem okay with flying, Tori."

"Are you kidding." she said. With excitement in her voice. "I've never flown before and when you contacted C. J. the other day and I knew we were going to do this, I couldn't wait." She said.

He smiles at her comment.

I look at her, then him, and say, "I don't want this to get out."

"What's that," Tori says.

"That Sasha Cain has a fear of flying."

"No one will ever know, Sasha, I would never do that to

you," she says. He agrees.

Soon C. J. was in the cockpit, and had invited Ty to set up there with him, to play co-pilot. He started the engines, bringing them to life with a loud whirring sound. After letting them warm up for a few minutes, we left the hanger and began to taxi out onto the tarmac to go down the runway, and take-off. And that we did. Before I could think, the little jet picked up speed at an incredible clip, and all I could do is close my eyes as we lifted off. I could hear the engines stain with power, as C. J. pushed them and pointed the planes nose up, gaining altitude and speed for several minutes before leveling off. All the time this was going on my eyes were closed, and I was thinking—God don't let those engines quit.

I feel an arm wrap around me. It's Tori and she just smiles, and says, "we're going to be fine."

"I just see us crashing into a ball of flames, that's all."

She smiles at me, but I will admit her curling up next to me had a calming effect.

"Remember when I told you I'd never drank much, or gotten drunk often?"

"I remember."

"Well now is one of those times, I wish I was drunk."

She laughs and so do I, causing me to let go of some more of my anxiety about flying on this very old airplane.

We stopped in Kansas City to pick up the cargo, and were there for an hour before we took off again. This time I wasn't quite as jittery as when we took off earlier. I kept my eyes open and actually began to enjoy it. I'm not sure why, though I knew that I was going to land again, and would have to fly home. Maybe that had something to do with it, I don't know.

******

Landing in Reno was like being on another planet. When we landed and exited the plane, it was hot, and not New York hot but desert hot. C. J. said the temperature is one hundred and five and it was only noon. The first thing I noticed as I stood next to the plane with Tori was that the sky out here is still actually blue. Even bluer than at the estate in the Catskills, and if that wasn't enough, the air is still breathable. Even though it's hotter than blazes, the air was cleaner and much fresher. All I could do is take deep breaths and so did Tori, causing us to both giggle.

Ty was at the front of the plane with C. J., telling him that we would be in the desert and would call him when we we got back to Reno, for the return trip home.

We found a place nearby that still rents cars and trucks, we got hold of a later model SUV, by later I mean it was built probably twenty five years ago. And back then it was the latest and greatest car on the road, with all kinds of gadgets and toys in it. Things meant to occupy everybody but the driver. It was internet capable, with an onboard computer, and self driving mechanism that made the car able to drive itself. As Tori has explained to us those things like that don't work so good any more. So today, Tyler is our driving mechanism.

NANCY HOWARD

TWENTY SIX

The drive to our destination took about an hour or so. We knew when we got there that it was near the old, but still operational top secret military installation, known as Area 51. It's been here for decades, and for all these years under scrutiny as a place where there has been alien contact. Or that we have been reverse engineering captured alien technology. A hundred years ago Area 51 was always in the news cycle, but not in 2124, no one cares.

Our journey doesn't actually take us there, because Tori's computer has had a strong signal from the desert nearby. After a while she tells Ty to stop the car.

"We're here," she says.

I look out and see nothing but open desert with distant mountains and an old chain link fence that is down in most places. There are a couple of old wooden shacks painted white with graffiti spray painted on the walls about a hundred yards away. The doors to both places are closed, and they look like they've been abandoned for years. But there is no sign of anything that would indicate that this WASP organization is anywhere near.

"You sure," I ask?

"Well as sure as I can be. This signal is really...really...strong."

"Let's get out and walk around," Ty suggests.

We do, and follow Tori as she walks around slowly looking at her computer, trying to solve the mystery as to why the signal is about to blow her laptop to bits.

"It's got to be nearby," she says. "And whatever it is, it's making my computer go wild."

"WASP?"

"I...don't know...or something. Damn," she exclaims! "I've never...Wow!"

"What happened," Ty asks? We walk over to her.

"Guys listen to me. Whatever it is that's out here, it just now blew up the hard drive on my laptop. We need to be real careful."

"What? Who?" I said.

"You know what could have done it," he questions?

She shakes her head, and says, "I have no idea. Whatever it is that's out here is so powerful it just killed my computer."

"So if it's WASP, where are they," I ask. "I mean look around, we're out in the middle of nowhere."

"Tori do you think us being so close to Area 51 could have had something to do with frying your hard drive," He asks?

"No, I don't think it was them, this is close to us. Real close. I think whatever is emitting a signal this strong, is right underneath us."

I look at her, curious, "beneath the desert floor?"

"Yeah, that's what I believe. And I know you think that

sounds crazy, but I'm sure that's where it is."

"I believe you," I said. I've learned to never question Tori's assessment of technology. I turned my attention to the two shacks, "I wonder what's in those shacks?"

"I don't know, but it looks like they were part of the oil and gas industry a longtime ago and got abandoned," Ty said. "So you want to go exploring?"

"I do. You?"

He shakes his head, yes and then asks Tori, "you okay with doing that Tori?"

She says, "yeah, let's just be careful guys, something crazy is going on out here. I don't have a good feeling about it at all, so let's just be real careful,"

I say, "we will." Doing my best to reassure her, though I will admit I've never seen Tori exhibit this much apprehension about anything since we left Westerville.

We walk over to the old cabins, there are two of them, one is larger than the other, and we decide to try to get into it first. Just as we reached the door we heard a helicopter approaching, and looked up to see if we could spot it. It was coming over the mountain tops to the west of us.

"Military," Ty says.

"But this is not part of 51 is it?"

"No, but we are really close and they're probably doing recon and checking us out." he says.

"What do you know about 51," I ask him?

"No more than the two of you do. I've just always heard the stories, you know. That over the years a lot of funny stuff was happening out here."

The choppers approached quickly and flew over our heads going directly east. We watched them as they flew out of site.

"Want to wait for a few before we go in here," I ask?

"No, let's go on in," Ty says. "No telling what they were looking for, and I'm sure everybody at that base knows we're here."

I nod to him and pull my gun out of my holster. Ty pulls his out, too. I open the door and go into the old building first, not knowing what to expect. Then Tori, then Ty. We couldn't see in the windows because the tint on them was so dark, obviously to shade the inside from the blazing sun. But what were these sheds used for? What was their purpose way out here in the middle of nowhere?

Inside the shack has some light from the sun that's getting through the windows dark tint. Looking around, the place is a total wreck, and it's hotter than Hades inside. Causing us all to sweat even more than when we were outside.

The place hasn't been used for years. The furniture is dried out, broken and falling apart, and the paint is peeling off the walls. The three chairs in the place are broken and the desk has been smashed in half. There is only the one door that we came through.

Ty is behind what's left of the desk looking down. He has located a trap door near the back of the shed—over in the corner.

"I wonder where this leads, too," he says.

He bends down and opens it up, and looks down. We go

stand next to him. We can see some sort of ladder that allows one to climb down and into a dark pit.

"Do you guys really want to go down there?" Tori asks with apprehension in her voice.

"Well we came here to find WASP and put them out of business, and if that's where they are, then yeah. And if you don't want to go down there with us, you can stay up here, we understand. I'll give you my other gun and an extra magazine to protect yourself with." I say to her putting my hand softly on her shoulder.

She shakes her head and says, "No, I'll go with you guys. I don't want to get separated from you. Besides I'd go nuts with worry about you if I stayed up here by myself."

We look at her and shake our heads, and begin our descent down the ladder. Ty went down first, then Tori, and then me. He gives us both a hand as we reach what appears to be the bottom.

We looked around and could see we were inside some sort of structure, but weren't sure what it was. It's creepy and dark, but at the same time light. We could see clearly where we were going. But it was what we were walking on that bugged us. We couldn't see any type of floor at all beneath us—like there wasn't any. Like whatever was below just dropped off into the depths of the earth, but felt solid to walk on.

I take hold of Tori's hand. She's shaking a little, and so am I. Ty is right behind us, his gun pointing around in case of danger. I am doing the same with my gun hand. Pointing everywhere, trying to prepare myself for any surprise that might be waiting on us to do us harm.

THE ALLEY OF EVIL

We walk about ten minutes and soon all around us we see these pods with light on them. And of lines of light that appear to stream up and out of sight, that encircle each one of them. We notice that from time to time one of the pods goes up rapidly and never leaves that shaft. Like an elevator. The whole place is like that, and now I wonder where is WASP? Who are they and why did they build a place like this to run their human trafficking operation from?

"Sasha," Ty says.

"Yeah."

"Do you have a feeling that we're being watched?"

"Yeah I do, I've had it since we got down here."

"Somebodies watching us," he says.

"But how?" Tori says. "There are no cameras anywhere. You know guys I think we should turn around and go back. I said, I don't have a good feeling about any of this."

I stop and turn to look at Ty, and we all turn around to look back for the ladder we came down on and it's nowhere in sight.

"Where did it go." I ask? They didn't answer, shrugging in bewilderment.

We walk on for a few more minutes and see more pods, and more shafts of light. Then suddenly three of them appear right in front of us out of nowhere, and some sort of force begins pushing us onto them. It was strong. At first we tried to resist it, but the more we resisted the stronger it became. Soon, this force or whatever it was won out and we were all standing on the pods. In the same instant they zoomed us up and into the darkness of this place.

I wonder what is going on? If Tori's computer signal for WASP is here, where are they and what are they doing in a place like this? Where the technology seems to be suspicious and at the same time very advanced. Is this some new and advanced technology that the government is working on? And the shacks with the trap door. Why was it placed inside of them, where it was?

The pods stop, and the force pushes us off. Then they descend down, leaving us standing on what seemed to be thin air. I look at the other two. Tori and I are hanging onto each other for dear life. Then we look in front of us and all around, and what we see is mind boggling.

We see these beings, creatures, all around us. They seem to be milling around not looking at us at all. They're walking—not like humans walk, but they seem to be floating along. They are gray in color, all of them with small bodies and very large heads. Big black coal like eyes, and no ears. Their very large heads are on thin necks and are elongated in the back. They seem to be wearing no clothes at all.

They all look the same and are about five and half feet tall. There are bunches of them everywhere we look, and I couldn't begin to shoot them all even if I wanted too. Then in front of us several of them parted out of the way and we could see one of them sitting in a chair that's gliding toward us and then stops ten feet in front of us. The creature in it gets up and walks toward us. I point my gun at it, and it stops.

"Whatever you are, don't come any closer," I warn. Not knowing if I could kill it or not.

It looked at the three of us moving it's large head back and forth slowly, as if to be studying us. We could also see that the creature's eyes seemed to have many thousands of eyes within the bigger one. Opening and closing, it's creepy as hell, but at the same time fascinating.

Finally, the creature speaks to us in a monotone voice with no inflections at all, in English, that is non threatening. The voice is neither male nor female. "You have intruded onto my vessel. Why?"

"We're...looking for a...criminal organization called WASP that has led us here. They deal in human trafficking," I said. I know I stammered, but how do you answer what appears to be an alien?

The creature pauses and scans us with it's many eyes. Again, creepy as hell. "Yes we know about you and your activities, but we weren't exactly aware of your whereabouts until we got rid of your primitive little machine."

"You're the ones that destroyed my hard drive," Tori says.

"Yes."

"You knew about us," Ty comments.

"Yes, we've known about the three of you for sometime, we knew that you were trying to disrupt the experiment."

"Experiment," I ask?

"The experiment that you speak of called human trafficking."

"You were conducting an experiment in human trafficking?" Tori says in disbelief.

"Yes, that is correct."

"So who are you, and what are you," I ask?

Again a pause from it, like a robot would do as it searches for an answer to a question. It also seemed to be a bit occupied by my gun being pointed at it.

"I am Two-Tar, in your primitive language. And to answer your other question we are Talasians. From a planet called Talasia in what you would call the numeric sector ten. Our world is in what you call the Andromeda Galaxy."

"The Grays," Ty says. "And my God, Andromeda is two and a half billion light years away.

"That is true," Two-Tar responds.

"The Grays?" Tori asks him.

"Yeah for thousands of years there are those who believe that these guys tinkered with our DNA causing us to be like we are today. That's true isn't it Two-Tar?"

It nods.

"So does that make us your cattle, Two-Tar?" I ask it poignantly.

"Yes, you could say that. We are millions of your earth years more advanced than you. You're very primitive, so much so, we generally don't consider you an intelligent life form."

"Well you're talking to us, primitives now," Tori said.

"It's because I have the ability to do so. I can come down to your level to talk with you. Unlike you, you do not have the ability to go down to the level of the insects on your planet and converse with them. You and your species are not advanced enough to do that."

I look at him and say, "so you're WASP?"

"No, I never said that. This is WASP?"

"What is?"

"This vessel, my ship, it is called WASP in your English language."

"You said earlier that we disrupted your experiment. How so," Ty asks?

"We've spent much time developing a scientific way to see how your human species acts and reacts to the buying and selling of other human beings. So we infected your computers with what you call a malware virus to get the thing started. People would go to the site and find out all about the program. We've paid thousands of people at all levels a lot of your dollars to kidnap and run our prisons. We made it look like we were a big crime syndicate just doing business."

"How long have you been doing this experiment," Tori asks?

"Hundreds of your Earth years," Two-Tar answers.

"A criminal business that ruined a whole lot of lives," I said.

"I do not understand, criminal. The whole thing was merely a scientific experiment to us."

"Ha," I laugh out loud. "A scientific experiment, that hurts others.

"That amuses you, Ms. Cain."

"No, Two-Tar, I'm not amused at all. What I'm not amused by, is you and your so called advanced race, enslaving thousands of girls and boys, to make a point. A fucking experiment that was meant to amuse you and help you pass time."

"Time is of little consequence to us, and the experiment

here was necessary in order to facilitate it on other worlds where we are involved."

"So you have more than one herd of cattle," Tori says.

"That is correct."

Then he asks me, "Ms. Cain, why do you continually point that weapon at me?"

"Hmm...well, Two-Tar to answer your question, I don't trust you."

"Trust? That doesn't register with me."

"So let me get this straight. You're so advanced that trust is nothing to you," Ty says.

"I did say that. You see we did away with those thoughts and emotions long before we came here."

"How long ago was that," Tori asks?

"At least ten thousand of your earth years."

"Were you one of them Two-Tar, that originally came here," she asks?

"Yes, I am over fifteen thousand of your years old. We Talasians have all but defeated death as a natural end to life."

"But you can be killed," I comment.

"Yes, that is still a possibility," he says.

Then his manner changes toward us and he says, "I am growing tired of your immature verbal questioning of me and as to our intentions here on your primitive world, that I have clearly stated." He pauses briefly. "You, all three of you have had the intent of destroying the experiment for months.

"As stated earlier we've known about the three of you for sometime and have been tracking your activities. We were unaware that you had come here, until our sensor mainframe located your computer Ms. Nicks and destroyed its hard drive."

Then he looks at me and says, "you do realize Ms. Cain that I can eradicate you with a thought."

"And Two-Tar, I can pull this trigger and eradicate you just as you have that thought, too."

He seemed surprised at my audacious answer, and he must be bothered by my weapon being pointed at him or he wouldn't have mentioned it again.

"You and Ms. Nicks along with Mr. Baines here have set out to destroy all the work that we have done on the experiment," he says. With what could be construed as anger in his voice, because his inflections changed.

"The WASP experiment," Tori says.

"If you will." He states to her, sharply.

Then I say, "so you intentionally set up your so-called experiment to enslave humans."

"I have said, that is correct."

"And in all the time you've been running this little experiment of yours, you've managed to ruin thousands upon thousands of lives. Do you realize that?" Tori says.

"It doesn't matter to us, since, like I said earlier, we do not recognize you as a viable intelligent species."

"But you've spent the last several minutes talking to us, and we're part of that species," Tori said, curtly.

"And I also stated that I have come down to your level, because I am that advanced, and can do so," Ms. Nicks.

With my gun still pointed at him, I say, "Well we came here

to stop WASP and that is still our intention, so put an end to your experiment or I will start shooting, eradicating you and some of them before you can eradicate me. And you will be my first victim."

"I assure you that our trafficking experiment was purely scientific."

"Well scientific or not. Shut it the hell down, or I will start shooting, even if you kill me. I will get you first."

I'm saying this in hopes that he'll take my so-called threat to him seriously and shut down the experiment. I am fully aware of the fact he could kill me with a thought.

Tori says to me, "Sasha, I hope you know what you're doing."

"No, I don't. All I'm trying to do is get him to listen to a little primitive reasoning."

"It could be dangerous," Ty says. "But it also might work."

After watching us talk, Two-Tar says, "Ms. Cain I assure you that there is no need for you to exhibit your abhorrent behavior toward us. Which we've been studying and are well aware of."

"Abhorrent. What the hell does that mean?" I ask Tori.

"It means you're violent." She says smiling at me. I smile back at her, and raise my eyebrows after hearing her say that.

Two-Tar has paused his conversation with us, he seems to have left us, and while we can clearly see him standing in front of us, he just moves his head slightly from time to time.

"Why's he stopped talking to us," Tori asks?

Ty says, "He consulting with the others. You know they're so advanced that they can communicate telepathically. So I'm sure the others we see around him have been listening to our conversation."

"They're like a collective," she says.

"Exactly. He's not the only one whose come down to our level."

"There's a lot of them and I doubt I could kill many before Two-Tar killed me and the two of you," I say.

"You're right, but they knew we were here all along," Ty says.

"Why," Tori asks?

"Not sure, but I'd bet they've suddenly become curious about us, for some reason."

"Maybe they're beginning to think that we're more intelligent than they think," Tori says.

"That could be," Ty says.

We just stood there for several minutes while the Talasians discussed what I said.

"You think they're going to do as Two-Tar said, eradicate us," Tori asks?

"They could and no one would ever know," Ty says. "But no, I don't think they will, because resorting to violence has to be a last resort for them to solve a problem. And they just learned something about you, Sasha."

"Yeah, what's that?"

"That resorting to violence is your first way to solve a problem. That's why I said this might work. Let's see what they do."

"Sure is taking them a longtime," I said.

"Yeah, like he said, time is of little consequence to intergalactic travelers the likes of them."

"What could they be talking about," Tori asks?

"Well you've got to understand that they have put a lot of effort into this. We are very inferior to them, like lab rats. And some of those he's talking with are arguing that very point. They don't want to shut the experiment down because of what they consider to be an inconsequential human female with a gun pointed at them. Which in reality they don't consider you a threat at all, Sasha."

We shook our heads at Ty's comment.

After a couple more minutes of waiting, Two-Tar, starts talking to us again.

He looks at all three of us, moving his head back and forth slowly. For a split second I didn't know for sure if he was going to do, as he puts it, eradicate us or not. But he began to speak, "very well, Ms. Cain. After much discussion among us, it is agreed that we will shut the experiment down. But only after you stop pointing that weapon at me, and them."

I looked at Tori and Ty with a wide grin on my face, and said, "well what do you know? Two-Tar and his Talasian buddies want to deal with us primitives."

Ty and Tori laughed at my comment—Two-Tar is waiting for my answer."

"Okay, cool, I'll do it. But you've got to prove to us that you are shutting it down. You know To-Tar in an act of good faith."

"Your word faith does not register with me, but if you will look up here I will show you that we are indeed keeping our end of the bargain."

We looked up and to his right where he is pointing and this picture appeared in what's like a television or computer screen. And image after image began to go by very rapidly, and in just a few seconds the screen disappeared.

He looked at us and said, "there done. All of the prisons have been closed and the kidnapped people have been returned to their homes and families. None of them will even remember this experience, I assure you."

I lowered my gun and returned it to its holster.

To-Tar looked at me and said, "thank you." He seemed relieved that I wasn't going to shoot him.

Then Tori asked him, "To-Tar there are four girls that are staying with us on the estate, did you return them?"

He paused before answering her, like he was again searching for the answer. "No, because they're no longer being held prisoner, so they are still there."

He looks at all of us with those creepy eyes, and says, "now I must return you to the surface, because we are leaving your world."

We saw him bow his head and close his eyes and pods appeared beneath us, with the shafts of light or whatever they are. We have also been pushed closer together by the same force as before. We put our arms around each other, holding on tight as the pods suddenly rise.

Then something crazy happens. I was holding on to Tori, and Ty then I wasn't. My pod began to go adrift moving away from them, rising rapidly, and shaking violently as it went. I've completely lost sight of Tori and Ty. As the pod I'm on lays on it's side, and begins to spin around, jostling me all over the place. Causing me to hit the sides where the light shafts were. I wasn't getting hurt because the shafts seemed soft but resilient to me going through them.

    I begin to get scared. Not only is the pod going crazy, but I feel a powerful rumbling beneath me. I'm getting dizzy, and breathing hard, like I've been running a sprint. Adrenalin is pouring into my system and is making me sick to my stomach. I can do nothing about my situation, as the pod continues to violently shake and spin out of control. And the rumbling beneath me grows stronger and louder, making whatever is happening to me worse.

    I feel like I'm about to pass out, then everything goes black and the shafts lose their light. It's at this time I figure that I'm a goner, that I'll never see my Tori or Ty, or any of my friends again. I'm going to be killed by that alien Two-Tar. I should have shot him anyway. I can't catch my breath as I feel the pod suddenly rise upward again, this time at an incredible speed. It is totally dark inside, I can't see anything, as I speed to whatever will lead to my certain death.

    Just as that thought races through my mind, and just as suddenly as this all began I am instantly thrown into light and into the air. I'm not sure if I'm dead or not, I don't think so, because I am still breathing, hard. I'm not sure if it's sunlight that I see, or I've gone onto the next realm, to be chased for eternity, into that alley by those five shadows.

    Then I land on the ground, but not hard, and I know that

I'm not dead because I land on my side. It's a soft landing where I feel no pain at all. I lay there for a few seconds trying to get my wits about me. Then I set up slowly and that's when I hear Tori screaming at the top of her lungs.

"Sasha!...Sasha!" She yells. "Sasha Cain, where are you? My God!...No baby, you can't be dead. No! No!" I hear her crying out.

I quickly get up and realize I'm on the other side of the rented SUV we drove out here. I walk around the back of it and call out to her, "Tori. I'm here, turn around." She's in Ty's arms, sobbing, as he's trying to comfort her.

She sees me and exclaims, "Sasha!...My God you're alright!" She runs quickly over to me and we jump into each other's arms. Ty is not far behind and hugs me, too.

"I thought, we thought, you were dead," she exclaims! "What happened to you? We saw your pod just disappear into the darkness."

I then told them about what I'd just experienced, in the pod and how it rolled out of control to wherever, until I ended up being flung into the air and landed behind the SUV.

"Sounds as though old Two-Tar was getting back at you," Ty says.

"Yeah, that's exactly what went through my mind when that all happened."

"So maybe he's not as advanced as he thinks he is, if he tried to get revenge. Which is what it sounds like he was doing with you."

"I agree." Then my attention goes toward the huge chasm in the ground in front of me, where WASP took off.

"Did you see them leave," I ask?

They shook their heads yes and looked at each other.

"It was...the most incredible thing I've ever seen, Sasha," Ty says.

"Yeah?"

"Yes," he says. "We were deposited here next to the SUV sitting down, as the ground began to shake violently, then that thing came up. As it rose the dirt on top of it just seemed to slip away and those two shacks just collapsed into nothing. Tori and I are holding onto each other for dear life, as we watched this happen. We felt the ground around us tilt downward, still shaking, and for just a few seconds it felt like we were going to slip toward that chasm. Then the damn thing rose up and hovered about fifteen feet above the hole and it did something truly amazing."

"What was that."

"It elongated, completely changing its shape entirely. It was so big is went back over us a hundred feet or more, before turning ninety degrees." He pauses and shakes his head. "Then Sasha, it shot out of sight and was gone in less than two seconds. I've never seen anything like it."

"It must have been huge to have left a hole like that in the ground."

As we walked back to the car to leave, over our shoulders and to the west we hear trucks, lots of trucks. We all turned at the same time and could see four of them headed in our direction, and coming fast.

"Troops," Ty says. "Let's get out of here."

THE ALLEY OF EVIL

TWENTY SEVEN

We run as fast as we can to get to the car, and quickly get in. I tell Ty to toss Tori the keys, so she can drive. She's quickly behind the wheel and starts it up, then whips it around and out onto the road. Tori is one hell of a driver and I trust her driving skills way more than mine or Ty's anytime.

The troop carriers are coming fast and are accompanied by four other military vehicles. HumVees, with heavy machine guns mounted on the top of them. As they close in on us, Tori floors the SUV—giving it all it has has. It has to much get up and go for them to catch up to us, and we quickly out distance them.

Ty and I have situated ourselves in the back of the car so we can defend ourselves. I pull out a semi automatic rifle and Ty does the same. They're not getting any closer, they're falling back, not able to match Tori's speed. They hadn't started shooting at us yet, so we didn't shoot at them.

Then out of nowhere I see motorcycles, lots of them, coming at us from both sides across the desert floor. There must be at least forty of them. They are all heading straight for us. The riders have guns and are shooting them at us. Ty and I wasted no time, and began firing back at them. As they more than match our speed, coming up alongside of us.

I Shout, "Tori, give it all you got, and don't stop whatever you do."

She doesn't answer, I feel her push down on the accelerator, propelling the SUV to its limit. We have the bikers behind us, for just a few seconds, before they begin to match Tori's acceleration—the troops are still chasing us, too. Ty and I are shooting at the bikers, but they're hard to hit because of the speeds we are both traveling. He and I take out one, two, or more, but I'm not keeping count. I empty the magazine in the rifle and reload. They're still coming at us full tilt, shooting at us at the same time. Then I see a second wave of bikers come out of the rocks we pass to our right.

"Damn, where the hell are they coming from?" I yell to Ty.

"Don't know, I can't believe that they're all after us."

"Yeah that's what I'm thinking."

I feel the SUV swerve as Tori's driving skills take over. She makes a sudden violent move to her right in an attempt to take out a biker pointing a gun at her. She moves to veer into him. He veers with her then regroups and come alongside us again. She swerves again, suddenly, this time making him pay. She hits him hard driving the right side of the SUV into the bike. Causing it to launch into the air. I watch as the rider and bike crash violently.

Tori heads into a small canyon speeding through towering rock formations on both sides of us. The canyon has stopped the bikers from coming alongside in threes and fours except for one that comes up to us on my side shooting away. I quickly point the rifle at him and make him pay with one shot.

I turn around and look out the front of the SUV, and see a

curve coming up on us fast. We're traveling at a very high rate of speed. I yell to her, "can you make that going this fast?"

"Piece a cake. Watch this," she says. Just then I feel her let up on the accelerator at just the right instant, as she coaxes the SUV to the left and we speed around a bend in the road, going downgrade. Then she floors it again as we come out of the turn and head into the open desert. She's pushing the engine with all it has left doing her best to put space between us and the bikers. They are speeding out of the canyon and gaining on us again. The troops are no longer visible—they either can't match the speeds we're going or they've given up the chase completely.

As I watched her take that turn, I was amazed at her intense concentration as she drove around it. I've known this beautiful girl that I'm engaged to for eight months, and she never ceases to amaze me with some new skill. She is indeed a great driver—she took that curve like it was, a piece a cake.

After another half mile of the bikers coming up to us once more shooting at us, then they did something crazy, they suddenly stop, like their frozen place. The troops who have also come out of the canyon a mile or so back have stopped, too, in the same manner. It's just then that I realize we are slowing down. What's going on?

"Tori, don't stop, keep going," I say to her.

Then she stopped the SUV completely and I turn around and was about to ask her why? When she says, "guys you gotta come and look at this."

"What the...," I say." I see now why she's stopped the car.

We look out the front.

Ty says, "our old friend Two-Tar?"

"I don't know."

We turn around and look at the bikers, they haven't moved, and neither have the troops. In front of us and hovering about thirty feet off the ground is this huge metallic object. It's saucer shaped and shiny in the late afternoon sun of the Nevada desert. We take another look at our pursuers—they've still not moved an inch, so we decide it's safe to get out of the car and see if this is indeed the Talasian ship that we dealt with earlier.

We walk around to the front of the car and stand, just as we did that we saw five Talasians appear in front of us. They approach us, walking, but not like we walk. It's like they're taking steps, but they are floating along the top of the ground.

I say, "To-Tar?"

"Yes, it is I," he replied.

"So what brings you back so soon," Tori asks?

"I came back to apologize to you and to you in particular Ms. Cain. I was a bit reckless with you in that pod earlier, as I became…shall we say a bit vengeful toward you."

A bit vengeful! You damn near killed me.

"Yes and I'm sorry for that, I hope you accept my apology."

"You heard me, and I do."

"Yes I did hear you. We are as you learned earlier, telepathic. It is not like us, to be vengeful, because we gave up vengeance as a way of retaliation millennia ago. I was quickly reminded of that by my council, who you see here with me. So I hope you are not hurt in any way."

"I'm good."

"I hope the two of you were not hurt in any way?" He asks Tori and Ty and they say to him that they were not hurt.

"That is good because we also have another reason to come back and talk with you. As I eluded to earlier we have been coming here to your Earth for centuries, but have had only limited contact with your species. Though we did find one person to be a most remarkable man, Leonardo DaVinci. He was very engaging. A genius, as you earthlings would call him."

"You knew DaVinci?" Ty asks, with amazement.

"Yes and quite well, too." He pauses briefly and looks at his council and begins again, "What we would like to do is form a...what you humans call a partnership."

Tori asks, "why us?"

"Well, you each of you has a different skill set that can be helpful to us when we do come back, especially you Ms. Nicks. Your computer skills are beyond reproach."

I give her a great big smile as she blushes at To-Tar's comment.

Then I ask, "No more trafficking?"

"None."

We looked at each other and shook our heads and said yes to his proposal.

"Very well. You do know that while we may be able to help you ease some of the issues that distress your planet today, we cannot get directly involved and change the course of your history. The only time we would get involved is if you are about to have a nuclear conflict. We would stop that if we are near and can do so."

"How will we know you're in the area and are going to...stop by," Tori asks?

"You, Ms. Nicks, will receive a message on your computer. And from time to time it may be necessary to contact each you telepathically."

"You can do that," she asks?

"Yes and at great distances I might add."

Then I turn around and look at the bikers and Troops who are stuck in some sort of state of suspended animation, and ask, "can you help us with all of them?"

"I already have, they will be like that until you are all safely back in Reno. So until we contact you, I bid you good-bye."

We nodded to him—Tori said she's looking forward to it. Then they disappeared and in an instant the ship again changed its shape like Ty said it had done before, and shot off out of sight in less that two seconds.

We turned around and looked at our assailants and got into the SUV and left.

******

Two hours later I'm strapping my seat belt on, as I wait in great anticipation for the plane ride home. Ty has again gone up front to play copilot for C. J. Tori sets down next to me and latches her belt. We look at each other and kiss gently, something that seems like we haven't done in forever.

"God, Sasha, I'm glad that's over."

"Me, too."

"I can't believe what happened with Two-Tar and the Talasians."

"Yeah, he came back and apologized to me. Are you all right with the pact we made with him?"

"Yeah, I mean how do you turn down an alien, who wants to partner with you?"

"True."

Then I looked out the window and felt the plane move. Tori was up and looking, too, leaning across me as we taxied out onto the tarmac. We looked at each other and smiled, then kissed again. Soon we felt the little jet turn and head down the runway picking up speed and just like that we were airborne. I sat and wondered about the Talasians. They fly all the time—everywhere never staying put in one place for long. They travel the universe. Ty called them intergalactic travelers. I would sure like to know how they do it.

After several minutes looking out the window I turned my attention to Tori. I looked down at her, she's already fast asleep—head on my shoulder. She's curled up in a near fetal position next to me, her right leg thrown over me. I look at her and I think about how lucky I am to have her—how much I love and cherish her.

I watch her sleeping so beautifully, something I did every night when we were locked up in that tiny jail cell all those months ago. I would lay next to her back then, facing her and watch her. Listening to her rhythmic breathing, until it would put me to sleep. Her peaceful sleep gave me such a peace that I can't explain, just as it does now. She told me once that she could do that while we were there, because she knew I was there with her. That I, Sasha Cain, would protect her. But she still does it to me. It gives me such a peace watching her sleep, as we speed toward home. And I, too, soon drift off and am fast asleep.

THE ALLEY OF EVIL

EPILOGUE

Today is Sunday and we are back at the estate. It is early September and while the days are still warm, we can feel the cooling chill of autumn coming on. The days have certainly grown substantially shorter, and the leaves are just on the cusp of beginning to change color.

Tori and I are off to the little beach to do some swimming, and relaxing in the sun—yes, the sun. And to think, just two months ago she and I were incarcerated against our will in that jail cell. We were both placed in there for doing nothing wrong by people that can no longer hurt us. Now that seems like a lifetime ago, as she and I gain confidence together and get even more control of our lives.

As for that awful nightmare that plagued me for so many years—it's gone, too. I hope for good. I had it one more time and the figures did what Dr. Yost said might happen. They ran right past me and into that dark alley. The alley of evil, that still haunts and scares me if I think about it.

Tori has opened up to Dr. Yost about what Behar did to her and the rape. It's a good thing—she would talk to me about some of it, but would always stop short of telling me everything. I'm just glad that she getting help for it. I want it for my Tori more than anything.

After our return home we told everyone what WASP was and what happened. We also told them all about Two-Tar and pact we made with him, and how we got him to close down the experiment.

Speaking of the Talasians, they left all that money in the basement, so cash is not a problem for us. I'm not sure why they did it other than they have no use for it. Money must be one of those things that doesn't register with Two-Tar or his council.

Tori and I of course have a wedding to plan for, and are gradually doing that. She has her ideas as to how she wants it to play out, and I just let her plan, because I want her to have fun doing it. I am not much help to her at all. I'll admit that. But she has the four other girls who live here at the estate to help her plan, and they're all having fun with it. I've told her I will not wear a wedding gown, it's just not me, or for me. I have however agreed to a nice dress and some wedges. I have promised her one thing for sure, I will not wear guy clothes made for a girl. Period. She's agreed.

And if all that is not enough, I have for some reason become the unofficial head of this little group of people who live here on the estate. Every decision that is to be made is run by me, for some reason. Like I have some sort of special authority. I don't, trust me. But hey I do it, because they're all important people to Tori and me.

Then there's Penn and Cash, my good buddies. They still call me boss even though I've insisted on them calling me, Sasha. That request of course falls on deaf ears, so I just play along with them. And speaking of those two, I finally have learned their first names. I just always called them Penn and Cash. But I have since found out that Cash's first name is Roland and Penn's is Joseph. How dumb of me.

I lay down on the beach recliner with the warm afternoon sun on me. Tori is in the recliner next to me. We are in our bathing suits, both bikinis, that at first I felt uncomfortable wearing,

She's also insisted we wear these big floppy hats with wide brims today. Mine is yellow and hers is hot pink. Tori's looks absolutely cute on her, but mine looks totally ridiculous on me. I hate hats, but she wants me to wear this one, so I will for her.

"You know, Sasha, they used to call tomorrow, Labor Day in the country before it changed."

"Yeah I've heard that."

"Maybe someone should start to do that again, just like the Fourth of July."

"I hear you. Maybe what I said right after we found all that money in the basement that we should start a revolution with it, and do those things. Make this country by the people and for the people like it used to be. Not just for the plutocrats."

"Yeah, maybe we should, but only after we do one thing."

I look at her questioning.

"Have our wedding."

I laughed, and said, yes to that, causing her to giggle.

We're soon joined on the beach by Janet, Davy, Maria and Shelly, with their poles, net, and ball. They challenged Tori and I to a game of volleyball. We looked at each other and couldn't resist.

NANCY HOWARD

-ABOUT THE AUTHOR-

Nancy Howard is a writer, author, and avid cyclist and lives in Colorado. She's also the author of Logan's Promise, and Our Place By the Sea.

Other Books By Nancy Howard
Logan's Promise (Available August 17, 2020)